The Las

Nick Louth is a million-copy bestselling thriller author, and an award-winning journalist. After graduating from the London School of Economics, Nick was a foreign correspondent for Reuters, working in New York, Amsterdam, London and Hong Kong. He has written for the *Financial Times*, *Investors Chronicle*, *Money Observer* and *MSN*. His debut thriller, *Bite*, was a Kindle No. 1 bestseller and has been translated into six languages. The DCI Craig Gillard series and DI Jan Talantire series are published by Canelo, and in audio by WF Howes. He is married and lives in Lincolnshire.

Also by Nick Louth

Bite
Heartbreaker
Mirror Mirror
Trapped

DCI Craig Gillard Crime Thrillers

The Body in the Marsh
The Body on the Shore
The Body in the Mist
The Body in the Snow
The Body Under the Bridge
The Body on the Island
The Bodies at Westgrave Hall
The Body on the Moor
The Body Beneath the Willows
The Body in the Stairwell
The Body in the Shadows
The Body in Nightingale Park

Detective Jan Talantire

The Two Deaths of Ruth Lyle
The Last Ride

THE LAST RIDE

NICK LOUTH

First published in the United Kingdom in 2024 by

Canelo
Unit 9, 5th Floor
Cargo Works, 1–2 Hatfields
London SE1 9PG
United Kingdom

Print ISBN 978 1 80436 781 0
Ebook ISBN 978 1 80436 782 7

This book is a work of fiction. Names, characters, businesses, organizations, places and events are either the product of the author's imagination or are used fictitiously. Any resemblance to actual persons, living or dead, events or locales is entirely coincidental.

Cover design by Dan Mogford

Cover images © Shutterstock

Look for more great books at www.canelo.co

Printed and bound in Great Britain by Clays Ltd, Elcograf S.p.A.

For Louise, as always

Chapter One

He heard it first as an aggressive revving engine, not the familiar distant drone of traffic, but the distinctive Saturday-night racket of boy racers heading to the emptiest parts of the moor. Angrier, louder, insistent, it prised him from his dreams, accompanied by the booming bass beat of music. Ever closer, like an incoming projectile. There was a screech. Then a heartbeat of absolute silence, before an impact that made the house shake.

It took him time to move from the chair where he slept downstairs to the window and draw the curtains back on a scene of hell. He had witnessed some terrible things in his life. He was one of the glider-borne assault troops in Normandy at D-Day, aged nineteen, and fought hand-to-hand with the Germans in and around the city of Caen. He had seen his friends die, to either side of him, brutally cut down, as he stormed a machine-gun trench. But Brigadier William Llewellyn, ninety-eight, had never seen, nor heard, anything like he saw that night, in his own garden on the edge of Bodmin Moor.

–

At the same time, seven miles away, Detective Inspector Jan Talantire awoke with a start. For a moment, she didn't recognise where she was, staying in her mother's rented holiday cottage, in a rare weekend away from work. Jan's mother, Estelle, was a GP, still working as a locum aged seventy, and, after the death of Jan's father six years earlier, now embarking on a spree of new relationships. Of the dozen suitors that Talantire had heard of, only Geoffrey, moderately wealthy, self-confident, a yachtsman, had survived to this stage, which patently included lovemaking next door. Being awoken by your mother's cries of passion isn't exactly how most thirty-eight-year-old women want to spend the small hours of Sunday morning, but at least that part of the disturbance had been relatively brief. It was the subsequent giggling and some male shushing which completed the intrusion. At least she wouldn't have to get some balled-up toilet paper for home-made earplugs like she had the previous night.

She yawned and turned over, then headed for the loo, feeling sleep slip away from her. On her return, she reached for her phones, sitting on the bedside table. As always, she first checked the work device. That said as much about her limited social life as about her years of workaholism. It was 2:23 a.m. She tapped into the control-room message feed, and found a serious road traffic accident just reported a few miles away from the cottage where she was staying, in a remote area on Bodmin Moor. A first responder, an ambulance and a fire appliance were on their way to the RTA, but there were no police units nearby. Plymouth was the closest, but had no patrol cars to spare for an hour.

She put the phone down, reminding herself that she wasn't at work until Monday. Instead, if yesterday was anything to go by, she had to look forward to her mother appearing at breakfast, bubbly as a schoolgirl, and smirking like the cat that had got the cream. Yesterday morning,

Geoffrey, a lean and craggy fellow with a seaman's deep tan and a luxuriant snowy thatch, had made champagne cocktails for each of them at ten a.m. Talantire had been more than happy to meet her mother's latest new man but had fervently hoped that this bacchanalia would have been got out of the way first. It made her feel like a gooseberry.

She tiptoed downstairs in pyjamas and opened the back door. The cool breeze of the night was welcome after the humidity and heat of the day, and she stepped outside in bare feet, staring up at the dazzling stars overhead. In the far distance, she heard a siren, the urgent call for attention. It decided her. She would go.

She rang into the control room and, after giving her location, was told she was easily the closest officer. The 999 trace was just beyond the tiny hamlet of St Trenewan, seven miles away, maybe a ten-minute journey. It was a part of Bodmin Moor she knew well. The brief call had come from a mobile, female screaming against a background of music, cut off in less than a second before any info from the caller had been taken, then, a minute later, a pendant alert from a device registered to an address nearby, Bodmin Rectory. It was followed by a message which mentioned a serious car accident. Her attendance, the operator said, would be appreciated.

Fortunately, Talantire always travelled with a decent medical as well as forensic kit in her go-bag, which went with her whether she was in a work vehicle or her own Ford Focus. She was also a fully trained crime-scene photographer, and that would be useful when the forensic accident investigators got to work.

She made her way back to her room and slipped into jeans and T shirt in less than a minute. She penned an apologetic note to her mother saying she'd been called away to an emergency and left it on the kitchen table. After making a rapid mental checklist, she jumped into the car. She nosed out onto the main road from Liskeard to Bodmin, heading west. Using the hands-free phone, she tapped into the emergency services radio channel. A first responder was fifteen minutes away, but the ambulance arrival was likely to be at least forty minutes. Not much worse than average, but a world away from the target response time for a category-one call like this. Eight minutes!

With a deep breath, she sped away into the empty night, heading for Bodmin Moor.

–

St Trenewan, once a thriving agricultural settlement, was just one long and unusually straight road, with eight houses all on one side of the road, the edge of the moor on the other. It followed the line of an old mining track, along which lead and tin ore had been taken by cart from Colliford Lake down towards the coast at Looe. There was nothing in the hamlet beside a handful of homes. Neither a pub nor a Post Office in living memory, just a South West Water sewage facility, a disused bus shelter and, on the right, the great brooding shoulder of Bodmin, a mist-shrouded world of lost industrial heritage tangled with spiky gorse. Three miles further on still, the road ended at Colliford Lake, Cornwall's largest reservoir.

For all of its obscurity, St Trenewan had its little piece of local notoriety. It was the road accident capital of south-east Cornwall, with nine deaths and forty-six injuries over the last twenty years. The thirty-mile-an-hour speed limit on the approach to the hamlet was probably the most widely ignored in the county. The radar warning signal with its green smiley face seemed permanently lit to an angry red, as it was when Talantire sped through.

There might be no information from the 999 caller, but she knew. Four miles of straight albeit narrow road is rare in Cornwall, and one with so little traffic even rarer. For joyriders, it was a nirvana, made even more thrilling by the occasional dips and bumps. She knew from her days in uniform in Cornwall that the average age of those killed at this blackspot was seventeen – a pointless waste of young life and devastation for their parents. She had no doubt that that was exactly the type of shout she was attending tonight.

There were two bends at the very end of the road, within a mile of the reservoir. The first, Vinegar Hill Corner, caught most of the inexperienced drivers. The road rose slightly, then dipped suddenly over a culvert as it turned sharp left. The concrete retaining wall on the far side of the culvert had taken immense damage over the years. The erection in 2006 of a black-and-white chevron sign warning of the bend, and high-vis shock-absorbing pillars in front of the concrete, had done little to stem the carnage. She was a little surprised when driving through that it was not here where the crash had occurred.

She drove on as the road took a shallow, rising right towards Ore Spill Lane, before dipping sharply. It was then that she saw the lights of Bodmin Rectory at the next sharp bend, a tight left-hander. A telegraph pole within the walled garden had been snapped off, at least ten feet up, with a crown of five-feet-long jagged splinters, in the thicket of which was dangling a car door, folded at the frame, like a giant ring pull. She was surprised to see no apparent gap in the six-foot-high stone wall which enclosed the grounds, but the gates were open, so she drove in and stopped on the circular drive. The car clock showed 2:32 as she jumped out.

No fire brigade, no police, no ambulance. She was the first one there.

Very loud music was coming from somewhere. At first glance, all she saw was an elderly man kneeling close to the open front door of the house. But where was the crashed car? It was only when she peered much further left, down the side of the rectory, that she saw a pile of wreckage: white metal, wood and lots of glass. It was the twisted shell of a Victorian glasshouse, within which squatted the remains of an inverted car, barely recognisable but for the wheels on top.

Turning back to the man, she saw he was bent over a recumbent form. She rushed to the back of her own vehicle, grabbed the first-aid bag and ran over to them. She could immediately see that the victim was in her teens, drenched in blood, her eyes almost closed.

'I'll take over,' she said to the man, trying to make herself heard over the sound of Meatloaf's 'Bat Out of Hell', which was blaring from within the car. In brief gaps in the music, she could hear two mobile phones ringing and the soft chimes which indicated a seat belt was undone. With two phones that meant at least one other person was likely to be in the car. She could now see that the girl had a tourniquet on her thigh, a stick used to tighten it. Professional and competent.

'She was conscious for a couple of minutes after I got her from the car,' the man said, breathlessly. 'Her name is Lily, and she's thirteen.'

'Dear God,' Talantire said. She knew youngsters had so much fight in them and could survive incredible trauma with prompt treatment. But she didn't dare make that promise either to him, or herself.

'When is the ambulance due?' he asked.

'Soon,' she lied. 'Did anyone else get out?'

'I glimpsed somebody, near the gates, just for a second. She was running away from the car and went out beyond the wall.'

'A girl?'

'Yes.' The man looked so old and frail that he could die of shock. She didn't relish the prospect of trying to keep two people alive simultaneously. Still, someone of that age managing such a good tourniquet, that was impressive.

A car screeched into the driveway, and first responder Stef Metcalfe jumped out carrying a defibrillator and other kit.

'Jan, long time no see. You got here quickly.'

'I was staying at an Airbnb just a few miles away. Thought I'd pitch in.'

Talantire was relieved. Stef was a first-class medic and would free Talantire to co-ordinate the response. She rang the control room and asked for four more ambulances, assuming a car-full of victims. The latest ETA of the ambulance had improved, to fifteen minutes, with at least one fire engine from Bodmin also en route. Send more, she said. She then felt she could risk looking for other casualties.

Stef, meanwhile, had opened the buttons on the girl's blood-spattered blouse, set up the green pads of the defibrillator on her pale boyish chest and watched the read-out. 'Her heart rate is high, but her breathing is ragged,' she said.

'Will she live?' the old man asked.

'Yes, but she needs oxygen. She must have lost a pint of blood at least, and I'll need to raise her leg to reduce pressure at the wound.' She turned to the girl. 'Can you hear me? Clench your fists if you can.'

There was no movement, just the fluttering of her eyelids, from which one false eyelash dangled forlornly.

Talantire made her way over to the wrecked vehicle, which had inserted itself into a very substantial Victorian greenhouse, creating a new hazard all around the car: dozens of partially shattered, razor-sharp panes hanging like scimitars from cast-iron frames, waiting to impale anyone who approached. She began to take photos as she circled in.

There was a Mercedes emblem, an encircled triangle, on the boot lid. It was unbelievable that what had originally been a very sizeable car could fly so far, apparently over the wall rather than breaking through it, hit a telegraph pole halfway up, before deflecting thirty yards to the right.

She made her way gingerly into the shattered structure of the greenhouse, crunching a path around the vehicle, on mounds of broken glass mixed in with shattered plant pots and compost. Meatloaf finished, and the jolly voice of a disc jockey boomed out, wishing everyone a lovely summer night, promising that he would stay with them through the night until six a.m. Then he introduced the next track: 'Total Eclipse of the Heart'. She wished she could reach in and turn the damn thing off, so at least she'd have a chance of hearing if anyone was calling for help.

The Mercedes roof was crushed almost flat at the front, with ripped airbags spilling out from a small gap where the laminated windscreen, now crushed and folded in two, used to be. Only the rear window was unbroken. Where the front passenger door had been ripped off, there was just a hand-width gap between the crushed roof and the bottom sill. That gap should have been a yard. There was no sign of movement, and no sounds, apart from the ticking of the engine as it cooled down and the occasional beep of a text arriving on a mobile phone inside the vehicle.

She kneeled down and used the light on her phone to peer into the hellish interior of the car. She saw bodies, jumbled, and one bloodied palm still pressed against the back window, unmoving. She rang in again, detailing her suspicions of more youngsters she couldn't reach. She crouched down at the smashed driver-side passenger window through which Lily had astonishingly been retrieved. She called softly into the car, her knees resting on fragments of broken glass, and saw a couple of thumb-sized nitrous oxide canisters catch the light on her phone. Laughing gas. Abused by teenagers, and soon to be illegal.

There was a faint moaning sound, barely discernible over Bonnie Tyler. She stretched her arm inside and alighted upon a kneecap. She wasn't sure if the ripped material across it was by fashionable intention or the result of the accident, but the most important thing was the knee was still warm. She moved her hand down the slender denimed calf, which she took to be female, and found an ankle, sticky with something warm. Blood. She rested two fingers just below and behind the inner side of the ankle bone. There was a pulse, but it was weak.

Where was that ambulance? Where was the fire and rescue? They might all be dead in fifteen minutes. What could she do? How could she reach them? She felt totally helpless.

She called out: 'Anyone conscious? Give me a shout, we'll soon get you out.'

All she heard was Bonnie Tyler, promising that forever was 'gonna start tonight'. Well, how true that was for these kids. Life-changing injuries, at the very least. She thought of the anxious parents, the brothers and sisters, maybe those who were already ringing those inaccessible phones, normally never out of a kid's reach. Unanswered now. Forever was certainly going to start tonight.

–

When Talantire came back to Stef to report what she'd seen, in the distance she spotted the flashing blue lights and heard the thunderous roar of engines, the honk of air horns. They had been promised one fire engine from Bodmin and one from Liskeard, and here they both were. Her heart gave a little leap, and she caught her breath as she saw the Cornwall Fire and Rescue logo.

The first tender roared into the drive and three burly firemen jumped out, then from the second tender half a dozen more men, and one woman. Emma Thurlow, her former neighbour's daughter. A tall, raw-boned girl of twenty-one. Their arrival made Talantire's heart sing, and she wanted to hug each and every one of them.

Fire Chief Greg Hammerson, an enormous bear of a man, greeted them both like long-lost friends, then peered across at the vehicle and up at the shattered telegraph pole. 'Jesus Christ almighty, that was some impact.'

'There's three or four youngsters still in there,' Talantire said. 'At least one of them is alive, but unconscious. And maybe another one who got out, apart from the casualty here.'

'We'll do what we can, Jan. Stef, do you have an ETA for the paramedics?'

'Five minutes. Jan just rang them.'

Soon, the scene was swarming with men in olive drab uniform, high-vis stripes catching the light from the house. Some were unloading heavy-duty cutting equipment, gathered round the stricken vehicle. Stef returned her attention to Lily, who seemed to have stabilised.

'A and B pillars are crushed both sides,' someone called. 'C pillar intact to offside.' Talantire knew that they were referring to the car roof supports, front to back, which were supposed to be the safety cage to prevent occupants being crushed. But even the best engineering had its limits.

Hammerson made his way into the greenhouse and with gloved hands pulled down two or three of the most dangerous-looking shards of glass hanging above, then lay down on his side on a glistening bed of glass splinters and peered into the car. 'It's a helluva mess in there,' he said. 'There are at least three of them inside.' He got to his feet, and called for his crew to bring two hydraulic jacks. 'Right, everybody, we're going for a rear oyster,' he yelled. 'We're still within the golden hour, so there is a chance of saving any survivors. The vehicle is stable, but we've got to be careful about dislodging this lot,' he said, pointing to the dragon's teeth of glass. 'Now, occupants may be suspended from the seat belts, if they were wearing any.' He called across to the back of the second tender: 'Where are those lights, Emma?'

'One minute, boss,' came a distant reply.

'And where are the uniformed police?' he muttered, almost to himself. 'Right, everyone. Remember your training,' Hammerson shouted. 'I can already see some acute neck flexion against the interior of the roof. John and Chris, I want you to site the jacks carefully, get some lights in there. If we can create some space, at least we'll get a better chance of opening up the back.'

Talantire held her breath as the rescuers took their positions. She didn't dare imagine what they would find inside that car.

Chapter Two

By three a.m., there were twenty emergency vehicles and fifty people at the scene of the crash, along with a sizeable number of members of the public who apparently didn't have anything better to do in the small hours of Sunday morning. Arc lights mounted on cherry pickers bathed the crash scene with dazzling light and would be visible from miles away, easily the biggest glow over the moor.

A senior police officer had just arrived. Chief Inspector Bernie Campbell was a reliable, common-sense cop, the most senior Black officer in the county, the type you wanted on your side when the proverbial was hitting the fan. Talantire had worked with him when she was a trainee. Everyone was dreading his retirement, due in a couple of years.

'Hello, Jan. This looks like hell on earth,' he muttered, managing a thin smile below his steel-framed glasses.

Hammerson approached, and they high-fived, out of long familiarity.

'Bernie, this is probably one of the worst I've seen in thirty-five years,' Hammerson said. 'We're going to prise open the back in a minute, but one of the paramedics has already managed to get halfway in to get a proper look. Of four occupants, three are still in there. One dead, two still hanging onto life. The fourth was extricated alive by the householder.'

'That's almost miraculous,' Campbell said.

'It is, considering only one was wearing a seat belt. And he was the one who died. I think it says a lot about the quality of modern airbags that any of them are alive.'

They both shook their heads in amazement.

Talantire said: 'I can do some gel lifts and DNA samples, if you're having trouble with casualty ID. But seeing as it's like Waterloo Station, I don't rate my chances of getting much else. I've taken dozens of pics.'

Campbell nodded. 'The car was notified stolen on Thursday night, though that's obviously well below your pay grade for a CID investigation.'

'The insides are awash with nitrous oxide canisters, so they were probably laughing like hyenas as the car sailed through the air,' Talantire remarked. 'But, again, still legal.'

'Jan, let's treat it as a crime scene as best we can. Better to be too diligent right from the start than try to go back later for evidence that isn't there any more.'

'Absolutely,' she said.

'We could do with the assistance of your digital evidence officer, to look at the mobile phones we have recovered. I'm having a mobile Aceso Kiosk brought here.'

Talantire knew that her new and quite brilliant DEO, Primrose Chen, would be on shift in a few hours. 'I'll message her to see if she can come straight here. She only lives in Plymouth, so it's half of her normal commute.'

The screech of cutting gear cut off their conversation for a few moments, along with shouted instructions from Hammerson and the other fire officers.

Campbell gave an involuntary grimace as the angle grinders bit into metal.

'If you think that's bad, you could hardly hear yourself think for the music from the stereo, when we first arrived,' Talantire shouted. 'Hammerson's men snipped through the speaker cables, to see if we were missing any sounds from the car.'

'I've just received a couple of names,' Campbell said, looking at his phone. 'Both missing from the Penypul estate in Camborne, both from families well known to the police. Facebook is awash with activity, and there's a dozen more names to conjure who might have been in there. We've got two FLOs going to the addresses we've been given.'

Family liaison officers had some of the most difficult jobs in policing: breaking news of the death, in this case of a child. Talantire had spent twelve weeks in Penypul as a trainee community officer, a decade ago, and remembered some of the families. 'What names do you have?' she asked.

'Aaron Darracombe, aged fourteen, and Jordan Bailey, sixteen. A thirteen-year-old was rescued by the resident here, who we believe to be Lily Jago. She and her older sister Scarlett, sixteen, were reported missing by her mother late yesterday evening. Then we've got Leanne Moyle, sixteen. All from the same couple of streets.'

Talantire knew the Jago family very well. The older brother Kevin had been a hyperactive shoplifter a decade ago, as a ten-year-old. Scarlett she recalled as a sassy six-year-old, and Lily just a toddler. Their mother, Joyce, had managed on her own for a long time, stuck on benefits, unable to find a job that paid enough to fund a child-minder. There were a lot of unsavoury men the kids referred to as uncles, but no single stable male influence, and no real breadwinner. The Penypul estate may not have looked deprived, but with the collapse of the last remaining mine equipment engineering businesses in the 1980s, its austere pebble-dashed houses contained some of the most curtailed life chances in the county. The Darracombe family she knew less well. She had a vague recollection of one of the brothers being a delinquent, but not which.

'As we've got three left in the car, it probably won't take too long to narrow down who they are,' Campbell said.

Talantire nodded. She couldn't get to the wreck because of the firemen still working on extricating the injured and the dead, so instead surveyed the shattered telegraph pole, and the great tangle of wires that were draped along the garden wall. She tried to envisage the trajectory of the car, and its speed to have flown right over a six-foot wall into the garden of Bodmin Rectory. Could anyone have escaped from that? Maybe the householder's recollection was mistaken.

Half a dozen more nox canisters glinted in the light at the base of the pole. She donned her nitrile gloves and slid a few of the silvery capsules into a plastic evidence bag, hoping for dabs.

Feeling surplus to requirements, she exited from the garden through the gateway, and under the blue tape which was holding back a knot of onlookers. The first floral tribute had already arrived: a bunch of red roses in tissue paper tied to the road sign warning of the bend. She was amazed: how did you get fresh flowers at this time of night, without going out to your own garden with secateurs?

She made her way back along the road in the direction that the crashed car must have come. The line of onlookers' parked cars was now seventy yards long, all over the verge on both sides, and in all probability obliterating the tyre tracks the crash investigators would want to look at. Why had the Merc lifted off? Could it be speed alone, a dip in the road, or contact with a roadside object? With the mess that this lot had made of the verge, they might never know.

She walked right to the end of the row of cars looking for tyre tracks, then retraced her steps to the gateway. Two uniforms – one male, one female – were guarding the blue tape perimeter. Both were nursing hot drinks, presumably dispensed from inside the rectory. The steam from the mugs drifted up in the light of the arc lamps.

'I need you to clear the public's cars from the verge for at least a hundred yards,' Talantire said. 'You presumably have some cones?'

'Chief Inspector Campbell asked us to stay here to stop the rubberneckers, so you'd better take it up with him,' the male said with a touch of insolence. 'Ma'am.'

Talantire couldn't see Campbell, so tried ringing his direct line. It went straight to voicemail. She left a message, then stared again at the shattered telegraph pole. This time, she walked along the outside edge of the rectory wall in the other direction, beyond the crash site and the final two parked cars. There was a gathering mist over the moors, which the glare of the arc lights illuminated in a ghostly fashion. She continued to follow the outside edge of the wall, from the corner where it turned away from the road and marked out the garden from the boggy moorland beyond. In the light from her phone, she saw shards of shattered plastic, a headlamp rim, more canisters. Jewels of window glass glinted back at her in all directions. This was clearly where the debris from the impact with the telegraph pole had sprayed. She continued to follow the edge of the wall another thirty yards parallel to the side of the rectory until she was level with the protruding metals struts poking above the wall. She was directly opposite the remains of the glasshouse.

Campbell returned her call, but she almost missed it. The urgent shouts of firemen, and the rending of metal assailed her senses, so she strode across the moorland, away from the wall, with one hand over her free ear to give her a chance.

'I think we need to get cars off the verge,' she told him, and explained about the tyre tracks. She continued to walk away from the noise, splashing through mud, and brushing aside sharp gorse.

Campbell made some excuse about resources and added: 'Okay, but I've got bigger fish to fry, right now Jan.' He hung up.

The land was boggy here, dotted with spiky shrubs: hawthorn, blackthorn and gorse, with some of its yellow-petalled flowers still surviving. Ahead of her, the brooding ridges of the moor stretched away under the gathering mist.

Talantire sighed and pocketed the phone. Then heard it ring. Pulled it out. No, it wasn't her phone. The ringtone was similar, and was very close by. She followed the sound, deep into a brake of gorse, now some thirty yards beyond the wall. Using her phone light, she scanned the bushes. The sound stopped for a few seconds, and then there was the tone of an arriving text. She took two more steps and stumbled across a body.

A teenage girl, her blonde hair glittering with glass fragments, lay face down in the mud, one bloodstained leg caught in a gorse bush, the other, minus trainer and sock, twisted around it. The phone was a few yards further on, and the girl's outstretched hand looked as if she'd tried to reach it. The classic teenage reflex.

Talantire crouched down and pressed her hand against her long slender neck, with its fuzz of fine pale hairs. Warm. And a pulse.

'Can you hear me?' she asked. She lightly tapped the girl's hand, a slender beautiful object, perfect pristine fingers with pale green nail varnish.

No response.

She stood, filled her lungs and bellowed: 'Live casualty! Thirty yards north of the wall.'

A fireman's head popped up above the brickwork.

'Here,' Talantire shouted, waving her phone. 'Paramedic, please!'

Once she had the acknowledgement, she turned back to the girl, and recalled her first aid; ABCDE. Airways, breathing, circulation, disability, exposure. She slid her fingers under the girl's face to lift her airways from the mud, and they came away sticky with blood. She made a slight upward inclination of the nose and jaw, without moving the neck, but saw that her nitrile gloves had left a smear of blood on her chin. In repose, this was a timeless face on the verge of womanhood, one that would have inspired Botticelli. She reached inside the girl's mouth with a finger, and made sure the tongue was forward. There was blood, lots of it, in the mouth, but she was breathing.

'It's all right, it's going to be all right,' she crooned into the girl's ear, far from certain there was going to be any truth in that reassurance. 'Can you wiggle your toes?'

No response. Her breathing was barely discernible, and the pulse seemed faint.

She considered trying to turn her into the recovery position but feared spinal damage. Was this the girl the householder had glimpsed? Or was she thrown from the car? To be thrown thirty yards indicated a very high-speed collision, with severe head and neck injuries almost inevitable. She felt tears prick her eyes. The girl radiated an ageless, innocent beauty, a pristine prototype for all humanity. And now Talantire realised who she was.

Almost ten years ago, on the Penypul estate. A six-year-old child under her supervision crayoning on scraps of paper, while another officer took her mother into the kitchen to break the news of her eldest son's near-fatal drug overdose while in Winson Green prison. She remembered to this day, the child pricking up her ears at her mother's soft sobs behind the door. Talantire had guided the girl's errant and distracted hand, her soft biscuity warmth drifting up to her, as she had helped her write her name amid the images of hearts and puppies: Leanne.

Leanne Moyle.

She *had* to live.

Two green-clad paramedics with a bodyboard were with her within a minute, and she surrendered the girl to their expertise. But first she grabbed the pink iPhone. The last received call was still showing. It was marked 'Mum'. She made a note of the number, before the message disappeared. There was no handbag, no purse, no form of ID, just whatever was on the phone. Her whole life, if she was like every other teenager.

Chapter Three

In the Penypul estate, at the bottom of Church Close, where it joined Wheal Terrace, there used to be a pond in which children splashed about looking for pennies. Bryony Hill had drowned there aged three in 2013, and the following year it was filled in by the council. The oak sapling planted there in memoriam – in concrete with minimal soil – had died in weeks from lack of water, but there was always a bunch of plastic flowers tied there, and a mouldering teddy bear.

The estate was hemmed in by moorland at the top and the London to Penzance railway line at the bottom, but within it was a theme park of killer hills, made for daredevil bike races, gravel-surfing on toboggans for the lack of snow, and impromptu skateboard and parkour competitions. Talantire had witnessed the sound of heavy gear changing and hard acceleration from inside the adjacent Ressell Rise homes of the Moyles and the Jagos. So steep was the road that Joyce Jago could look out of the side window of her kitchen and keep an eye on the Moyle kids playing next door in the upstairs back bedroom.

The deceitfully named Church Close had the worst hill of all, leading up at a one-in-four gradient to the scout hut, where the road stopped and a set of steep stairs continued on to St Cuby's parish church. All this made God hard to reach and quick to escape from, as older residents said, explaining the estate's wildness. In one storied episode, the Hill family, all five young 'Hillocks' as they were known, and their drink-addled dad Pete, rode a wheeled settee, liberated from the front garden of number 48, all the way down to Carr Avenue, only to collide with the kerb opposite and hit a Ford Escort. So frequently were parked cars on that road damaged that it became known as Avenue Carr, because so many residents needed to. The eldest Hillock, Jason, nine, wore his dentures with pride afterwards, as he had learned to fly. Pete, pre-equipped with false teeth, was rumoured to have swallowed his own.

She recalled a funeral, when trying to get the coffin of Uncle Tony Moyle out of the house, up Ressell Rise and into Church Close, the shuffling steps on the steep path and then the tiny rarely used church, its graveyard a tangled mess of Jagos and Moyles and Kernows, gravestones as tipsy as their descendants. Another time, she recalled the arrest at home of Scarlett's estranged father, drunk as a lord and seeking to find and damage his wife's rumoured new boyfriend. Above the mayhem, she saw little Scarlett, just seven, lining up her dolls at the bannisters to watch this stranger being frogmarched out, never to return.

–

Talantire made her way back into the garden just as three ambulances were departing with casualties, blue lights flashing. She caught up with Hammerson, who was overseeing the removal of the hydraulic jacks which had prised open the rear of the vehicle.

'I just need to get some forensic samples, if you can give me five minutes,' she said.

'All right.' He turned to his crew and bellowed: 'Stand back, everyone, for five minutes, take a breather.'

'Any survivors from inside?' she asked, as casually as she could.

'Yes. The front passenger, male, has sadly passed away, but the other three are alive but critical; the male driver's left leg was severed when the engine block moved into the passenger compartment. A female in the back is unconscious, with head injuries. The young girl who was extricated at the start is intermittently conscious, and they're all being moved to the specialist unit at University Hospital Plymouth.'

'So with the one that I found on the moor, there were five of them crammed in there.'

'Seems so,' Hammerson said. 'Christ, I could do with a fag.'

'And I need a coffee. But I'll get my samples first.'

Talantire retrieved her forensic case and set to work on the outside of the car: fingerprint gel lifts from the boot lid, each door handle, or those that she could find. On the oily underside of the car, someone had placed a pink high-heeled sandal, dotted with blood, its strap torn. She found the car roof on its edge by the garden wall where it had been cut and removed. She took gel lifts on each edge above the door frames, hoping for fingerprints. The inside of the roof told its own story: the white material badly ripped in places, bloodstains caked with matted hair, and bejewelled with window glass, like some ghastly art project. In the stickier patches of human blood were a couple of teeth, a hooped earring, a lipstick, an earbud and some tablets. The pills were mauve, with a little smiley face. She was pretty sure they were MDMA: ecstasy. She placed evidence markers and took pictures. Youngsters,

23

possibly high on drugs, in a fatal car crash. Now there definitely was a CID angle.

–

Having retrieved as much evidence as she could, Talantire headed indoors, where the dining room had been turned into an evidence collection point. Three police officers were busy with plastic evidence bags, writing up what had been found. This included a wallet, a pair of broken sunglasses, the remains of a charm bracelet, a hairband, a smashed wristwatch. Finally, a matching pink sandal to the one she'd already seen, but this time crushed flat. Despite her best efforts, the documentation wasn't quite up to normal crime-scene standards, with photos but only her few markers for the location of each find. The three phones recovered so far sat apart. Campbell had decided against officers answering the calls which came in sporadically on them.

While the dining room was a hive of activity, the drawing room was closed off. A female officer just emerged, finger to her lips, carefully shutting the door behind her. She smiled at Talantire and said: 'Mr Llewellyn's finally dozed off, poor old chap, sitting in his armchair under a blanket. I had to take his tea out of his hand, so he doesn't let the mug drop. It's been a bit much for him, I'm sure. His carer is on the way, and we've managed to get hold of his niece who lives in Liskeard.'

–

Talantire, finally able to secure a coffee for herself, made her way out of the house. A woman, wearing a cardigan over what looked to be a dressing gown, was standing by the police crime tape. With her was a large, bearded man, wearing a sweatshirt and jogging trousers, and there were raised voices with two police constables. The name Jade kept being mentioned. The woman must be the mother of one of the girls.

'I've rung four times, so I got Gary to drive me over from Camborne to speak to you in person. I'm terrified she was in that car, because she knows them, and she's not come home. And she's reliable, she always texts me if she's not coming in. Are you sure you've not found her anywhere?'

Talantire approached and introduced herself. The woman, whose name was Meghan Kernow, seemed relieved that anybody wanted to hear what she had to say. 'We can go and sit in a patrol car with a little privacy,' Talantire said.

She found a vehicle, with a constable sitting in it scrolling through his phone. She asked to borrow the car and also if he could find them both a cup of coffee. With only a little resentment, the young officer surrendered the vehicle and made his way into the house, followed by the bearded man. Talantire ushered Meghan into the back and sat side-by-side with her. A fortyish-woman with a tired face and straggly hair, her hands were trembling, and she kept wiping away tears.

'Thank you so much,' she said, resting a beringed hand upon Talantire's own. 'I felt I was wasting my time and that no one was listening. Jade needs her epilepsy medication, twice a day, and I don't think she's got any with her. This is her latest lot.' She took from her bag a packet of tablets which showed an unbroken seal, marked Sunday. Meghan then showed her a picture of Jade on her phone. She was a striking-looking girl, with intelligent brown eyes and thick golden curls down to her shoulder. Behind her confident smile, she had the mien of a determined and wilful woman, with few teenage self-doubts. Seventeen going on twenty-seven.

Talantire got out her phone, indulged Meghan repeating a few more loops of complaints about police not taking her report seriously, then urged her to take a deep breath and start from the beginning. Only then did she turn the voice statement app on and give the details of who she was interviewing.

'Let's start with the good news,' Talantire began. 'We've got everybody out of the car, five of them, and your daughter was not among them. However, you say your daughter is missing and that she knows some of the occupants. Is that correct?'

'Yes. She is best friends with Leanne, because they used to go to school together. She also knows Scarlett pretty well, though they fell out recently.'

'When did you last see your daughter?'

'Tea time yesterday. I knew she was going out, which was good. She and her boyfriend broke up four months ago, and she'd been a bit moody until the last few weeks. So now she was socialising again I was pleased for her, and her mood had brightened.'

'But you had no idea where she was going?'

'No. She gets annoyed if I even ask.'

The patrol officer returned with two mugs of coffee, which he passed to the two women in the back of the car.

Meghan calmed down a bit, and Talantire was eventually able to get a bit more structure into the evidence: Jade had left home at six, had texted her mother just after nine, and there was no message after that. She took a note of the missing girl's phone number and messaged the details to Primrose with a request to get a cell tower trace.

'In an hour's time we'll know where that phone is,' Talantire said. 'And as we know with youngsters, they are never far from their phones.'

'Yes, but what if she has a fit? She needs her medication to stop the seizures. And she is a hundred per cent reliable about taking it. That's why this all seems so wrong.'

Talantire's own disquiet mirrored the mother's. Five in the car accounted for. Could there have been six?

–

After completing the statement, Talantire took a break and wandered out of Bodmin Rectory to get away from the noise and the carnage, to think and deal with her own memories of working with the victims. The remarkable thing about these wild kids growing up on the Penypul estate was that they were never far from trees and streams, hedges and woodland. Places to grow up outside like real children should. They played in the streets, in each other's gardens, in sheds, dens and the inside of abandoned cars up the road at the entrance to Torrick's farm, which was always half blocked with discarded fridges and other stuff that you had to pay to get rid of at the tip.

Penypul was where the trainee Talantire had learned something important: that the police are not really an organisation designed to deal with crime. They are in fact just the heavy-end branch of social services, clearing up the consequences of families with chaotic lives, weighed down by poor life choices, mental health episodes and a big dose of bad luck. Crime, in the way that it is measured, is only the scar visible to society. But the wounds beneath are within families, and that's where the hurt is.

Not that she was immune to that herself.

If her mother's own attention had not been so focused elsewhere, she might have listened to Jan, then an eight-year-old, murmuring complaints about Mr Pye. Len Pye – uncle Lenny, as he called himself – was the next-door neighbour with a wife dying of cancer, who used to babysit Jan, and sometimes her older brother Richard after school. This happened when her father was working away and her mother had a late shift at the hospital. She recalled the embrocation smell of Lenny's house, the big waxed jacket hung by the door, being asked to sit on his lap while they watched TV. Lenny was a retired naval officer, with a huge pale head with white hairs greased like wire crossing a scabby scalp, which showered dandruff in all directions. He had told her many tales of running away to sea, becoming a fifteen-year-old merchant seaman on the Arctic convoys to Russia in World War Two, and later sailing to the West Indies on the *Ark Royal* aircraft carrier. He was treated with huge respect by her mother for the dedicated care he gave his bedridden wife who had bone cancer. Talantire remembered like it was yesterday the revulsion of his touch, which only happened on the occasions when her brother wasn't there. While watching TV, Uncle Lenny had combed Jan's long dark hair, which he said was beautiful and set off her big blue eyes. She'd had a premonition of distaste even at that time, while being literally groomed.

She often wondered how many Mr Pyes there might be, operating behind closed doors, creating the kind of damaged kids who would later come to police attention, here and elsewhere. She herself was one of those kids. Perhaps it was only luck that had brought her to the right side of the law. It could easily have gone the other way.

Chapter Four

It had been a hard night, and everyone was exhausted, but there were urgent matters to resolve, so an eight a.m. multi-agency meeting was called in the Liskeard Police Station, chaired by Chief Inspector Campbell. Crammed into the small meeting room were Fire Chief Greg Hammerson, and Kate Brownlow, the head of Social Services for Camborne and Redruth. With them were first responder Stef Metcalfe, and Devon and Cornwall Police media chief Moira Hallett. On Zoom from Plymouth were two male NHS Trust managers, and from Nottingham they had private-sector accident investigator Doug Blackstone. From Camborne, they had the head of community policing, Sergeant Beatrice Dodds, a flinty, no-nonsense type who Talantire had worked with before.

'Right, everybody,' Campbell said. 'Thank you all for being here for an early start. This is an active ongoing inquiry, still in its early stages. There are several young people on life support, and as you can see from the crowds by the crime scene, this is a massive public relations challenge. There is much to do, and it needs to be done quickly but professionally.'

There was a lot of nodding from the bigwigs from the NHS and, indeed, Hammerson.

'Here's what we know. On Thursday night, a Mercedes was stolen from an address in Truro, and was reported as such first thing Friday morning. That same vehicle was caught on ANPR cameras on the A30 heading west into Redruth at 3:21 on Friday morning. There was no sign of it for the next thirty-six hours. Then, at 11:53 on Saturday night, it triggered the same cameras, this time heading for Bodmin, at speeds of up to 110 mph. It took the A38 to Liskeard at 1:46 on Sunday morning, according to the last ANPR camera. We now know it turned off north towards the hamlet of St Trenewan. As many of you are aware, this is the county's worst joyrider accident blackspot, because of the long straight running up to Vinegar Hill Corner. The car left the road at 2:17 this morning, was in collision with a telegraph pole and came to rest upon its roof thirty yards away inside a glasshouse at Bodmin Rectory.' He glanced at Talantire and Stef Metcalfe, before saying, 'We were extremely fortunate to have a very prompt response by DI Talantire, who was off duty, but came in during our time of need, aided by our excellent first responder here. They not only performed essential medical interventions at the scene but were able to quickly direct the breadth of response required.'

Campbell then described the technical extrication of casualties conducted by the fire service, and said: 'We have now identified all five casualties – three of whom are residents from the Penypul estate in Camborne. The injured are Leanne Moyle, sixteen, who was found on the moor, Scarlett Jago, sixteen, Lily Jago, thirteen, and the driver of the vehicle, fourteen-year-old Aaron Darracombe. Jordan Bailey, sixteen, who was sitting in the front passenger seat was declared dead at the scene.'

'But I understood the front passenger was the one who actually *was* wearing a seat belt,' Kate Brownlow said.

'Yes,' Hammerson replied. 'But an unrestrained rear passenger hit him from behind. It's all too common, and was made worse because the occupants had removed the front headrests, so it was a head-on-head impact.'

'Why would they do that?' Alan Stucklingford, one of the NHS chiefs, asked. 'It's dangerous to remove the headrests.'

'It's not unknown,' said Blackstone, the crash investigator. 'It does facilitate seat swapping and physical interaction between front and rear, and it allows the rear occupants a better view of the road ahead. It's fair to say that a joyrider is the opposite end of the health and safety spectrum from a health professional. Danger to them is the thrill, not something to be avoided. It's why they do it.'

Stucklingford conceded the point with a grimace.

'What is the condition of the injured?' Kate asked.

Campbell gestured to Stucklingford, who looked down at his notes. 'Latest I have is that Lily remains semi-conscious and in a serious condition, while Aaron, Leanne and Scarlett are critical, unconscious, each with head injuries, and in Aaron's case the loss of a leg below the knee.'

'Their families have been informed, and of course our thoughts have to be with them,' Campbell said. 'This is a very distressing time, naturally. However, there is another girl missing.'

Talantire had wondered if he had been going to mention this.

'Jade Kernow, seventeen, was reported missing several hours ago,' Campbell said. 'Beatrice, can you fill us in on this?'

'There's not much more I can tell you,' she said, looking down at her notes. 'Jade lives in Truro, fifteen miles away from the others, but she is a former classmate of Scarlett Jago. Her mother knew that she'd been out last night but hadn't returned this morning. She's epileptic, and hasn't any tablets with her, so it's quite urgent she's found.'

'Actually, her mother drove over to the scene,' Talantire said. 'I interviewed her, but it seems unlikely her daughter was in the car – at least at the time of the accident.'

'It might be a coincidence,' Hammerson said. 'Hundreds of kids go on unplanned sleepovers, particularly on a Saturday.'

There were some nods of agreement around the room. Many of them had teenage kids.

'Quite possibly, but we'll know in an hour or so, I'm sure,' Campbell said.

'We have some additional information, via social media,' Beatrice added. 'There were several TikTok videos posted by Leanne last night, and shared on Facebook. We're only just wading through them, but here's one.'

The Zoom screen immediately switched to a bumpy view of the interior of a vehicle, packed with youngsters trying to make themselves heard over the deafening sound of pop music. The view shifted shakily to show three girls – one blonde, two dark-haired – their faces pressed together, pouting towards the camera. It was clear they were crammed together in the back seat of a car. A male hand intruded and got batted away amid gales of laughter. The footage was only eight seconds long and had been uploaded at 11:36 on Saturday night, three hours before the crash.

'Can we identify the three?' Campbell asked.

'Yes,' Beatrice said. 'I know them all. They are Scarlett, Leanne and a girl called Holly Skewes.'

'Can we be sure that this is from the correct car?' Talantire said.

'Ah, good point,' Campbell said, raising a finger in acknowledgement.

'It probably is,' Talantire added. 'I can see a removed headrest on the parcel shelf behind the girls.'

'About this Holly, was anyone suggesting she was in the car at the point of impact?' Hammerson asked.

'No, in fact we know where she is, and are getting a statement as we speak,' Beatrice responded.

Talantire raised her hand. 'If we can confirm Holly was in the car, or at least the car we've seen on video, for part of the journey, she may be a vital source of information. Not only for the circumstances of the accident, but also witness to whether any drugs were supplied or taken by the driver.'

'What drugs?' Hammerson said.

'These,' Talantire said, holding up a small plastic bag, which contained a dozen or more mauve pills. 'I found a number of tablets at the scene – two of which were embedded in bloodstains on the inside of the roof panel, which indicates they were in the car at the point of impact. They have a known imprint – this little smiley face – which is indicative of an MDMA tablet.'

'Ecstasy,' Campbell said.

'So many inappropriate happy words for such a grim event,' Kate said. 'Joyriders, ecstasy. My caseworkers in deprived areas like Camborne are constantly struggling to get kids away from such temptations.'

'Here's another video,' Beatrice said. 'Posted on Scarlett's own Instagram, TikTok and Facebook pages, earlier on the Saturday.'

The video of Scarlett showed her dancing in her bedroom to a Shakira number. A leggy girl, with a model's body, short skirt and cropped top, she had all the professional moves: pouting to the camera, writhing sideways to the Latin beat with her back to a mirror which gave her a double image, jiggling her breasts, swinging her long, black ponytail and rhythmically swaying her hips. She added her own rap lyrics. 'Here's what I've got to say, to those who call me names, they're jealous of me now and they feel no kind of shame. I do what I want, yeah, it ain't no kind of stunt. Rhyme up that line, yeah? You motherfucking...' As she finished, her face moved near to the camera, her dark eyes and heavy eyebrows fixing the viewer, before a final snarl as it ended, leaving the inevitable closing word absent.

Hammerson's mouth was hanging open, whether transfixed by the jailbait sexuality or by the violence of her expression wasn't clear. 'I've got a daughter two years younger than that,' he breathed, shaking his head. 'Is this what I've got to look forward to?'

Campbell smiled at him. 'You can't live your children's lives for them, the last thing they ever want is advice.'

'Well, if Scarlett survives, there may be a change of heart,' said Kate. 'It might be the silver lining in this awful cloud.'

Talantire pointed her pen at the screen. 'This video may be important. Scarlett clearly has enemies and she is warning them. We need to know who they are.'

'I saved this one until last,' Beatrice said. 'It's from Scarlett's TikTok account but was posted on Leanne's Facebook page just before midnight.'

The video began with the *Mission Impossible* theme tune and a view towards the back parcel shelf of the same car. It was screeching around the brightly lit car park of the local Asda, turning doughnuts, tyres smoking. Lily was lifted up horizontally along the rear seats by a forest of girls' hands and gradually passed left across the camera and fed out through the open rear window of the car. The skinny adolescent slid her arms, head and then shoulders out of the window, and then slithered further until she was sitting on the open window, her legs held by the other girls.

'That is so dangerous,' Kate said, her hands steepled across her face. Even Hammerson had a hand across his mouth.

The view changed as someone passed the phone out to Lily. There was a quickening and dizzy arc of the large, almost empty car park as the Mercedes circled at speed. The engine was screaming almost as loudly as Lily, and smoke from the tyres obscured the view. Lily turned the phone on herself, leaning outwards like a windsurfer, from the centripetal force. The car then headed to one end of the car park and turned around for a full dragster-type acceleration. The phone gave a quick view of Holly Skewes, at the opposite window, red hair flying in the wind, beckoning across to her. The phone was passed to Holly, who then videoed Lily crawling across the roof to the driver's side, while the car raced at insane speed around a service road behind the Asda.

'Never seen this on film before,' Hammerson said, shaking his head in horror. 'They have no fear.'

Lily was spreadeagled face-down across the roof, as the car turned a sharp right, her arms held in Holly's free hand, and one trailing foot by another girl, who, as she gradually emerged, turned out to be Scarlett. The last view was of Lily's legs, held vertically by Holly, giggling, and somehow wriggling back into the car headfirst. A huge cheer could be heard.

'Could you see that, Doug?' Campbell asked the crash investigator.

'Yes. If we need to, we should be able to get the exact location from the car's infotainment system, which would have logged GPS data,' Blackstone said. 'Even if the system was smashed to pieces by the impact, significant data, including GPS position, should still be retrievable from the manufacturer's servers.'

'Moira,' Campbell said to the PR chief. 'We are going to stick to the minimum of information at the moment, but undoubtedly the press will scour Facebook and find names.'

'Yes, it will undoubtedly emerge as "named locally",' she replied. 'I'm going with "in intensive care" and "life-changing injuries", which we at least know will be the case with Aaron Darracombe, right?'

'That's right, Moira,' said Stucklingford. 'Paramedics had to remove the remains of his lower left leg at the scene. He remains in a critical condition.'

'So that about wraps it up,' Campbell said, tapping his papers on the table.

The NHS people and the fire chief were already beginning to stand up.

Talantire called out: 'What about Jade Kernow? Do we pursue the missing girl separately?'

Campbell turned first to Hammerson, and then to the screen, where Beatrice was still online. 'Do we have anything on Jade?' he asked her.

'The team has just finished interviewing Holly Skewes. She hadn't seen her that day and she wasn't in the car.'

'Well, I don't think we need to worry about it too much then,' Campbell said. 'I would suggest community police follow it as a separate incident.'

'Hang on a minute,' Talantire said, turning to Stef Metcalfe. 'Mr Llewellyn, the witness, said he saw a girl running from the scene. That could have been Jade.'

'That's right,' Stef said. 'He said it was just as he was opening his own front door.'

'Wasn't that Leanne, the girl on the moor?' Campbell said, as he stood up.

'I think Leanne was thrown out of the car, I don't think she ran,' Stef said. 'I don't think anyone could have got out of that mangled car.'

'All right,' Talantire said, trying to make herself heard over the scraping of chairs. 'I'm going back to speak to him.'

–

Half an hour later, Talantire sat with PC David Cawthorpe on the sofa in the elegant front room, as the old man's niece, Daphne, and his carer, Bridget, bustled around in the kitchen making tea and coffee. 'You want more biscuits, Bill?' Bridget called out.

The old man adjusted his position slightly, his liver-spotted hand straying to the hearing aid which looped over the top of his right ear. He was wearing a neatly ironed white shirt with a V-neck pullover and blue military-style trousers, with creases sharp enough to cut. His black shoes were polished to a high sheen.

'She asked whether you'd like more biscuits,' Talantire said.

'No, I've had enough.'

'Did you get some sleep?'

'No, not much. I kept thinking about those poor youngsters. So awful.'

She looked down at her notes. 'So I'm sorry, Bill, I realise you already said this to the officers as they arrived, but can we start again at the top, because I want to make sure we get this exactly right. I want to make sure we get your name right too.'

'Formally, I'm Brigadier William Morgan Llewellyn, DSO DFC and Bar, retired. Everyone calls me Bill, except my few remaining army colleagues, who know me as Taffy.'

'I understand you are ninety-eight years old?'

'I am indeed, sixth of June. It was my birthday on D-Day.'

Talantire nodded. 'So what was the first you knew about the crash?'

'I heard an almighty noise, which woke me up at 02:17 hours.'

'You're sure about that?' asked PC Cawthorpe. 'You told me 2:19 earlier. I realise it must've been very confusing.' He smiled at the old man, who visibly stiffened.

'I suggest it is you, Constable, who is confused. I told you it was 02:19 hours when I emerged from the house to attend to the accident. It was 02:17 hours when I awoke.'

'My mistake, sorry.' He visibly shrank back.

'Granted.'

'Tell me about what you heard?' Talantire encouraged.

'Well, it took me right back to Normandy. It was a whoosh, then an almighty impact. It sounded exactly like a German 88mm anti-aircraft shell, which, as you probably know, they used to great effect as an anti-tank weapon. I could also hear very loud popular music. It took me half a second to realise where I was, and I got up to go to the window.'

'Which bedroom is that?' Talantire asked.

'I sleep down here, on the upright chair,' he said, pointing to a large wing chair. 'Since 2008 when I had a burglar. Need to defend the damn place. Anyway, I can't easily get upstairs now, even with my walker. I sleep fully dressed, as you see me now. I like to think I'm always ready, but I didn't think it would be for this. So I walked to the window and flung open the curtains. I saw the broken telegraph pole and some debris. It was only when I peered to the right-hand side that I saw a white Mercedes saloon upside down in the middle of the greenhouse. Even inside the house, I could hear awful, awful screaming, louder than the music.'

'And that was when you tried to ring for help,' Cawthorpe said, looking at his notes.

'Yes, I picked up the receiver but couldn't get a dial tone. There isn't even a whisper of mobile reception in the house, and often not in the garden. I pressed my emergency pendant, and it seemed dead too, presumably because of the damage to the telegraph pole. But I left them a quick message, saying it was a car accident.'

'In fact, it did register at the call centre,' Talantire said. 'They tried to speak to you, but it seems you didn't hear.'

He shrugged. 'Anyway, I headed out into the garden, on my walker. No sooner had I opened the front door, when I saw movement, and someone slip out of the gateway.'

'Not near the car?'

'No, but running away from it.'

'Can you describe the person you saw?'

'My impression is that it was a woman, or girl, with long hair. The proximity light above the porch was on, which showed the movement sensor had been activated. She turned her head to me, then back towards the car, and then ran off, through the gate.'

Talantire scrutinised Bill's face while Cawthorpe made looping longhand notes. There were still a few wisps of carefully combed hair across his liver-spotted pate. He was solidly built and hadn't yet lost bulk, which so many elderly people do. And he was with it. She had very rarely come across a witness with such precise and accurate recall.

'Did you see or hear any other vehicles?' she asked.

'No.'

'Are you sure? Joyriders often like to race each other.'

'Yes. There were no headlights, no other music, no revving.'

'What did you do after seeing the girl?' she asked.

'Well, I could hardly chase her. She seemed to be fine, so I headed off to where the screaming was coming from. Fortunately, the proximity light was still on, so I could see. Looking at the state of the car, I found it almost impossible to believe anyone could have survived. It was on its roof, flattened at the front, and as I approached the rear door I could see blood splattered all over the inside of the glass. And this screaming was awful, and upsetting. However, after my time in the hellhole of Caen, I can tell you there is a qualitative difference between the sound of the dying, which is often an unearthly death rattle, and the more recognisable racket of the lightly injured and the terrified. This was of the latter variety. So I decided to take immediate action. I took out my Browning, and crouching down, used the butt of it to break—'

Cawthorpe ceased his notetaking and looked up. 'You have a gun?' he asked.

'Yes, just an old 9mm service weapon. Here it is.' The old man lifted up his jumper to reveal a holster, from which he pulled a gun and placed it on the coffee table between them.

'I'm sure you must be aware,' Talantire said, 'that the possession of a firearm is a serious offence. Do you have a licence?'

'In 1939, His Majesty gave us all a licence to bear arms in defence of this country. He never revoked it, nor indeed did his daughter. I retain it, purely should I ever be called upon again to defend our proud realm from foreign invaders. I hasten to add that I have never fired it in anger.'

'Well, I think we ought to take care of it for you,' Talantire said.

'As you wish.'

'Is it loaded?' she asked.

'Yes, but the safety catch is on.' He pointed to a lever at the rear of the device, then, with quick, skilled hands, slid out the magazine from the stock, to reveal a dozen or so bullets. He passed across the weapon, butt first. 'Totally safe now.'

He watched as she brought out an evidence bag from her pocket and gingerly eased the weapon into it.

'I'm afraid there may be legal consequences for possessing it,' she said, almost apologetically. 'We can't overlook something like this.'

'I think when you look upon the circumstances of the accident, you will be glad that I was in possession of this weapon.'

'Okay, let's get back to your statement,' she said, looking at her notes.

'Right. It took me a while to get down on my aged knees, and it took me two or three goes to break the glass. Almost as soon as I had, I saw a pale bloody hand reaching out towards me, and a change in tone of the screaming. I said: "I'm going to get you out. Can you move?" The screaming stopped, to be replaced by a kind of breathless shuddering. I lay on my side and peered into the car. It was a truly horrible sight.' He paused and retrieved a cotton handkerchief from his pocket, with which he dabbed at the corners of his eyes. 'Apologies for this,' he said.

'It's natural,' Talantire said with a smile.

'What did you see?' Cawthorpe asked.

'Apparently dead teenagers, heaped together, but moving from between the bodies, there was this hand – a tiny feminine hand, streaked with blood. For the first minute, I just held it in both of mine, and with my forefinger traced a pulse that I counted to be at least 120. I asked how old she was, and she said thirteen. "What is your name?" I asked.' He paused and dabbed his eyes, a sound came, an L, and caught in his throat.

'Sorry, what was that?' Talantire asked.

'Lily,' he replied, hoarsely. The old man swallowed hard and his hands began to shake. He dabbed his eyes again but could not stop a single tear track which ran down the side of his nose. 'Lily was the name of my fiancée. A beautiful girl, the love of my life. She died on the twenty-fifth of November 1944, killed by a V2 missile. I couldn't save her because I was fighting in France. I still think about her every day. I could never marry anybody else.'

Cawthorpe was staring open-mouthed, his pen poised in his hand.

'So, you see, I had to save Lily,' Bill continued.

Talantire nodded. 'Of course, you had to.'

'I asked Lily if she could move towards me, and she did try. I broke more of the glass, and took off my pullover so that I could hold it over the sharp edges which remained in the frame. I reached in through the window and slid my own hand along Lily's arm, until I found her shoulder. I asked her if she was in pain anywhere, and she said only in her leg. I then told her I was going to try to pull her out. Then she asked: "What about Scarlett?" I told her that I'd try for her later, but she said: "No! I don't want to leave my sister behind." I told her that was very brave of her, but that she would help them most by being able to get out safely. I said that an ambulance was on its way, though I was far from certain that was the case.'

'And you say you could still hear nothing from emergency services on your pendant?' Cawthorpe asked.

'No. I tore the damn thing off because it didn't work. I suppose because of the telegraph pole being damaged. It took me a minute or two, and I cursed myself for not having the strength I did when I was a boy, but I gradually pulled Lily out through the window. She had a deep wound to the upper leg, and from the amount of blood there, I assumed it was a femoral artery. She asked me if she was going to die, and I said, "Not if I have anything to do with it." I carried her away from the greenhouse, towards the portico, and laid her down. I took off my regimental tie and used it to tourniquet her leg, and a cane from the greenhouse to twist in it, to increase pressure. It made her scream, unfortunately, and she held on to me and then lost consciousness. I then put her in the recovery position, and checked her pulse, which was fast but fainter than before.'

'It sounds like you saved her life,' Talantire said.

'I hope so. Anyway, it was at that point that you arrived.'

'Can I just go back to the other girl you saw, the first one,' Talantire said. 'She was definitely able to run, not limping at all?'

He sat back and steepled his hands. 'No, she looked uninjured – or should I say she moved easily.'

'Can you describe her in any more detail?' Cawthorpe asked. 'Like what colour her hair was? Or her clothes?'

'I'm so sorry, it's really hard to recall. However, I do remember one thing. This short skirt… I mean, I'm not just remembering because it was short, but I think it had two brass zips down the back. It was my last view as she ran away.'

'Did you see anybody else moving about?' Cawthorpe asked.

'No.'

'Thank you,' Talantire said.

'I was just wondering, I suppose that's why it stuck in my mind. Why would a skirt need two zips?'

Talantire grinned. 'I don't think it's related to function, but to looks.'

'Ah, I see,' he said, with a nod. He clearly didn't.

Chapter Five

Primrose Chen arrived at 9:35 a.m., a little earlier than Talantire expected. She was dressed in ripped jeans and a bomber jacket, with her thick dark hair in a pony-tail tucked up and through a baseball cap. Talantire had never seen her without her trademark fawn hijab and was slightly surprised at the edgy informality. More like a joyrider, even.

'Thank you for getting here so quickly.'

'It's fine, ma'am, I didn't have to get up any earlier than usual, as it saves me ninety minutes of the journey,' she said, with her slight American twang. A native of Malaysia, her father had worked for the Royal Navy, but had then moved the family to the US, where he split from her mother. Primrose had returned with her mother to Britain, and had become her carer since she had lost mobility.

'The kiosk is over here,' Talantire said, leading the digital evidence officer to a patrol car.

A male uniformed officer inside had already set up the briefcase-sized unit, and exited the front passenger seat so that she could use it. Three mobile phones were in evidence bags ready on the seat. Primrose quickly opened the least damaged one – a Samsung model – extracted the SIM card and pressed it into the device.

Once it was clear that Primrose had everything she needed, and was able to use her secure key card to log on, Talantire left her to it. When she had first begun her career, extracting data from mobile phones required some careful liaison with the service providers, and could take many hours, if not a day or two, but now it was possible to extract call records, photos, videos, text messages and most associated metadata in just a few minutes. Digitally-savvy youngsters like Primrose were the key to a huge increase in police productivity, which was something that her own boss, Detective Superintendent Michael Wells, never ceased to enthuse about.

Talantire emerged to find that uniforms had finally got a grip on public order. A cordon had been put on the road half a mile away in both directions, verges cleared of parked vehicles, replaced by rows of blue-and-white police cones. There were no sightseers at the gates any more. All but one of the fire service tenders had departed, and there were perhaps only a dozen professionals on site. Apart from Primrose, she was the only woman.

A fire officer and most of the rest of the police had clustered around a van which had just arrived. She caught the delicious smell of hot food and spotted at the open back a tray full of bacon sandwiches and sausage baps, all wrapped in foil. Thermos flasks of hot drinks had been provided too. She made her way towards them, hearing the sound of laughter, the release of tension in the black humour that allows stressed professionals to cope. And that was another reason for clearing away the great British public. It doesn't look good to see cops chuckling at the site of tragedy. Talantire had never actually heard a joke that began with: 'Did you hear the one about the dead joyriders?' but onlookers, and worse still the press, might assume there was one.

She arrived just in time to get the last sausage bap, otherwise it would have been the dreaded Cornish pasties. Post-operational nosh always seemed to be the least healthy type. High-fat, high in carbohydrates, plenty of processed meat. Of salad, fruit or vegetables, there wasn't a sign. At work, she often brought her own lunch in, as she noticed Primrose did. Barnstaple Police Station had a kitchen but no refectory, and officers often roamed the industrial estate in search of food outlets.

She stood with the men, and noticed an immediate dampening effect on their jollity. They became a little more formal, a little less jocular. Perhaps it was her seniority, almost certainly it was being female. 'Don't mind me, lads,' she said, biting into her bap.

But they did, and whatever it was they were discussing came to an end. The men drifted away and got busy. She could smell smoke on the breath of one of them. Smoking while wearing uniform was banned in theory, but rarely enforced so long as the officer wasn't in view of the public or close to a police building.

Now, with full daylight, she returned to the place on the moor where she had found Leanne Moyle. Among the shards of plastic and broken glass, she found a ripped sock and tiny faux-leather backpack with broken straps and a smear of blood on it. She photographed everything before bagging it. She saw her own footprints, and then, looking more closely, noticed they were not the only ones. There was a line of two or three prints on one muddy track, with a definite narrow deep heel, indicative of a female shoe. Her own footprint had obscured one of the prints, indicating that it was made before she had arrived to rescue Leanne, so sometime before three a.m.

These were not prints that could have been made by the casualty herself. Leanne had been wearing trainers. So who was this? Who was here in the small hours of the morning, on Bodmin Moor wearing high-heeled shoes? Was this the missing Jade?

–

Sergeant Beatrice Dodds arrived at the smallholding at the bottom end of the Penypul estate near the stream. The Skewes' accommodation was two mildewed caravans and a shed, within a fence made of wooden pallets linked together by wire. Two goats were tethered inside a small wooden enclosure and bleated plaintively as Beatrice made her way gingerly from her patrol car to the main caravan, accompanied by a group of friendly chickens. There was a white painted tree surrounded by flowers in the small front garden, and from it was strung Tibetan-style prayer flags that rippled in the breeze. She climbed the steps of breeze blocks to the front door, and rapped sharply on it.

Skye Skewes, Holly's mother, opened the door.

'I just need to take a statement from Holly,' Beatrice said.

'That's fine, I was expecting it,' Skye said, and invited her in. She was a waif-thin woman with long, unkempt dark hair, and a complexion which spoke of decades in the sun. She was braless under her tight green T-shirt, which revealed the loss of one breast, presumably from cancer. Her daughter, a tall and more solidly built girl, appeared behind her.

The whole caravan was a mass of dreamcatchers, wind chimes and joss sticks, though the latter failed to mask the odour of cat pee. Three skinny felines stalked the room, one of them making use of the litter tray underneath the coffee table, in which Beatrice was careful not to place her feet.

Beatrice got out her notebook and smiled encouragingly at the teenager. Holly's pallid face was twisted with grief, and her big brown eyes brimming with tears, but with a little encouragement, she gave a clear account of the evening. She had started at the chip shop, and named various other youngsters who she had seen around. Her brother, Paul, and his two friends on bicycles were there, pulling wheelies. A couple of the neighbourhood lads had roared past in their own cars, as they often did to impress the girls. It was only just before ten, by Holly's reckoning, that she saw the white Mercedes she had heard about.

'I mean, this was a proper car,' she said. 'Not one of those rusting wrecks that most of the local lads have. Proper shiny, and a bit of class to it.' Her eyebrows rose, in approval. 'I hadn't believed Aaron when he messaged me to say that he got a Merc. When it come past, I thought, "yeah, let's get a ride".'

'So you say that was around ten?'

'Maybe just after?' the girl said, the rising tone betraying a lack of confidence in her answer.

'So you got in?'

The girl nodded.

'Who else was in it at that time?'

'Leanne and Scarlett, and Jordan's younger sister, Wap. She sat in the front with Aaron while Jordan drove.'

'Wap?'

Holly's mother leaned forward and explained: 'Jordan's younger sister is actually called Rhapsody, she's got a lisp. And when she was little she couldn't say her own name.'

'Yeah, everyone took the piss out of poor little Wapsody,' Holly said, with a slight twist of a smile.

'And how old is she?' Beatrice asked.

'Year eight,' Holly's mother replied.

Thirteen, Beatrice thought. What Russian roulette occurred that night: who had left the car, and who was in it at the time of the crash, who lived and who died. All so young.

'What time did you leave the car, Holly?'

'About eleven?' Again, the upspeak answer was hesitant. 'I got dropped off by the Asda, just down the road.'

'There was no sign of this girl?' Beatrice said, offering her phone for Holly to look at.

'That's Jade. I have seen her, before she moved away, but she's always too high and mighty to talk to me. She used to go out with Finlay, but she wasn't in the car.'

Beatrice knew that Meghan Kernow had moved house from Camborne to the western end of Truro a year earlier.

'She's missing, Holly. Who are her friends?'

'Leanne is the main one. I don't know any others round here.'

'Now there's something else I need to ask you about,' Beatrice said, with a note of gravity. 'Some drugs were found in the car.'

'We only had balloons,' Holly retorted. 'Nothing else.'

'No purple tablets? No ecstasy.'

'No, I never had it. I never saw it.'

'Are you sure? They were found in the car.'

'I'm sure.'

Beatrice wound up the interview. She was far from convinced the girl was telling the whole truth. Getting at what had happened wasn't going to be straightforward.

As she stood up to leave, Beatrice disturbed a wind chime, which jangled plaintively. Walking out of the caravan, she saw something on her shoe. Overspill from the cat tray.

–

Talantire was waiting for the CSI team. They had promised to be there by nine but were running an hour late because of a more urgent commitment: a stabbing at a house in Plymouth. When the van finally arrived, she showed the two officers the section of the moor where she had found the injured Leanne Moyles, and the associated heeled footprints. Talantire had herself sealed off a fifty-square-yard area of moorland with police cones that she had borrowed from the verge and some crime tape.

'Here,' she said, crouching at the edge of the enclosed area. 'This is the first footprint and it shows that the woman was following the outer edge of the wall from the roadside.'

The male forensic officer leaned over by her side. 'I can take casts of the best prints, if that's what you'd like.' He sounded unsure of the purpose.

'I think this could be evidence of the missing girl,' Talantire said. 'So, yes, let's get a cast.'

She walked back to the patrol car, where Primrose was still working away.

'Hello, ma'am,' she said, formal as ever. 'I've got requests in for cell site analysis on all three phones, and on the number that Mrs Kernow gave for her missing daughter's phone.'

'That's great, I would suggest you start with a download of all the data from the nearest tower to here, which I'm told is Colliford Lake South,' Talantire said. 'That will show everyone who's been in the area. If we confine it to an hour before and after the accident, there shouldn't be that much data.'

'No, I guess not. This is such a lonely, uninhabited place.'

'The old man who lives here says that mobile reception is really bad, and he can't get a signal in the house.'

'Yeah, but I guess on the open road, there are bound to be places where the signals kick in,' Primrose said. 'You only need a few milliseconds of connectivity to pass across the ID of the handset to the tower. I think by midday we will know exactly who was in the area.'

Talantire's phone rang. It was Sergeant Dodds, head of community policing in Camborne.

'Go ahead, Beatrice,' she answered.

'I've just interviewed Holly Skewes. As you recall, she was in the car earlier in the evening. It now seems she left while the car was still in Camborne. She recognised Jade, but isn't a friend.'

'I take it Jade hasn't turned up?'

'No. We've spoken to her ex-boyfriend. He hasn't seen her but is really concerned about her whereabouts.'

The community police sergeant said that she had secured elimination samples of DNA from a toothbrush at the home of Jade Kernow, and some fingerprints from the handle of her hairbrush.

'I'm getting the swabs couriered over to the lab. My inspector says they are to go normal, not express, unless you can provide the budget for it.'

This kind of penny-pinching was a daily hassle for Talantire, indeed anyone in CID. The basic lab service could take two days, but the same-day express service, three times the price, would get answers in hours. Jade was missing, and Talantire seemed to be the only person outside her family who was worried by it.

She rang her own boss, to get permission for the express DNA tests.

Detective Superintendent Wells, working from home as he usually did on a Sunday, was unpersuaded. 'Look, Jan, the girl is seventeen and has simply failed to show up after a Saturday night.'

'Her mother is distraught. It's quite out of character. She hasn't got her medication with her. We have to take our cues from the family. Some kids stray and others don't.'

'I disagree. We need to follow our own internal guidelines. Some mothers are just worriers; we simply don't have the resources to take every frantic phone call seriously.'

'She drove here in person from Camborne,' Talantire said flatly.

'Whatever, I've looked at your own interview notes,' he said with a long, drawn-out sigh. 'As her mother says, Jade Kernow is level-headed and sensible, with a strong streak of independence. She probably met some young man and stayed overnight, nothing more. Yes, her phone's off, but she might still be asleep, or whatever it is that teenagers get up to when they stay overnight with somebody.'

'Sir—' she began.

'Look, if she had been thirteen, it would be a different matter. If she's still missing by seven o'clock this evening, then okay, I'll give it an operational priority. I've got teenage kids, Jan, and I can assure you that by Sunday evening, however wild the weekend has been, they will return home for food.'

'I still think we need the tests express, sir,' she pressed.

'You're in good standing, Jan, after the Ruth Lyle case, but don't push it.'

'Okay, sir.' Wells was a reasonable boss, enlightened, intelligent and handily based two hours away at Middlemoor – Devon and Cornwall Police's headquarters in Exeter. That distance gave Talantire and her team a certain amount of freedom from supervision. Being micromanaged was one of Talantire's pet hates and she'd struck lucky with Wells. He was the kind of manager who would have allowed police officers to work from home, were it possible. That certainly seemed to be where he spent most of his time, according to rumour. But she would have to let this go, at least until after seven o'clock.

'You came in despite being off duty last night, didn't you?'

'Yes.'

'Thank you for your dedication, but I'm puzzled why anyone would voluntarily get out of bed at two in the morning to go to work. Unpaid.'

'It's a long story.'

'That's as may be, but I can't give you overtime, I'm afraid.'

'I hadn't expected it.'

'Well, just leave it to Campbell, it's his case. There's no significant CID angle. Look, just take the rest of the day off, because I need you in bright and early tomorrow morning to look at this epidemic of rural quad bike thefts.' He hung up.

Wells hadn't actually told her to give up on the missing girl case, merely to put it on the backburner. Talantire decided that still gave her all the freedom she needed to pursue it for now, at least in her own time. While she was thinking how to do that, Primrose leaned out of the patrol car window and called to her.

'I've got something I need to show you.'

Talantire slid into the driver's seat next to her and looked at the Aceso Kiosk screen. 'Here is a selfie, on Leanne's phone, taken on the night of the accident. I've only had a glimpse at the photos, but isn't that Jade with her?'

Talantire peered at the image, which appeared to be taken in a crowded car. 'Yes, that's right.' There were other individuals partially visible, including a mass of dark frizzy hair to the left. She didn't remember there being anyone in the car with hair like that.

'Is that the same car?' Primrose asked.

'It's hard to be sure, but if Leanne was there and the time is right, it probably is.'

'Ah, and we've just had the data dump from the cell tower,' Primrose said.

Talantire pulled out her iPad and logged into it herself. The spreadsheet simply listed a series of numbers on one tab, and on another much more complex one, the times and durations they were within range of the tower. She got Primrose to display the list of mobile numbers from the phones in the car. Each of them showed up, as expected: Aaron, Jordan, Scarlett, Leanne, Lily. She then looked at her notepad for the missing phone from Jade. She cross-referenced the number to the data.

'It's there!' Talantire exclaimed.

'So she *was* in the car after all,' Primrose said excitedly.

'Or nearby. We got a selfie which appears to show her in the car, and now cell data which seemingly reinforces it,' Talantire said. 'Though she wasn't in the car by the time I got there.'

'Maybe she was thrown out, like the other girl.'

'If so, it's hard to believe she could have just got up and walked away,' Talantire said. 'Certainly Leanne couldn't.'

'But you found those high-heel footprints?'

'I did, and I'm mystified.' She turned to Primrose. 'Look, Wells wants us to put this case on the backburner. I've got a hunch that there is a lot more going on. I would suggest that you head off to Barnstaple now for your normal shift. If you have a spare moment, I would appreciate anything that you can get from looking at those phones. It's something that the forensic accident investigators will want eventually anyway.'

'Okay.'

Talantire thanked her, then took a final look at the crash scene: the greenhouse, now completely flattened, and the broken telegraph pole, on which BT Openreach were now working, removing damaged wires. The wreckage of the vehicle had been righted, ready to be removed by transporter for forensic analysis. The roof was still on its side against the brick wall. A uniformed female evidence officer working for Campbell was walking backwards and forwards between the house and a police van, carrying trays of plastic and paper evidence bags. At some stage, she would check the log and find that she didn't have any of the mobile phones belonging to the casualties. It would probably be a good idea to let her know that CID intended to retain them, at least for a while.

Now Talantire had an important hunch that she needed to check.

Primrose called out to her, breaking her reverie: 'Are you going back to Barnstaple too? We could go together.'

Talantire smiled. 'No, I'm off duty now. So I'm going to Camborne. I want to speak to Jade's former boyfriend.'

-

While she drove, Talantire rang Beatrice on the hands-free. She had already arranged to meet her outside the Truro home of Finlay Roscoe, Jade's ex. Beatrice filled her in on his background. Considering his mother was the head teacher at a junior school, the nineteen-year-old was a naughty boy: he had come to the attention of the police at the age of eleven with some antisocial behaviour and involvement in an arson attack on the very school where his mother was teaching at the time. Fortunately, the conflagration was not too serious, but it marked him out for social services and community policing. Academically a poor achiever despite his parents' best efforts, he had been a persistent truant. The theft of a bike and possession of cannabis followed in his mid-teens, but it was a community project that put him back on the straight and narrow. A scheme to get non-academic youngsters interested in car repair turned out to be a brilliant success. He left school at sixteen, but through the project found work as an apprentice at a local garage, Yelland's. From then, everything had turned around and continued to improve after the Roscoe family moved house from Camborne to Truro a year ago. He was now a trainee manager at a pub company.

It was all that Talantire had the opportunity to digest before she arrived outside the four-bedroom detached house of his parents, in one of the smarter areas of the city. Beatrice was waiting in a patrol car outside.

'One thing I haven't had the chance to tell you,' Beatrice whispered as she pressed the doorbell. 'The car involved in the accident was registered to this address.'

'What?'

'It was stolen on Thursday, from here.'

Talantire could barely begin to process this bombshell before the door opened.

Finlay's mother, Shona, welcomed them at the door, and ushered them into a comfortable modern lounge, where the coffee table was decked with biscuits and cake and a steaming pot of coffee.

Shona was a solidly built woman with a piercing voice, who bombarded them with questions about sugar and milk and dietary requirements as if they had come to share a meal. The woman was a buzzing ball of anxiety.

'Isn't it absolutely terrible about the accident,' she said as she began to pour coffee. 'Those poor young kids.'

Talantire shifted her gaze to the settee, where Finlay, a broad and bearded young man, sat with folded tattooed arms and a slightly smug expression. Next to him was his lean, dark-haired father, David, interlaced fingers tight enough to show white at the knuckle.

'Yes, it is a terrible accident,' Beatrice said. 'And our hearts go out to everyone involved. As you may know, we've already spoken to several of the families.'

'I know, Facebook is full of it,' Shona said.

Talantire observed the small talk with a keen interest. The parents were clearly terrified. Reputationally perhaps, because of her role as a head, and maybe because of the misuse of their car, but mainly because of the son, their only child, and what he might or might not be accused of. Finlay himself seemed somehow detached. It wasn't quite a smile hovering on the edge of that light brown beard, but perhaps a look of satisfaction. He certainly didn't look worried.

'We just need answers to a few questions,' Talantire said, keen to move the conversation onwards. 'As you know, Jade Kernow, who I believe is your former girl-friend, has been reported missing. I don't think at this stage there is any cause to be alarmed, but do you have any idea where she might have been?'

'No idea. We broke up months ago.' He tightened his arms and his expression, daring Talantire to disbelieve him.

'Well, she wasn't in the car – that was the main worry, wasn't it?' Shona said, smiling to everyone in turn. Her husband nodded in vigorous agreement. 'We did so adore that girl.'

Talantire wasn't going to say anything about who was in the car, but noted Shona's use of the past tense.

She must have noticed because she added, 'When they broke up, we never saw her much again.'

'There was that one time at the Asda,' David said.

'Oh, yes. We talked to her in the car park while she was waiting for her mum to fetch a trolley,' Shona explained.

'She seemed quite down,' David added.

'Tell me about the break-up,' Beatrice asked Finlay.

He gave a kind of slow shrug, which rippled his tattoos as well as his shoulders. 'We'd been arguing a lot, about this and that, and it just kind of petered out.'

'Jade's mother says her daughter was really upset, inconsolable,' Beatrice said, glancing down at her notes.

'She was a very emotional girl,' Shona added. 'She was in tears at the Asda; we couldn't really get her to talk, could we?'

'No,' David said.

'And when was that?' Beatrice asked.

'That would have been about three months ago?' Shona asked the two men in her family.

'Dunno, I wasn't there,' Finlay said. But his father nodded.

'Was that after it became known you had begun a relationship with Scarlett Jago?' Beatrice persisted.

Talantire could see now the line that her community police colleague was pursuing. If Scarlett and Jade had fallen out over Finlay, maybe the choice of car to be stolen was not random.

'Wasn't exactly a relationship,' Finlay smirked, seemingly eager to parade his prowess. A shadow passed over his mother's face. 'More a one-night stand.'

'Which particular night?' Talantire asked. It hadn't escaped her notice that Finlay hadn't shown the supposed concern about Jade's disappearance that Beatrice had mentioned.

'It was a couple of nights before Jade and me broke up.'

Both parents looked aghast.

Beatrice intervened: 'Two-timing a woman isn't illegal, though it's hardly something to be proud about, Finlay. But why I'm here today is to try to find out if Jade's state of mind had something to do with her disappearance.'

'I'm not the person to ask,' Finlay said.

For once, Talantire had to agree, it was Jade's friends who would have the inside track on how she felt. Unfortunately, many of them were lying close to death in a hospital in Plymouth.

'Finlay, where were you between the hours of midnight and three a.m. last night?' Talantire asked.

'Staying at my new girlfriend's place,' he said. How he was enjoying this, Talantire thought. And how the parents were dying inside. The father had one hand fluttering over his face.

'What's her name and address?' she continued.

'Ellie Symmonds. She lives just opposite,' he said, jerking his thumb over his shoulder.

'Number six,' Shona clarified.

'And she will confirm that?'

'Yeah, as will her little brother. We woke him up and he banged on the wall.' He smirked again.

Was it possible for Finlay's parents to shrivel any more? Shame is a peculiar sentiment, sometimes more powerful at one remove than in the instigation of the act. Emotional arson in which love is the accelerant.

'We need to do a DNA swab to eliminate you from our inquiries,' Beatrice said, bringing out a sample kit.

Finlay shrugged again but conceded, leaning forward for Beatrice to run the cotton bud around the inside of his cheek.

She was about to put it away again, when Talantire added: 'We need both of yours too, to eliminate you from any samples found inside the crashed car.' She could see in her peripheral vision that Beatrice seemed caught off guard. Damn, should have spent some time co-ordinating.

'This is all a bit rich frankly,' David said, his blue eyes blazing. 'I reported the bloody theft first thing Friday, and knew where it was because of the tracker. But as of yesterday afternoon, and after chasing three times, the police said they hadn't even allocated the case. No one's been round here to help us solve the crime, now you lot want to get samples off us.'

'We appreciate your frustration,' Talantire said levelly. 'I don't suppose it's helpful to spend any time detailing our resourcing issues, but we are where we are. DNA samples will definitely help us isolate anyone else who has used your car. It allows us to subtract known and legitimate users of the vehicle from all the rest.'

'I get it,' David said. 'But still.'

'We'd like to see your car too, Finlay,' Talantire added. It was another thing she should have mentioned to Beatrice but hadn't had the opportunity.

It was the first moment the lad seemed alarmed. 'Why? I walked over to Ellie's, didn't I?'

'Finlay, stop arguing,' his father warned. He led them outside to the drive, where a silver Audi hire car and a metallic blue three-year-old Peugeot sat either side of an aged black Vauxhall Nova. Talantire clocked the Nova immediately for lads' wheels: cut-down chassis, and although she couldn't see it from where she was standing, she was pretty certain it would have an illegally modified exhaust. She made a note of the registration number and took a photograph.

'It's all legit,' Finlay complained.

His mother turned on him. 'With one person dead and four in hospital, your thoughts should be with them, Finlay. I think it's time you grew up.'

Talantire wholly concurred. The two officers said their thank yous, walked down to the street and debriefed in Talantire's car.

'I'll chase up the girlfriend opposite,' Beatrice said. 'What's your interest in his car?'

'I'm just going to run it through the ANPR system. If he's been lying to us, we need to know where he's been. There are three cameras between here and Liskeard, and I hope for his sake that he didn't trip them last night.'

Chapter Six

Talantire got home to Barnstaple by two, just a few hours left of a precious Sunday afternoon to have to herself. She felt emotionally drained by what she had seen last night and couldn't stop thinking about the youngsters who had been caught in that car. She drank a bottle of water and then tore off her work clothes, dumping them on her bed. She went to the laundry basket and pulled out her running gear. One more use wouldn't matter.

It was a five-minute turnaround from her arrival to leaving again, following the alleyway that led down to the B road over the back. The path ran between the side of a disused petrol station and an industrial unit, and as she splashed through the first muddy section, she considered it was untypically warm for a British summer's day, and humid with it after a heavy shower an hour ago. She fell into a stride quite quickly, feeling energised and positive. She passed two walkers coming the other way, just by the finger post. She usually took the low short path along the edge of Watchett Woods, but this afternoon fancied the steeper track through the centre of the Forestry Commission area – the one that was too muddy year round to attract many of the dog walkers. It then led on to the uncompromising stony track as it rose over to Oxcombe, and then a long haul up Modge Hill, which always tested her hamstrings. The full loop was a little over four miles.

It was only when she got to the top and stood hands on hips gasping for breath that she allowed herself to think about Jade Kernow. She had no idea whether the girl had turned up or not. She couldn't contest Wells' judgement that most seventeen-year-olds absent over a weekend would turn up by Sunday night. But there was something about this girl, and her mother's insistence that she was reliable, that had tied a knot of anxiety in Talantire's gut.

She gazed over Barnstaple, and the distant sheen of the River Taw, winding out westwards to the sea. Then she headed for home, eating up the distance on the downhill section.

Back home, she showered, washed her hair and dumped the now filthy running gear back in the laundry basket. Only when she had dug out a ready meal of lasagna from the fridge did she turn back to her phone and scroll through work messages.

The first was from Chief Inspector Campbell to all those at the meeting, which declared that Police and Crime Commissioner Lionel Hall-Hartington had decided to give a press briefing at five p.m. about the accident. That in itself was uncontroversial, but rather than use the conference facilities at Middlemoor, the commissioner had insisted that he wanted to do it at the site of the crash so that, behind him, the mangled remains of the car could still be seen. Campbell's message coolly labelled this approach 'unusual', clearly code for unwise. Police protocol in managing the message in serious incidents was well established: keep it simple, keep it clear and use passive language to drain the emotion from the situation. She had heard police press chief Moira Hallett make this case time and time again. Instead, by using the wreckage of the car as a prop, presumably to warn the public about the dangers of speeding, the commissioner risked inflaming public opinion. Hallett had replied to the post simply by using an emoji of an anxious face with hands over its eyes.

The next message was from the road safety officer who had checked the ANPR cameras for her. While Finlay Roscoe claimed to be staying overnight with the girl opposite, his car told a different tale. It had been racing east along the A30 at around one a.m., just a few minutes after the stolen Mercedes full of joyriders. However, it did not show up any further east than the town of Bodmin. It had not triggered the final camera before the turn-off north to St Trenewan. Nevertheless, this seemed to blow a huge hole in Finlay's alibi, something that surprised Talantire not one bit.

The final message was a short one from Sergeant Dodds. Jade was still missing, her phone still switched off. If the girl didn't show up by seven p.m., just over two hours hence, an official missing persons inquiry would begin.

This was getting serious. Even Wells would admit that now.

—

Talantire was sitting on her sofa, a mug of coffee in her hand, when she turned on BBC regional news in time for the police briefing. The commissioner stood in the gateway of Bodmin Rectory, with members of the families to one side and the almost unrecognisable remains of the car visible behind him. It looked more like a funeral, with the Honourable Lionel wearing a black suit and black tie, his thinning grey hair fluttering in the breeze above his jowly gammon face, as he read from a prepared statement.

'Ladies and gentlemen of the press, behind me here we see the tragic consequences of car crime, which, as many of you will already know, has led to the death of one young person, and four others fighting for their lives. In every town and city and village up and down the country, young lives are being squandered.'

This wasn't a police briefing, it was a political statement. She could just imagine that Moira had tried and failed to get him to stick to the usual script. Hall-Hartington had been elected only just over a year ago. As a prominent Devon dairy farmer, county councillor, political contributor and the owner of the nationally known Sleepy Monk cheese brand, he felt he had his 'finger on the pulse'. She had actually heard him say that, when he addressed staff at Barnstaple Police Station. She just hoped he wouldn't use that phrase now, in front of anxious relatives, where at least one pulse was gone forever.

He didn't, thankfully. But he didn't quite take questions either, leaving them to Chief Inspector Campbell.

The first question was fairly predictable: 'A young woman called Jade Kernow is still missing. Is it your understanding that she was in the car when it crashed?'

Campbell's discomfort was obvious. 'That is something we are still investigating,' he said.

'Something that you lot are only just *starting* to let me investigate!' Talantire shouted at the TV.

The report cut back to the studio, and Talantire pointed the remote and killed it, before tossing the device onto the settee. Shouting at the TV news, maybe it was another thing she had inherited from her late father.

She gulped down her lasagna, tossed her plate into the washing-up bowl and ran back upstairs to change into her work gear. She wasn't due on shift until nine a.m.

tomorrow morning, and was already booked into a big serious accidents meeting at ten. But she couldn't wait that long. They'd missed at least eight precious hours to find the missing girl thanks to the caution and procrastination of senior cops. Messrs Campbell and Wells may have followed the rules, but they hadn't spoken to Mrs Kernow. Jade could now be wandering on the moor, with concussion, or lying somewhere having had a seizure. She could have fallen into a ditch. It was still possible to get exposure up there even in midsummer, especially if you were injured. If she ended up dead, for whatever reason, because of the delay, there would be hell to pay.

–

Beatrice answered Talantire's call on the first ring, and had fresh information. Finlay's girlfriend supported his alibi, unsurprisingly, but there was no proof Jade's ex-boyfriend was in the house all night. He could easily have taken his car, which was parked just a few yards away at his own home. Beatrice said she hadn't rung Meghan Kernow for a couple of hours, but she would have been notified if Jade had turned up.

'That's fine. I've just got some other questions to ask her,' Talantire said. 'Have you disclosed that Jade's phone was up at Bodmin Moor the same time as all the others?'

'No. I didn't see how it would help at this stage.'

'I agree,' Talantire said. 'I don't want this kind of information leaking out into the wider community, and once you tell the family, you can forget about confidentiality. It just becomes a rumour mill.'

Talantire thanked her and hung up, then tapped out the Kernow family landline. It was answered immediately by

Gary, one of Jade's uncles. She began to introduce herself, but he interrupted.

'Have you found her?'

'No, I just want a little bit more information about her.'

'I'll put Meghan on.'

'What are you lot doing?' Jade's mother said without introduction. 'There was no mention of her on the police press conference until the press asked.'

'I know, it's just we have certain rules—'

'My only child is missing and no one cares!'

'We do care and that's why I'm ringing you. I'm on the case and will stay on it, I promise.'

'Why has it taken until now?'

'Look, Mrs Kernow hundreds of people go missing every day, and the vast majority turn up. There are certain thresholds to meet—'

'—Bureaucracy.'

'—for someone to be classified as missing.'

Talantire gave up trying to justify the delay, in the face of Meghan's anger. There was no point telling her that she had wanted to start the search eight hours ago, even less point in telling her that she was actually making this call in her own time, while she was off duty. Listening to this terrified, combative and ultimately courageous woman, she soon became aware how desperately this family needed a family liaison officer to reassure them and act as a single point of contact. But until the case was official, there couldn't be one.

'Meghan, what was Jade wearing when she went out?'

'I don't know. I had a quick look through her wardrobe, but she's got so much stuff. Gary, you saw her on the way out, what was she wearing?'

'No idea,' he called out. 'I don't notice that kind of thing.' It was clear that the phone was now on speaker mode.

Talantire was dubious. What man doesn't notice what an attractive seventeen-year-old girl is wearing? 'Was she wearing jeans, Gary?' Talantire asked.

'No, a skirt. Light-coloured, I think.'

So he did notice. 'Did it have two zips?'

'No idea.'

'What shoes, Gary?' Meghan asked.

'Was it trainers, something flat?' Talantire chipped in.

'Heels, I think,' he said.

'Keep thinking, Gary, we need details,' Talantire pressed. 'I want to know what jewellery, if she had a wristwatch, particularly if she has a fitness tracker because we can trace those.'

'No, she wanted one, but we couldn't afford it,' Meghan replied.

'Can you email me some more pictures?' Talantire said, reading out an address.

'You can use the one we put on Facebook,' Meghan said. It was clear that the police delay in taking Jade's disappearance seriously had prompted the family and their friends to take matters into their own hands. Jade's mother told her how they had been organising searches: to Bodmin where the car crashed, to places in both Camborne and Truro where Jade had spent time in the past, and the Camborne Hockey Club building where she had been a star goalkeeper. A funding page had been set up and an online campaign begun that afternoon entitled 'Find Jade'.

It was Talantire's turn to feel ashamed.

'Look, Mrs Kernow, what you've done is brilliant and resourceful. But I need you to share your information with us. It can save time all round. There is also a danger if you do go somewhere where she has been, you will muddy the evidence.'

'What are you saying?' Her suspicion was clearly aroused.

'We'll be looking for DNA samples, as you know, to match the ones we have taken from your home, but also traces of other people in the places where she's been. Now, if all your friends and family are tramping around Cornwall looking for her, it might be a problem if one of them was—'

'You think one of us did it!'

'I didn't say that.'

Talantire overheard Meghan: 'Gary, she thinks we might have done it.'

Gary swore, and grabbed the receiver. Talantire held the phone away to diminish the volume of invective and swearing. This wasn't going well. She'd always been told she would never make an FLO. Too impatient, too direct. A hothead. She really needed to retrieve this situation, somehow.

'Please don't hang up,' she said. 'Let me explain.'

She sat through another two minutes of verbal from Gary. Thinking back through what Beatrice had told her, she now recalled that Gary, sometime 'Uncle Gary', was Meghan's one-time boyfriend, next-door neighbour and a taxi driver. Finally, he calmed down enough to let her speak.

'I apologise for what sounds like casting aspersions on the energy and enthusiasm of your friends and family, but in order to do my job and to help you, there is some information I require. Would you be kind enough to pass me back to Meghan?'

The transfer completed, Meghan answered with resignation: 'Yes?'

'First, could you send me a list of all the places that you think Jade might have gone. I'd like a list of her friends, with contact numbers if you have them, and as much about her movements over the previous week as you are able to supply.'

'I gave most of that to the local cop, Beatrice.'

'Okay, we will be allocating you a family liaison officer as soon as possible. She will be someone that you can talk with to find out the latest. Now, what I'd like to do as soon as possible, Meghan, is to go over to Bodmin Moor with you and see if we can find her. It will be light until ten thirty or so.'

'Yes, I'd like to do that,' she said, finally calmer.

They arranged to meet by the rectory at 8:30 p.m. But first there was a visit to be made.

–

Talantire arrived at Welby Ward at Plymouth Derriford Hospital at seven p.m. She was allowed into intensive care to see Lily. The thirteen-year-old was intermittently conscious and not able to speak. The ICU nurse said that she was doing the best of the four survivors, but was still very poorly.

Talantire introduced herself and talked to the family by the nurses' station for a few minutes. Lily's stepfather, Pete, a stocky, bald man, arrived with several coffees and offered his own to Talantire. She politely declined and asked if they minded if she tried to elicit some responses from their daughter. 'I know she's not able to speak yet, but I understand she's been able to manage some yes-or-no answers.'

'She uses her thumb,' Pete said, smiling proudly. 'Up for yes, down for no.'

'That's great. This will literally take two minutes and then I'll leave you to be alone with her.'

A female doctor emerged from the curtained-off bay and invited them to return to Lily's bedside. 'Her vital signs are improving a little,' the doctor said.

They all gathered around the bed, where the pale young girl appeared to be asleep, slender arms on the covers, dark hair swirled across her forehead. A whole series of machines were connected to her by tubes, adding to her sense of vulnerability. 'There's a police lady here,' her mother said stroking her hand. 'Come to wish you a speedy recovery.'

Her eyes fluttered a little, but remained closed.

Talantire got out her iPad and pulled up a picture of Jade, one that Beatrice had got from the parents.

'Hello, Lily,' Talantire called softly. 'Can you hear me?'

There was a slight stirring from the bed.

'Lily, do you know Jade Kernow?'

There was no response, although her right hand trembled.

Talantire repeated the question, and saw the thumb of the hand moving downwards.

'She doesn't know her,' Lily's mother said. 'But Scarlett did, so she'd probably recognise her.'

Again, the past tense.

'They hated each other,' blurted out the younger brother. 'Because of Finlay.'

This was heading down the track of hearsay. Talantire wanted to stick to Lily's own knowledge, so she propped up the iPad where the girl could see it. 'Can you see this, Lily?'

Her eyelids fluttered. The thumb twitched upwards.

'Do you recognise this girl?'

The thumb stayed up, then dropped. Talantire noticed a kick in the traces on one of the machines, perhaps a faster pulse or heartbeat, something like that.

'Lily, was this girl in the car with you when it crashed?'

The thumb jumped back up, for a moment or two. Lily gave a huge sigh and started to shift in her bed as if turning over, the arm relaxed and the fingers splayed outwards.

'Thank you, Lily. I hope you're soon on the mend,' Talantire said. She said a whispered goodbye to the family and exited towards the car park.

This was probably not reliable, from a girl who was half conscious. But if Lily was right, Jade *had* been in the car, and had somehow survived the crash. So where was she now?

There was one obvious answer. Somewhere on Bodmin Moor.

Chapter Seven

The video began with laughter and a view from the back seat. The older boy – Jordan – was driving, a glimpse of the speedo showing eighty, until the view was cut off by Aaron easing up close. Soft bongs indicated that neither driver nor passenger had seat belts on. The younger lad reached his own foot across Jordan's lap, and slid it between his legs, down into the footwell. Now half sitting on Jordan's lap, he continued to move until he was able to grab the steering wheel. 'Now the tough bit,' Jordan said. A pair of female hands slid out the driver's headrest, then removed it left, out of view. Jordan began to ease himself up and along the back of the seat behind Aaron, heading left. The camera wobbled, and the dashed line marking the middle of the road, visible through the windscreen, jerked from side to side as the two youngsters attempted to move around each other. It took a few more seconds but the manoeuvre was accomplished.

Talantire clicked off the video.

She had been walking back down the hospital corridor when Primrose had messaged her with this, the latest evidence of the recklessness of youth. It was 7:30 p.m. on a Sunday and Primrose had already created a CID database from hundreds of gigabytes of video data from the phones of Jordan, Leanne and Lily and in the last hour had added some data from the damaged phone of

Aaron Darracombe. Scarlett's phone had proved too badly damaged for anything to be retrieved directly from the SIM card. In her accompanying message, Primrose said she had sent a request to get a data dump from the servers of Scarlett's service provider. That wouldn't be back until the morning, so she was now heading home for some sleep.

Talantire rang her back, catching her while she was still at her desk. 'Primrose, did you get a chance to request data for Jade's phone?'

'Yes I did, but I have been told by Wells to prioritise the phones of those in the car.'

'Well, in the last hour, Jade has become a live missing persons case with high priority. I'm heading off to Bodmin Moor now to meet her mother.'

Primrose sighed. 'Well, if I'd had her actual phone, I could have put it through the kiosk, but I'm kind of stuck otherwise. I'll come in first thing tomorrow,' she said brightly. 'If I can get the overtime.'

Talantire thanked her and ended the call. She was in the hospital car park when she got a call from her boss. Detective Superintendent Wells, noting the time, conceded that her hunch had been right, and that Jade Kernow really was missing. 'The good news, Jan, is that I have fought to have you made deputy SIO for this case, rather than someone from the Plymouth crew, and I've allocated your usual team of DS Moran and DC Nuttall.'

Deputy SIO? Talantire wondered who was being put in charge.

'There is an incident room being set up in the church hall in Liskeard,' Wells continued. 'I want you there first thing tomorrow morning, but I'm not waiting for that. We are going to have an immediate night-time search of the southern half of Bodmin Moor by heat-seeking drones. If she is out there, we will find her.'

Then he said something that ruined all the good news.

'That search and the whole broader policing operation will be run by Commander Brent West, who just moved back from Avon and Somerset Police. It's a high-profile case and he will be SIO. You will report to him.'

Her heart plummeted. *This cannot be, this just cannot be. Not him, anyone but him.*

—

At 8:30 p.m. on a humid summer evening, Bodmin Moor looked beautiful. Low, watery light caught pale tussocks of grass and dark green gorse, peppered with yellow flowers. The fresh westerly wind drove along fingers of mauve and purple clouds.

Talantire parked just beyond Bodmin Rectory, very close to where she had found the unconscious Leanne. Police tape had been removed from the bushes now that casts of the footwear had been taken.

Mrs Kernow arrived a few minutes later with Gary, both with hooded raincoats and walking boots, though Gary sported a leather cowboy hat and a bootlace tie. Talantire, in her police-issue anorak, looked up at the swirling July clouds. The weather was forecast to deteriorate, with high winds and intense showers.

As they were approaching, Talantire felt her phone buzz.

A text from Beatrice Dodds, in answer to some questions she had asked earlier. She quickly scanned it. Uncle Gary, whose real name was Gary Heaton, had a whole host of traffic-related offences over the years, something

Camborne Community Police had already hinted at. But Beatrice had now dug up something sinister. More than twenty years ago, Gary Heaton had been caught up in Operation Ore.

Shit. There was no time to do anything now, as the man was standing right in front of her.

'Hello,' Talantire said, brightly, shaking the man's hand, while pocketing her phone.

He gave a wordless grunt in reply.

Meghan Kernow ignored her, instead staring across the unending vista of Bodmin Moor. 'How are we going to find her in all this?' she asked.

'It's not just about finding her, but finding something of hers, something to prove she was here,' Talantire said.

She led them to the fan of debris that had ejected from the car when it crashed into the telegraph pole just the other side of the wall. Window glass, pieces of plastic from the car and a couple more of the mauve smiley-faced tablets could be seen. They worked over the ground again, each of them crouching to examine various fragments.

'I got something here,' Gary said, holding up a hooped earring. He wasn't wearing the nylon gloves she had given him.

'No! Don't touch it!' Talantire called, making her way over.

'Can't get the gloves over my rings,' Gary said, showing the metal Day of the Dead-style skull rings on his middle fingers.

'Why not take the rings off?'

'They won't come off.'

'Don't touch anything, then.'

She took the earring and scooped it into a plastic evidence bag. She couldn't help noticing that it was damaged.

There was a spot of blood at the point where it had broken.

The three of them gradually spread out across the moors, methodically walking a hundred-metre-square area beyond the north wall of the rectory. No further heeled footprints were visible, though there were plenty of other footprints, mainly of walking boots. The land around was riven with gullies, most of them shallow and dry at this time of year, but some still deeper and muddy and, like much of the area, surrounded by thick tangles of gorse.

'Jade didn't have a driving licence, did she?' Talantire asked.

'No,' Meghan replied. 'She was saving up for driving lessons but hadn't begun. She'd also have to go for a year without a seizure.'

'How would she have got to Camborne from your home?'

'There's a bus from Truro that takes about an hour, or Gary would give her a lift. But he didn't.'

Talantire called over to Gary, who was some distance away, swatting his way through bushes with a stick. He made his way over.

'Gary, you said you last saw Jade at seven, when she left the house, right?'

'Yeah. I asked her if she wanted a lift anywhere, and she said no.'

'My community police colleagues say there was no sighting of her in Camborne, at least not in the Penypul estate on the night she disappeared.'

'Yeah,' he said neutrally. 'We went over there this afternoon.'

Talantire was still keeping from them her suspicion that Jade had been in the car. But if so, had she been picked up near home or had she travelled to Camborne? She decided to change the subject.

'I understand Jade is quite sporty?' Talantire asked Meghan.

'Yes, she's goalkeeper for the county hockey team and a keen swimmer. She raised £20,000 for her charity trip to West Africa when she was fifteen, by swimming twenty-six miles over a month. She got up before six every day before school to use the pool. Look.' Meghan showed Talantire a video on her phone. It showed Jade emerging from the pool at the end of her marathon swim, beaming a huge smile, as classmates and spectators cheered.

'It's really tragic that she got malaria when she was there,' Gary interjected.

'She fell ill on her return, with a massive fever, and then a seizure. She almost died. It had got into her brain,' Meghan explained.

'Cerebral malaria,' Talantire said.

'Yes. That's why she has to take tablets for the rest of her life. The malaria triggered epilepsy. It put her back a year at school, along with lockdown, which is why she's a year older than most of her classmates. Her confidence has mostly recovered.' Meghan looked to the horizon, her eyes watering. 'She's a brave girl, you know. But I can't bear the thought of her out there alone,' Meghan sobbed.

Talantire rested a friendly arm on Meghan's shoulder. 'We will find her.'

'Will we? Shouldn't there be hundreds of officers here, not just us?'

'I agree, but as I mentioned, it was only an hour or so ago that the case was finally assigned as a priority.'

Meghan looked utterly affronted.

'If it's any consolation, I've been told that a team from Exeter with heat-seeking drones will be scouring the whole southern part of Bodmin Moor overnight. If she's here, they will find her. But I think we've done all we can here for now.'

As she watched them depart to Gary's green Renault taxi, Talantire turned again to Beatrice's text about him. It was an ominous development. Operation Ore began in 1999 and was one of the first big international anti-paedophile cases. It was a sting operation run in conjunction with the FBI, that retained the details of everyone who had used a credit card to pay for access to child abuse images on a US website. Tens of thousands of British nationals, including MPs, senior civil servants, head teachers and judges, were caught, along with similar numbers from many other countries. So large were the numbers that only the most serious cases were ever prosecuted, where the credit card details were paired with child abuse images found on the computers of the accused. Gary Heaton was one of the minor names. His credit card had been used, but no abuse images were found at his home. He was simply cautioned and put on the sex offenders register for five years.

And now here he was, joining in the search for his 'adoptive' daughter Jade.

-

Just after ten, Talantire headed back to Barnstaple. She'd gleaned useful information and worrying suspicions but found no fresh evidence. She rang Beatrice and asked her to prioritise a search for Gary Heaton through to CEOPS

– the child protection arm of the National Crime Agency. 'I think we need to search the house thoroughly, get his computers,' Talantire told her.

'He'll probably have dumped them,' she said. 'The moment Jade's disappearance became a case.'

'Beatrice, we really should have been onto him from the start,' Talantire said.

'Well, he was only in his early twenties when he was caught up in Operation Ore. His name came off the register after five years. He didn't meet Meghan Kernow until six years ago, when Jade would have been eleven,' she replied.

'Predilections don't change,' Talantire said. 'Can you find out any other women he lived with and if there are any other issues relating to children?'

'Yes, I'll get onto it,' she said.

'Perhaps you can run checks on all the relatives from the families of the car-crash victims too. Leave no stone unturned, Beatrice.'

Talantire thanked her and killed the call. Now she had to let Brent West know. That was one call she wasn't looking forward to, so she deferred it until she got back to Barnstaple.

As she drove home across the moor on the A30, under a glorious salmon-hued sunset, she ran through the various possibilities of what could have happened to Jade: Lily had affirmed she was in the car, and if so, she must have been thrown out of the front passenger side door at the point of impact with the telegraph pole, just as Leanne was. It was that door which hung, bent in half, from the top of the shattered pole. She'd need to talk to the road accident experts to be sure about the trajectories, but it seemed to her that if Jade was still in the car when it fell on its roof in the greenhouse, she couldn't have got out. Only Lily, skinny as a ferret, had been able to slither out with the help of Bill Llewellyn. But, either way, Jade should have been seriously injured. It didn't square with Llewellyn's very clear account that a girl ran across his garden just moments after he emerged from the house.

What if there had been another car? It was an obvious possibility, even though Llewellyn was quite clear that he saw none. Joyriders like to race. If Jade had been in another car, it would explain why she had perhaps come to investigate the crash, was able to run and had shown no signs of injuries. It might also square with the mast data which showed her phone having been in roughly the same place at the same time as the crash victims. That was all well and good, but why didn't she stay and call the emergency services? And where was she now? There was no motive for her disappearance. What fate could have befallen her that was unconnected to the crash?

–

At midnight on a Sunday evening, Barnstaple's industrial estate was as quiet as a grave. A few articulated lorries parked up for the night, the faces of drivers visible in the light from their mobile phones. The leisure centre was closed, the burger vans shut for the night. Talantire slid her Ford into the compound of the police station, noting just a few subdued lights. She lugged her briefcase from the car, in the other hand a polythene bag full of evidence envelopes from Bodmin Moor. She barged through the main double doors with her shoulder and exchanged greetings with the overnight desk sergeant, Ollie Todd.

'Any progress on the missing girl, ma'am?' he asked.

'Nothing substantive, I'm afraid, Ollie,' she said, clambering up the stairs to CID.

She was just about to barge open the door at the top when Richard Lockhart held it open for her. He had a finger to his lips, so, following his cue, she eased herself quietly in.

DI Lockhart, known as the Prince of Darkness for his predilection for the night shift, was the office heart-throb. A lilting Welsh voice combined with saturnine good looks and deep brown eyes.

'She's asleep under there,' Lockhart whispered.

Talantire followed his gaze and saw Primrose Chen, curled up in a nest of blankets, underneath a desk behind the photocopier. She looked angelic and childlike. It reminded Talantire of finding Leanne Moyle on the moor, less than twenty-four hours ago.

'She told me she was going home,' Talantire said quietly.

'I just came in from a shout over at Westward Ho! and disturbed her when she was praying. She was very apologetic, but I told her to carry on and put in a good word for me too.' He smiled that irresistible grin.

Talantire crouched down and pointed to a line of masking tape on the carpet, just behind Primrose's desk. 'This is her prayer marker, to line up towards Mecca,' she whispered. 'The cleaners keep pulling it off. I don't think they quite understand what it's for.'

'She really is the sweetest creature, and so technically adept,' Lockhart said, leading her over to his desk at the far end of the office. 'But I'd heard that she had some difficulties with Sergeant Venables.'

'Yes, he's a total arse, but she refuses to put in a formal complaint. He was going to be transferred to dog handling, but he's allergic to dog fur, or so he says.' Talantire was hoping to be able to weigh in with her own evidence against the notoriously racist sergeant but felt she had to let Primrose take the lead.

Lockhart rolled his eyes. 'Well, I have just got some paperwork to finish off. Can I make you a coffee? Don't worry, it'll be from the kitchen downstairs, not the dreaded Doctor Crippen.' He eyed the ancient and notorious coffee machine in the corridor, refurbished under some hare-brained scheme from the crime commissioner.

'That would be lovely, Richard.'

While Lockhart tiptoed downstairs, Talantire logged into her terminal, wrote the dockets of all of the evidence bags into the crime log and allocated them to the out trays for the morning courier pickup. Apart from the earring, the Bodmin Moor reconnaissance had turned up some cigarette ends, a disposable vape, a small orange-juice carton and various other things which were probably unconnected to Jade but might yield DNA or fingerprints. Results would take at least twenty-four hours. She also looked over her notes about Gary Heaton. In person, Jade's so-called uncle didn't seem particularly strange or weird. He had been supportive to Meghan Kernow when she'd started crying after the discovery of the earring and had held her in a long hug. But that twenty-year-old snippet of information about Operation Ore was just so incriminating. You cannot look into a man's mind to measure his relationship with the devil, but a quick glance at his internet search history was the next best thing.

Talantire had half her paperwork done when the coffee arrived. 'A smooth Colombian roast,' he said, offering it in his own mini cafetière.

'Richard, you are an angel,' she said, sipping the delicious brew.

Thus fortified, she began to skim through the videos and pictures of Jade that Meghan had sent her, from which footage would be chosen for a public appeal: there was Jade as an eight-year-old in ballet class moving confidently across the stage; at eleven, she was playing the clarinet with panache; at sixteen, in mixed hockey bravely leaping out from the goal to tackle a much larger boy, in a flurry of loud clashing sticks, preventing a goal. Finally Talantire alighted on a video of Jade with Finlay Roscoe, which, according to Meghan's voice-over, was in the garden of her home.

'And here's the little lovebirds now,' Meghan said as she approached the couple who were entwined on a garden bench.

'Mum, knock it off,' Jade said, turning away. 'It's embarrassing.'

The look on Finlay's face didn't seem one of embarrassment at all. He looked happy, holding Jade's hand in his own and grinning into the lens.

Talantire savoured the last of the coffee and wondered: where was Jade right now? Was there any possibility that she could still be alive, drunk and hungover in some boyfriend's flat? Or would they soon find her body, stuffed in a cupboard, thrown down a mineshaft or hurriedly buried in a shallow grave?

Chapter Eight

On Monday morning, William Llewellyn awoke in a bed for the first time in several years, light pouring in through the partially drawn curtains, even though it was not yet five. He'd stayed last night with his niece Daphne and her family in Liskeard after eventually agreeing that Bodmin Rectory was for the moment no place for a man of ninety-eight. Some busybody from social services had visited him and said exactly the same thing, and eventually he'd relented, leaving his home in the hands of the police while they continued their investigation.

Last night, he had dreamt of his D-Day experiences – the first time in many years that the full horror of landing in enemy territory in an unpowered glider had intruded into his sleep. In the nightmare were not only his former wartime comrades, but a scattering of teenage girls, and among them, somewhat incongruously, was his fiancée Lily, her lovely heart-shaped face, framed by a dark Marcel wave, and those big brown eyes. The glider had drifted down in darkness, the ominous creak of the wings and no engines to drown out the ack-ack of the German anti-aircraft. Next to him, a young recruit with a rosary was saying his prayers. William gripped the silver cigarette case containing a photograph of Lily and her first love letter to him – a much-creased and thumbed talisman for a safe arrival. In the dream, the glider hit a telegraph pole and flipped over, splitting in two and spilling screaming soldiers into a marsh. The reality had been less dramatic, though scary enough – a long, slow scrape through an arable field, coming to rest against a hedge, part of Normandy's bocage.

He blinked away the gossamer threads of memory, the dream receding like melting ice.

But Lily remained.

Her grave was in Nunhead cemetery in south-east London, and he now realised he had not visited for several years, after he'd had to give up the car, and when his infirmity made navigating Britain's creaking rail services more onerous. He felt a wave of shame for neglecting the only woman he had ever loved. He reached for a tissue from the bedside box and dabbed his eyes.

He gradually eased himself out of bed, found his walking stick and made his way to the window. Being upstairs was something of a novelty but was aided by the stairlift that Daphne had put in years ago, hoping to persuade him to come and live with them. He had resisted, desperate to keep his independence. Now he might have to give up. A good soldier, after fighting his best, had to recognise the moment to surrender.

He stared out into Daphne's small rear garden, which butted up against the hedge of a neighbouring property. So close to each other, these modern houses, you could probably see the feller opposite cleaning his teeth in his bathroom if you picked your moment. So different to living on the edge of the moor, where every single day, the buffeted grass, the wild thorny ridges, the clouds and the slanting light drew on a different palate. The wildness, empty of humanity, with enough room for him to talk to Lily and hold her hand, without anyone saying anything.

'Oh Bill, what are you doing up?' Daphne said as she came downstairs swathed in a dressing gown and with a towel wrapped around her damp hair. 'You look all dressed to go out on parade.'

'I was hoping we could go to Plymouth Hospital, to see the young injured from the crash. I thought we could buy some flowers for the girls, and their families.'

'That's a lovely thought, Bill, but it's not long past seven in the morning. Harry is still asleep.'

'There's some tea in the pot for you,' he said. 'Though I think it might be cold by now.'

Daphne rested a hand on his shoulder and smiled kindly at him. 'I'll look on the internet to see when Derriford's visiting hours begin. I'm sure Harry won't mind driving. One of the benefits of retirement, eh? We can pick up some flowers from the supermarket.'

'That's very kind,' Bill said.

—

It took an age to negotiate the corridors at Derriford Hospital in his walker, but Bill refused the offer of a wheelchair. 'I'm a visitor, not a patient,' he reminded Daphne and Harry. At reception, he gave his name but was told that only family members could visit intensive care now. A shorter slot for more general visiting might be available in the afternoon. They went for a cup of tea to discuss what to do, when a man in dark blue scrubs came over to them in the refectory. 'Are you Mr Llewellyn?' he asked Harry. 'Who rang yesterday?'

'I am,' Bill said. 'Not him.'

'Lily Jago's family has asked to see you. Would you come this way?'

They followed the man along seemingly endless corridors, Bill once again declining the offer of a wheelchair. Finally, they went through a set of double doors marked ICU into a hive of medical activity, taken to a bay where behind blue plastic curtains an anxious-looking family was gathered around a bed in which a young girl was hooked up to various machines, her head bandaged.

'It's the brigadier,' exclaimed a teenage boy with a cap of wavy hair that fell over his eyes. 'I saw him on the telly.'

A woman by his side shushed him and then turned to Bill, introducing herself as Joyce Jago.

'Thank you,' she whispered. 'You saved our Lily.'

'I did what I had to do,' Bill said, looking at the girl.

They all turned to follow his gaze. Lily's eyes seemed to be almost shut, but her hand rotated slightly, and a small thumb, its nail showing traces of chipped pink varnish, lifted to vertical.

'She's thanking you,' Joyce said. 'She only came round a few minutes ago.'

The other side of the bed, her stepfather, Pete, held Lily's other hand in his own huge paw.

One side of Lily's mouth hoisted a minute smile, enough to see a glint of tooth.

Bill shuffled towards her, and the smile broadened. There was no sound, but the lip articulation was clear. *Thank you.*

An older woman sitting at the foot of the bed began to cry softly into her cotton handkerchief.

Bill had remembered that Lily had mentioned a sister when she was in the car. Scarlett.

'What about Scarlett?' he asked.

All eyes were downcast.

'She's having an operation to remove pressure to the brain,' her mother said. 'We've been told to prepare ourselves...'

The older woman shushed her. 'Joyce, have faith. Scarlett is a fighter.'

–

Bill made his way out of the hospital, escorted by Daphne and Harry. A car drove by and he heard a brief, familiar tune, one of the pop songs that had been playing in the car on the night of the accident. In that moment, he had a flashback to when he had first opened the door and saw the girl running away from the car, screaming. She fled through the open gates in the road, and then disappeared into darkness. He now realised that what he had told the police had been wrong – or at least incomplete. That darkness hadn't been just the shadow of the wall, it included a dark sleeve. And a momentary glimpse of a male hand from that sleeve, across her back, guiding her out of his view.

He must phone the police and tell them.

–

While Llewellyn had been waking up, Talantire was driving down to Liskeard with Detective Sergeant Maddy Moran for the incident-room meeting. Maddy's diligent detective skills were wrapped in a jovial and outsize personality. An instinctive judge of character, she was invaluable in interviews but often unnerved colleagues by her insight into them, as evidenced by this morning's topic of conversation: Commander Brent West.

'So who is this guy that's bothering you so much?' Maddy asked her. 'Someone from your past?'

'Unfortunately, yes. We had an affair seven years ago when I was based in Exeter.'

'Hmm, a sexual relationship with Brent West. Sounds like you were shagging an entire constituency,' Maddy said, chuckling, as she worked her phone. She soon came up with a picture. 'Blimey, is that him?'

'Yes, unfortunately he's very good-looking.'

'He looks like that James Bond – what's his name, not the current one. Two before that. Timothy Dalton. I mean, *phwooar*.'

Talantire managed a smile. 'Don't judge by appearances.'

'I'm afraid we all do, which is why I was called "Bouncy" at school. So what was the problem?'

'I'd rather not talk about it, sorry.'

Maddy waited a while before continuing her shameless push for further information: 'So did he finish with you or you with him?'

Talantire sighed. 'Me with him.' Her face tightened. 'And that's all I'm going to say.'

Maddy waited a few minutes, then, staring again at West's photo, asked. 'So what happened to that guy you were dating a few months ago?'

'Adam? I think he went back to his ex. Didn't I tell you?'

'You'd told me about him getting cold feet.'

'Well, whatever the reason, it was a shame. He was nice. In fact, he was the only decent prospect I met on the dating site in six months.' And she still thought about him. More than she had expected.

'Not as good-looking as Commander West, though,' Maddy said.

'Looks aren't everything, Maddy.' She changed gears aggressively at a junction, and accelerated down the main road towards Liskeard. 'You know, I thought Brent bloody West was out of my life for good years ago, but now he's set to be my boss.'

The car hit a pothole at speed and bucked. Talantire noticed Maddy's hand gripping the door handle, her knuckles white.

'He's unbearable Maddy. You'll soon find out.'

'Not if you keep driving at this speed, I won't,' she replied.

–

Liskerrett Community Centre was a traditional stone-built church hall in the centre of Liskeard. Inside, it was modern and comfortable. Numerous whiteboards, projectors, tables and chairs had been set up by the time that Talantire and Maddy arrived, amid the bustle of officers going back and forth to a couple of unmarked vans, bringing in kit.

DC Dave Nuttall had made his way separately, having given Primrose Chen a lift, and at this ungodly hour, they were nursing coffees and what looked like cinnamon buns. Nuttall was a reliable detective, and a jazz fan, and had devoted the years since his divorce to further increasing his collection on vinyl. He had thick-framed glasses, dyed dark hair slicked back and was in a creased and rarely seen suit rather than his trademark leather jacket. His white shirt was clearly straight out of the packet, a fold visible across the chest.

'Hi, Dave,' Maddy said, staring at the bun he was eating. 'Should you be eating this, given your dietary issues?'

'What dietary issues?' he asked, walking over to them.

'You're clearly suffering from an iron deficiency,' she said, staring at his creased sleeves and shirt.

'Arf, arf,' he replied, a dusting of cinnamon visible on his top lip.

While the uniformed attendees were largely male, the plain-clothes contingent were mostly young, attractive women.

'Your ex has assembled himself a team of totty,' Maddy whispered to Talantire as she returned.

'Am I surprised?' Talantire responded. She had spotted Brent West's giant black Ford Explorer in the car park and saw the man himself with a phone clamped to his ear just outside the community centre kitchen. He was wearing well-fitting jeans and a dazzling white shirt that showed off his tan. He was running his fingers self-consciously through his carefully trimmed dark hair.

'The picture didn't lie,' Maddy whispered to her. 'Such blue eyes!'

'Coloured contacts,' she hissed back. 'Don't be taken in. His teeth are bleached too.'

West spotted them and raised a hand in greeting and flashed a smile. 'Coffee,' he mouthed, gesturing to the counter.

'Attentive and charming,' Maddy continued, as she made a beeline for the refreshments.

It was one minute before eight when West clapped his hands, and his well-oiled team of helpers returned to various positions around the room.

Just as everyone was taking their seats, Chief Inspector Bernie Campbell walked in through the double doors, accompanied by Sergeant Dodds. They sat next to Talantire.

West gestured to the window, and one of the plain-clothes females hurried over to close the blinds. Two others were gathered behind the various bits of electronic kit on the central table.

'Welcome, everyone,' West began. 'This is the incident-room meeting for a missing persons inquiry for Jade Kernow. I think you've all had chance to look through the information dossier that I put together overnight.'

Bernie looked a little confused, but one of the smiling young DCs scurried over to hand him a carefully stapled set of printouts.

West continued: 'First, the latest update. The surveillance drone team here was busy overnight with the thermal-image XZ300M, covering twenty-two hectares of Bodmin Moor as far as Colliford Lake. We received four human signatures during that time, all male, most associated with identifiable vehicles, along with numerous animal images, deer mainly. We're chasing down the four individuals, but will follow up today with a volunteer search. I have to say my expectations are that Jade Kernow is not in this area any longer.' He gestured to Talantire. 'Jan, would you be willing to update us on the latest electronic intelligence on the location of the missing girl?'

She was a bit surprised, considering that he hadn't primed her he was going to call for her to speak, but she'd committed the details to memory. She walked up to the whiteboard and drew a timeline, vertically. 'The last signal from Jade Kernow's phone showed it was in the vicinity of Bodmin Rectory at the time of the accident.' She wrote an X at the top of the line. 'It had been approaching at speed in the moments before, on a very similar trajectory to phones of three of the occupants of the car. That indicates either that she was in the vehicle which crashed or in another very close behind. Jade doesn't drive, so if another vehicle was present, somebody else was probably driving. Unfortunately, the nearest ANPR camera is on the A30, more than twenty miles away. That final camera registered the Mercedes at 86 mph but no obviously pursuing vehicle. We therefore have no way of knowing from electronic means whether there was any other vehicle involved in a chase.'

West interrupted. 'When I drove through the village of St Trenewan, I saw there was a vehicle-activated speed sign, one of the smiley-face units. Jan, did you interrogate the history file of this device?'

Her throat went dry. 'Er, no. I didn't realise they retained any data.'

West smiled indulgently. 'It's not common knowledge that most modern units retain time and speed info for at least thirty days. When I passed by last night, I noticed it was an I-Safe Model 2 and contacted the local authority licence holder to remotely download the relevant data. Which you can see here,' he said, pointing a remote control at the projector. 'As you can see from the log file, two vehicles passed in quick succession three minutes before the accident. The first was travelling at 91.3 miles an hour and the following, three seconds later, was captured at 82.8.' He looked down at his screen. 'From reading your notes so far, Jan, the presumption has been the missing girl was in the crashed vehicle, hasn't it?'

'There was no presumption, sir. The witness at the scene heard no other vehicle, while a witness statement from one of the other occupants of the crashed vehicle said Jade was with her in the car.'

'But I understand that the householder in question could hardly hear anything over the sound of loud music from the crashed vehicle. And this "statement", from someone who you describe as barely conscious, was no more than a raised thumb in answer to a question. Had you considered that her memory might not be entirely reliable?'

Talantire felt like she was dying under cross-examination. 'Of course I had.' She could not help adding a note of steel to her voice. 'Furthermore, sir, I have received fingerprint results which show an exact match between those found on Jade Kernow's hairbrush and prints found both inside and outside the car.'

West seemed unaware of this. 'I see,' he said.

'So, sir, it is clear that, at some point, Jade *was* in the car. But perhaps not at the moment of impact.'

'What does the DNA say?' he asked.

'I'm expecting results by noon. I'll let you know as soon as we have them.'

'That's a bit slow, isn't it?'

'I had budget issues as the case was on the backburner at that time.'

He sighed expansively, with a glance at Campbell. 'Well, we are where we are. This inquiry is going to be put on a more professional basis now, and I expect rapid results.'

Talantire, Beatrice Dodds and Chief Inspector Campbell all exchanged glances.

'Commander West,' Campbell said. 'Would it not be better if we just moved forward in co-operation? This is not a forum for scoring points. We want to find a missing girl.'

'Yes, and that's why I'm here,' West replied. 'During the course of the day, with the help of Sergeant Dodds, we will be reinterviewing all of Jade's friends. I'm pleased to announce that we have now discovered that Gary Heaton, partner of Jade's mother Meghan, has some previous in regard to child abuse images. This seems, in retrospect, an obvious line of enquiry. His home – not the one he shares with her – was raided at six a.m. this morning, and he was arrested, then released under police bail. So far, he is denying everything, which is what you would expect. I'm minded to bring him into custody later on, depending how our lines of enquiry develop. I was a little surprised to see that we didn't already have a DNA elimination sample from him, so my team are putting that right.'

Talantire watched as Beatrice flushed at the implied criticism. There was something infuriating about West, who took credit for everything that went right and cast blame for everything that had been overlooked.

'Sir, I'm not convinced that Heaton is our man,' Talantire said. 'He was with Jade's mother at the time the car crashed; he was even messaging Jade.'

West smiled. 'We've easily got enough to hold him – and to show the press and the Great British public we've made progress. I do share your misgivings, but it gives us breathing space.'

'With respect, sir, the allegation alone will destroy his life. If he turns out to be innocent—'

'He was picked up by Operation Ore, wasn't he? How innocent can he be?'

She opened her mouth to protest further, but West held up his hand.

'Let's get back to operational matters,' he said. 'I'm not satisfied that the current last-known independent sighting, i.e. from those not involved in the accident, was as early as seven p.m. That means a full seven hours before her phone was last detected at 2:22 a.m.' He then turned to the digital evidence officer, smiling winningly at her. 'Primrose, I understand you now have a full list of all the messages sent to Jade's phone yesterday.'

'I do, sir,' she said softly, her eyes downcast and her hijab pulled tightly around her hair. 'I'll begin with the text messages, which are on slides two to fifteen, starting with the latest received, which was 4:15 a.m. on Sunday morning. There were later ones, but we don't have them because the SMS mailbox was full.'

The slide flashed up, and it was immediately obvious from the contents that Jade's mother had been frantically messaging her, as had Gary. The general tenor of them was: *Where are you? We are really worried*. The first three slides, thirty-six messages in total, were all received after the phone had been turned off at 2:24 a.m. Among them were two Primrose had highlighted.

'This one from "Maz" said "Are you still angry at her?" We don't know who the "her" referred to is, and I've passed across the number for Beatrice to find out who Maz is. Then onto the next slide, which is in the last dozen received before the crash, including this from Leanne Moyle, who, as we know, was in the car, and it's clearly mistyped. It starts OMG, and the rest seems like gibberish, seemingly random letters and spaces, finishing with uz.'

'The timing here, I think, is crucial because this was less than a minute before the crash,' Primrose said. 'When she was being driven very fast on a bumpy road.'

Maddy spoke up: 'At a guess, I'd say she might have been trying to write "Oh my God he's going to kill us".'

'Spoken with a little hindsight,' West said with a slight smile. 'But it's plausible. And if correct, it might well refer to the way they are being driven. We know that Aaron Darracombe, a fourteen-year-old, was in the driving seat.'

'It would indicate that Jade wasn't in the car at that point,' Talantire said, as she returned to her seat. 'Otherwise she'd have passed the message verbally.'

'Obviously,' West said and turned back to Primrose. 'What about the earlier messages?'

'There's a long thread of conversation with Leanne about music, at around nine p.m., on slides nineteen to twenty-four. I couldn't see anything significant here. However, there is a brief exchange with Jordan Bailey.'

'The front passenger who died,' West reminded the rest of the audience.

'Yes,' said Primrose. 'It says: "I'm there now, waiting. Is Scarlett with you?" to which he replies with two emojis – the first is a thumbs up, the next a wink.'

'A yes, in other words.'

'Then there's a final text from Jade, simply three letters: ICU.'

'Aha, "I see you". Okay, what time was that?'

'0:12 a.m.'

'Great. I want to find where that message was sent from, Primrose, can you do that for me?'

Talantire hated the transactional way West was carrying on, making this a personal request. It was the start of West's grooming technique, one she knew all too well.

'Yes. I haven't had chance to do it yet, but Jordan's phone had GPS location enabled. Scarlett's did too – but it's too badly damaged to use. Leanne's did not, neither did Lily's. I guess they didn't want their parents figuring out where they were. Anyway, rather than wade through all the cell tower data, which is fairly approximate anyway, I can just hack into Jordan's app. There was satnav on the car too, but the device was destroyed in the accident. Last night, I rang Doug Blackstone, the crash investigator, and he's going to see if we can get the data from the manufacturer's server. However, the GPS will be a quicker route as I might be able to get it this morning.'

'That's brilliant work, Primrose,' West said, as she sat back down.

'But there's something quicker,' Talantire interrupted. 'I've looked back through the statements given by David Roscoe, Finlay's father, who reported the theft of his wife's car first on Friday morning, then again on Saturday. He said they already knew where the car was, because they have the manufacturer's tracking app. He was furious that the police hadn't taken up the case, despite him knowing where the car had been. I'll ring Roscoe senior, to see if he can send us the data.'

'Good,' West said, then turned to the wider audience. 'Just to summarise, once we find where the car was when Jade claims to have seen it, we can home in on her location more precisely than with cell tower triangulation. That then becomes our final known sighting. From that, we can pivot the search away from all of the myriad places,' and here he parted his hands as if opening curtains, 'that she may have been earlier.' He then karate chopped for emphasis, one hand into the other. 'And then, ladies and gentlemen, we can hone down our search; with precision, with certainty and with speed.'

There was a spontaneous round of applause from some of the young female officers.

'Bloody hell,' Maddy muttered, rolling her eyes.

West turned to the chief inspector. 'Bernie, would you like to tell us where we are with the accident investigation?'

Campbell leafed through a sheaf of papers. New school in attitude but definitely old school in technology, he started to read out something he had clearly prepared: 'We have three unconscious accident victims: Leanne Moyle, Scarlett Jago and Aaron Darracombe. There is one semiconscious: Lily Jago. And, as we all know, one, Jordan Bailey, who unfortunately died at the scene. That means that we are very limited in witness statements, but we do have the benefits of modern car technology to record what happened.'

West's face betrayed some impatience at the laborious introduction.

Talantire watched as Primrose quietly got up and left the room.

Campbell continued: 'Mr Blackstone reports that both airbag control modules survived the impact and are serviceable. They recorded the car's speed at impact as 107 mph.'

There was a gasp around the room.

'It had accelerated from 93 mph in the previous five seconds,' Campbell continued. 'The car was in fifth gear and the brakes were applied only in the last half a second. There is a hiatus in some of the data, which Blackstone tells me implies the wheels were off the ground. At this time, only one of the seat belts was in use, on the front passenger, who we know to be Jordan Bailey.'

'You have a slide with this on?' West asked, gesturing to the screen.

'No, it's all here on paper.'

'In future, Bernie, I think it would be better to have this data in a more shareable twenty-first-century format, kapish?'

Campbell nodded, looking a little sheepish.

'Kapish? Isn't that Mafia speak?' Maddy whispered.

Talantire nodded. 'It means "do you get the message".' She turned to her companion. 'So have you gone off him yet?'

'Big time,' she breathed. 'What a monumental arse he is.'

'Anything else, Bernie?' West asked.

Campbell winced at being repeatedly addressed so informally in front of subordinates, but carried on. 'There is more data from the car infotainment system, and as Primrose alluded to, we can get the location, and much else. Blackstone said we should also be able to find out which doors were opened, and when the car was stationary throughout the journey, which might be useful to corroborate who got in and who got out in the few hours before the accident. This will entail interrogating the manufacturer's servers. Blackstone says he might be able to get an interim report to us by the end of the day.'

'Excellent. Can you get him to send it to me directly – copy in my assistant Samantha.' He gestured to a young and pretty plain-clothes officer, one who had been leading the applause. 'All right, everybody, thank you. Our next meeting will be a virtual one at six o'clock this evening on Teams. I'd like to do some breakout meetings now with some of the action teams I have pulled together.'

'Action teams,' Maddy muttered, as she and Talantire were summoned to a group around a table near the kitchen, with Beatrice Dodds.

At another table sat a bunch of uniformed officers who were making the final arrangements for conducting a search on the moor, together with two of the women who ran the drone surveillance unit. Primrose, now back with a bundle of evidence bags and her iPad in hand, sat at yet another table with West's assistant, Samantha. It was a hive of activity, but Talantire couldn't help feeling just a cipher in West's grand plan. She tried to tell herself that if it got results, what did it matter? But the humiliation stung, and she knew from some of the glances she was getting from Maddy that it was visible on her face.

Brent bloody West.

She had successfully avoided him within Devon and Cornwall Police for years, made easier by the fact he was seconded to the Avon force for a couple of years, and then to Interpol. She'd heard rumours of his rise, and hints of some of his affairs with female colleagues. She had hoped above all that keeping her head down meant she never had to run into him again.

How wrong was that. And how galling to be belittled.

She rang David Roscoe and left a message.

Primrose, meanwhile, buttonholed West as he was talking to Samantha and then showed him something on the device. He looked delighted, and briefly rested a hand on her shoulder. Talantire couldn't hear what he was saying, but from the glossy-eyed expression on Primrose's face, it must have been praise.

'Attention, everyone,' West said, clapping his hands. 'Primrose here has tapped into the GPS on Jordan's phone, which confirms – as if we had any doubt – that he was travelling at speed. Thus we can establish that at the time Jade texted "I see you" to Jordan Bailey at twelve minutes past midnight on Sunday morning, the car was just crossing a roundabout on the Truro bypass. So now, what I need *you* to do,' he said, turning to Talantire and Maddy, 'is to get CCTV from the petrol station, the Asda and the car dealerships which Google Maps shows in this area.' He then walked away towards another table. 'Once we get visual proof of Jade's presence in this area, we have a bulletproof final sighting, agreed?'

Affirmative murmurs rippled around the room.

'Yes, Mr West, no Mr West,' Maddy muttered in a childish whisper. 'It's like being back at school.'

'I did warn you,' Talantire said. 'He's even more controlling in private.'

Maddy turned to her and grimaced. 'Okay you've convinced me, he's an utter shit.' They high-fived. The two colleagues then cross-referenced the map that Primrose had messaged them and shifted to Street View to double-check all the premises that might look onto the road. They made a note of likely CCTV cameras and a set of traffic lights which would almost certainly have some cameras. They then handed the details to two of the admin women in West's team whose job was to ring round for CCTV footage, which could then be uploaded on the evidence sharing app GoodSAM.

Talantire was finding it every bit as difficult to work for West as she had expected. His patronising tone, the public doling out of praise or criticism, all rankled. She didn't mind doing basic investigative work, she'd done plenty in her career, but resented those like West who thought they were above it.

Chapter Nine

'So, like, there was this huge cat, with a long tail. And it was much bigger than a moggy. I mean, it was enormous, and had these big green eyes.' Fourteen-year-old Aaron Darracombe was speaking to camera, phone held at arm's length, in what looked like the inside of a shed. His fair hair was wild, his pale eyes wide with amazement. 'I was only six, but my dad saw it too, on midsummer's night. So every year until he left, we went back to try to find it, on Bodmin Moor between the big reservoir and the campsite at Siblyback Lake, the Hurlers Stone Circles and the Minions. They can live for decades, these pumas.' He turned around to a table and lifted up a photograph. 'This is what we saw, what it had eaten.' The print showed the dead body of a sheep covered in blood, its head and neck severed. 'No dog can do that. It's the Beast of Bodmin Moor!' He growled close to the screen and showed a hank of woolly fleece, black with dried blood. 'This is the bait, from the dead sheep we found, to bring the monster to us.'

The video ended.

Talantire's breakout team at the community centre lifted their heads from their screens.

'So this was on TikTok, reposted and shared a few times on Facebook, from some days before the accident,' Beatrice said. It was one of more than a dozen videos that she had found on the Facebook accounts of the various joyriders. Others they had seen included one from Scarlett kissing Finlay Roscoe, Jade's ex-boyfriend, with comments beneath it, including one from Jade which simply said: 'Slag'. 'We've got growing evidence of a rift between the two girls over Finlay.'

'You don't say,' Maddy muttered, earning a glare from Beatrice.

'Yet if Lily is right, and it corroborates the fingerprints of Jade we have inside and outside the crash vehicle, these two girls, seemingly enemies, were, at least for part of the evening, in the car together,' Talantire replied. 'So either the enmity had cooled or there was some other reason they were willing to share a car, at least for a while.'

'We need to know where Jade got out,' Nuttall said. 'If the car records which doors opened and closed during the journey, we might be able to work out how. I'll give the crash investigator a call.'

'Here's another thing that's interesting,' Talantire said, pulling up the fingerprint evidence she had been sent by the specialists in Exeter. 'I managed to lift a whole load of partial prints from the outside of the crashed car. Many of them are obscured by the glove marks of firemen, but this is one I got myself, early on. It's from the rear driver-side door handle. It's a thumb, the last discernible image over many previous ones on the button, and is matched by an index and middle fingerprint on the inside of the handle.'

'What are you trying to tell us?' Nuttall asked.

'It's a left-hand thumbprint and matches one from Jade's hairbrush at her home. The fingers are curled round the handle, over the top as we're looking at it.'

'That's right,' Maddy said. 'That's how you open a car door.'

'When the car is the right way up,' Talantire said. 'But the car was on its roof when I took this lift.'

'I'm sorry, I don't get what you're driving at,' Beatrice said.

'We're trying to work out when Jade was last in the car, or at least the last time she touched it.'

Three baffled faces stared at her.

'All right, come with me,' Talantire said, and led them out into the car park. 'Look at all the door handles of these cars.' She walked up to the nearest, a red Mini. 'On every driver-side door, the fingers slide over the handle like this and the button you press with the thumb is at the rear,' she said, miming with her own right hand on the Mini. 'You open the driver-side door in the UK with your right hand and a passenger-side door with your left. That's how it's designed to work to make it easiest to slip into the vehicle.'

'But you said that print was Jade's left hand,' Maddy said.

'Precisely. She tried to open a driver-side door with her left hand.' At this point, Talantire mimed the action on the Mini. 'You can do it, but it's awkward. You've got to fold your elbow underneath. However, if the car is already upside down, the button you press is now on the other side of the handle, and it's easier to try to open it with your left to get your thumb on it.'

'Aah,' Nuttall said. 'I see what you mean.'

'Run that by me one more time,' Maddy said.

'As we all know, the biggest problems with forensic evidence like fingerprints, footprints or DNA is that it tells you who was at a particular scene, but not when. So anything that allows us to know the exact time a dab was made is like gold dust. That is why the angle of this thumbprint is so important,' Talantire explained. 'It indicates that Jade Kernow was there at the scene of the accident, when the vehicle was already upside down. She tried to open this door.' She indicated the rear driver-side door of the Mini. 'And for its position at the time, the logical way to do that was with your left hand, not your right.'

'So Jade was the girl seen in the garden by the house-holder,' Maddy concluded.

'I've always thought so, but this proves it,' Talantire said. 'Moreover, there are half a dozen palm prints on the exterior of the car near this point which matched those of Jade.' She rested her hand against the rear pillar of the Mini, so the fingers pointed downwards. 'Not all are like this, but mostly. It's an unnatural position, and again it only makes sense if the car was upside down.'

Nuttall nodded and then said: 'So Jade arrived at the scene of the accident, attempted to open the least damaged door, and then when that didn't work slapped or banged her hands in frustration against the vehicle, calling to her friends inside.'

Talantire smiled. 'That's exactly what I think happened.'

'So why didn't she hang around?' Maddy asked. 'Why abandon the scene where her friends were dying? Why would she do that?'

'Maybe she was scared,' Beatrice suggested. 'Maybe she thought in some way she would be blamed for the accident.'

'I really don't know,' Talantire said. 'But I think we now have a firm last-known position for Jade, at 2:17 a.m. in the garden of Bodmin Rectory, trying to open the car door. If she ran away, we want to know why. What on earth was she running from, what was so frightening or more important than trying to rescue her friends?'

'Maybe we've got the answer,' Nuttall said, looking at his phone. 'The witness at Bodmin Rectory has just rung in. Says he now realises he saw a male arm around Jade after she ran away from the car.'

'That makes sense,' Talantire remarked. 'Jade could have run back to whoever this man was to get help.'

'But instead maybe he abducted her,' Maddy said.

'Did he notice anything about the man?' Talantire asked Nuttall.

Nuttall shook his head. 'No, just the shadow of a sleeve. I'll get the nearest uniform to visit, see if he recalls anything else.'

–

An hour later, the community centre had only one group left. Uniformed police had headed off to the moor for the search, Chief Inspector Campbell had gone back to liaise with the accident investigators. Commander West and his entourage were largely absent too, though the two admin assistants he had left behind didn't know where he was. Primrose Chen had taken the Aceso Kiosk back to Barnstaple, where she had her specialist software to go through more of the phone evidence. That left Talantire's group. Maddy Moran, Dave Nuttall and Beatrice Dodds had made considerable progress on CCTV. The petrol station and the supermarket had already forwarded footage from their own cameras that faced onto Truro bypass, and Nuttall was watching it on fast-forward, hunting for an image of Jade.

Talantire herself was continuing to examine finger-prints she had lifted from inside the car. There were a couple of Jade's from the top of the driver's seat, including to the right-hand side of it, which indicated that she had either entered or left the car from that side via the rear door. She found none of hers on the other side. Now what they needed to do was to find out exactly when that rear passenger door had opened: once presumably at the time when she got in, and again when she left prior to the accident.

'Gotcha!' Nuttall exclaimed.

The others crowded round his screen and saw a CCTV picture of a young woman, in a short skirt, heeled shoes and a lightweight jacket, standing by a bus stop. A face illuminated principally by her own phone, but also by a street lamp, made it clear that this was Jade. The footage matched the timing from the phone: 0:12 a.m. Nuttall ran the footage forward, showing Jade glancing to her right, and then the arrival of a white car. The number plate corresponded exactly with the crashed vehicle.

'I'll let his lordship know,' Talantire said, starting to message Commander West.

Nuttall reached up for the overhead TV and turned on the local news. A reporter was doing her piece to camera in front of a milling group of volunteers walking on the moor. 'Hundreds of volunteers and well-wishers today joined the Bodmin Moor search at first light for the missing Cornish schoolgirl Jade Kernow. The seventeen-year-old was last seen leaving her home in Truro on Saturday evening, more than thirty-six hours ago, and police say they are now seriously concerned for her safety. Her phone was tracked to the edge of Bodmin Moor, near where a fatal road accident occurred in the early hours of Sunday morning, but has been switched off since then. Jade was friends with several of those who were in the vehicle. Police are appealing for anyone who has information about Jade's whereabouts to contact them on the number that appears at the end of this bulletin. Jade's mother, Meghan, thanked members of the community who drove over from Camborne to assist in the search, saying, "My darling Jade is the light of our lives. If anyone has got her, or if she is out there somewhere, do get in contact with me or her uncle Gary, or call the helpline. Thank you to all those who came out today. I salute you."

Talantire watched the footage of volunteers in hi-vis tabards joining uniformed police as they combed the rugged moorland. Among them she recognised Jade's 'uncle' Gary, and her ex-boyfriend Finlay Roscoe, along with his parents.

Beatrice Dodds pointed out others she knew from the same community: the vicar of the local church in Camborne; Ivan Moss, an ex-offender who headed the local drug rehabilitation charity; Holly Skewes and her brothers, one of whom was thought to be the owner of an illegal e-motorcycle, which had been evading police on the estate for some weeks.

'Who's that?' asked Talantire, pointing at a tall hippyish man with Holly. He had grey dreadlocks, a goatee beard and was dressed as if for the beach, with flip-flops, shorts and a vest.

'That's Jelly Skewes, Holly's father, who's running the Find Jade website. He has some previous for cannabis dealing, back in the day when he was a Newquay beach bum. Now he makes jewellery for holidaymakers. Has a little shack at the beach.'

'Well, it's good to see everyone's involved,' Maddy said.

'The whole thing is just a massive feint,' Talantire said. 'Given that our lord and master Brent West believes she was driven off somewhere else.'

'I can see the benefit, though, of focusing the community on trying to help,' Beatrice said. 'It's like when everyone gave up their old saucepans for Spitfires in the war: it never really did any good, but it made people think that they were contributing something.'

When the Police and Crime Commissioner appeared on screen, Talantire turned it off. The last thing she needed to hear was some grandstanding speech by the Hon. Lionel Hall–Hartington.

–

'This is brilliant,' Talantire said. She was sitting at her iPad watching a GPS map on the Mercedes tracking app, using the log-in David Roscoe had sent her. It showed the location of the Mercedes from the moment it was stolen from their house at three a.m. on Friday morning right through to the time of the accident two days later. The car had been driven at speed all over the Truro, Redruth and Camborne area on the night of the theft. At 4:17 a.m. the signal disappeared near the Penypul estate.

'Someone's put it in a garage, or a multistorey, something like that,' Nuttall explained, looking over her shoulder. 'GPS is blocked quite easily.'

'It's probably a lock-up,' she said. 'There's hundreds around there, though we might be able to refine the map enough to find it.' Talantire turned around to him. 'So what have you been working on?'

'The Great British public.'

He showed her the incident-room message inbox and read out various titbits of information that had come through on the public information line, plus those passed on from the control room. There were several making accusations against individuals, but they all lacked detail, and most fell into the category of gossip. The information line crew at Exeter had marked up those of interest, but most simply told them what they already knew: that Scarlett and Jade didn't get on, and that 'Uncle Gary' had a wandering eye.

'Ah, here we go,' Maddy said. 'The DNA tests have arrived, finally.'

Talantire clicked open the email and the attached PDFs. She started with the results from the car. There were a large number of samples, and a match to Jade Kernow on quite a few of them, both inside and outside the car, which corroborated the fingerprints they already had. Interestingly, there were a couple of matches for her in the front passenger seat too, indications that the youngsters had been swapping seats a fair amount. Samples for Leanne Moyle, Scarlett and Lily Jago, Jordan Bailey and Aaron Darracombe came up in profusion, as expected. Holly Skewes, too, along with the original owners of the car, Mr and Mrs Roscoe, and their son, Finlay. There were three other unknown samples from the front and back seats and two other samples that were already on the DNA database. One was Jelly Skewes, from the front passenger seat, and the other was Tyler Darracombe, Aaron's older brother. None of the youngsters' traces proved anything. In the days after the car was first stolen, it was inevitable that all the local likely lads would have wanted to have a go in this expensive, sporty car. But Holly's dad Jelly was a surprise.

'Beatrice, what about this?' She showed her the sample result. 'Has Jelly got any car theft previous?'

'No. But he doesn't seem a likely acquaintance of the Roscoe family either. I'll ask them if they ever gave him a lift.'

Talantire switched to the next document, samples from Finlay's Vauxhall Nova: his own DNA was everywhere, naturally. There were traces of his father too, of Scarlett Jago, two other unknown samples and Jade. No surprises there; she had been his girlfriend several months previously, before the alleged one-night-stand with Scarlett. Tyler had been in the driving seat at some stage, too.

Talantire looked up the older Darracombe's criminal record. Nineteen years old, a conviction for car theft with a suspended sentence, possession of cannabis, a fine, and various bits and pieces of antisocial behaviour in his younger years. She scrutinised his mugshot: an intense-looking lad with a mop of tightly curled dark hair, tattoos up one side of his neck and a scowl that was presumably meant to be intimidating.

She looked across at Beatrice. 'Beatrice, tell me what you know about Tyler Darracombe?'

She smiled. 'A bit of a local tearaway, fairly petty stuff. His mother ran away from an abusive father, who has since departed the scene. The boys were brought up by their formidable grandmother, Roky.'

'Roky?'

'Yes. Her actual name is Roxanna. She's got a bit of previous herself. Affray, assault, receiving stolen property. Mostly a decade or longer ago. In truth, she's been good for the boys and has provided stability. The general feeling about Tyler is that he's on the straight and narrow now, having got a job at a local garage, though I wouldn't be surprised if he's doing some low-level cannabis dealing.'

'Is that Yelland's Car Repairs? The same one that Finlay Roscoe worked at?'

'Yes, though Finlay left a year ago.'

'Tyler's DNA turns up in the stolen car and in Finlay Roscoe's Vauxhall. Could he be the original thief, who actually stole the Merc?'

'It's possible. Of all of the names we have on the list, he is the one who clearly has the expertise. However, I'm a bit surprised he turned up in the Nova. There is bad blood between him and Finlay Roscoe, that's widely known.'

'Is it, indeed,' Talantire said. 'Shall we bring him in?'

Beatrice laughed. 'We won't have to go far. He is up there on the moor with the volunteers, I spotted him on the TV coverage. Let's take your car, he would recognise mine.'

–

Half an hour later, Tyler Darracombe was sitting with Talantire in the back of her unmarked car near Bodmin Rectory. Beatrice sat in the front passenger seat.

'It's very public-spirited of you to join in the search for Jade,' Beatrice said.

'Well, I can't do it no more after you dragged me in here,' he replied. 'And I'm going over again to see my little brother in Plymouth hospital in half an hour.' He took out an inhaler and sucked sharply from it, before wiping his nose.

'We appreciate that you are probably still in a state of shock because of the accident,' Talantire said.

'Yeah, I am,' he said, examining his fingernails which were bitten to the quick and showed traces of grime or oil. 'It was horrible, what happened to them.'

'Is there any word on the street who stole the car?' Beatrice asked.

'The woman cop asked me that before, and I told her, no, I hadn't heard anything.'

'Did you take a ride in it after it had been stolen?' Talantire asked.

His mouth opened, and he blinked rapidly but didn't say anything at first.

'Yeah, actually I did. When Aaron brought it round the house.'

'It's not what you told my colleague,' Beatrice said, looking down at her iPad. 'You said you "knew nothing about it". You lied, didn't you?'

'Look, I didn't know it was stolen.'

The two police officers laughed.

Talantire said: 'Your fourteen-year-old brother, not even old enough to drive, pulls up in a fifty-grand car, and you think he bought it?'

The trace of a smile passed across his lips. 'Well, I knew it wasn't his. I thought he might have permission.'

'Let's cut to the chase,' Talantire said. 'Your DNA is in that car.'

'Like I said, I got a ride in it.'

'Who else got a ride with you?'

'Leanne, Scarlett and her little sister. Aaron obviously, Holly. A few others.'

'Any adults?' She was thinking about Jelly.

Tyler frowned. 'Nah, not with me anyway.'

'Did you steal it?'

'Nope.'

'You're the only one we know who has the skill,' Beatrice said.

'Nah, lots of people know how to steal those keyless cars. It's a piece of piss. Me granny could do it. There's videos on YouTube on how to do it.'

'Yes, but it takes two people, Tyler,' Talantire said. 'One to hold a relay device next to the building where the keys are kept and another to jump into the car when it unlocks. You and Aaron, right?'

He shook his head and looked down at his nails, still smirking.

'C'mon, Tyler,' Beatrice urged.

'Wasn't me,' he said, now glancing out of the window.

'Where were you last Thursday night?' she asked.

'Don't remember.'

'Were you at home in bed?' Beatrice asked, helpfully.

'Yeah, that's right.'

'So, to confirm, you were in Camborne all night?' Talantire asked.

He shrugged.

'You own a poky little car, don't you?' Beatrice asked. 'A 2006 Ford Fiesta, with alloy wheels, racing trim, blue LEDs underneath. I bet it goes well.'

He examined his nails even more closely. 'Yeah, not bad.'

'Let anyone else drive it?' Talantire asked.

'No way,' he snorted as if it was the most preposterous idea he had ever heard. 'Wouldn't be insured, would it?'

'No, Tyler that's right,' she said. 'So perhaps you can explain why it was caught by a camera on the A30 between Camborne and Truro at 3:15 a.m. on Friday morning, roughly the same time as the Mercedes was stolen.'

He shrugged.

Talantire and Beatrice exchanged a satisfied glance. If only every criminal could be as dim as Tyler Darracombe.

'Right, Tyler, I think you need to come down to the station with us,' Talantire said.

He extruded petulance like a child denied access to sweets. 'My brother's dying in hospital and you won't let me see him.'

'We certainly will – after we've had a little bit of a conversation at Plymouth Crownhill. It's just down the road from Derriford Hospital,' Talantire said.

He folded his arms and looked out of the window. 'This ain't right. My family's been torn apart by this, and I'm devastated with grief.'

'You don't look that upset to me, Tyler,' Talantire remarked. 'Grief, just so you know, is what happens after somebody dies. Last we heard, Aaron was going to pull through.'

'You're a doctor, then?' he asked her.

'And you're a car thief,' she replied. 'C'mon, Tyler, we're going to the station.'

–

Plymouth Crownhill Police Station was two classic 1970s lumps of brutalistic concrete connected by a glassed-in aerial corridor. The interview rooms were suitably gloomy, the tape machines elderly and the coffee fitting only for those convicted of the most heinous crimes. Talantire set down her lukewarm plastic cup and peered across the table at Tyler Darracombe, squirming on the chair like the recalcitrant school truant he had once been. Next to him sat Nigel Sutton, a moustachioed duty solicitor, who she knew had been done for speeding just the previous week. Sutton was looking at papers in his lap. As he had arrived, she had spotted a sudoku puzzle magazine hidden among them. Cynicism about the criminal justice system was the default setting for all who worked within it, but all she could do was to think about why they were there: an innocent girl called Jade, missing now for more than thirty-six hours.

'Tyler Darracombe, you are not obliged to say anything. But it may harm your defence if you do not mention when questioned something which you later rely on in court. Anything you do say may be given in evidence.'

Tyler rolled his eyes as Talantire cautioned him.

She then said: 'Let's talk about Jade Kernow.'

'I don't know her.'

'So why did you come all the way over from Camborne to help look for her?'

'Because I'm a nice person,' he said, and then forced a smile which got no further than the bottom of his nose. 'Community spirit, innit? Me nan's here, on the way to the hospital.'

The solicitor stopped to write something in his lap. The pen movement was too brief to be anything but a sudoku answer.

'Excuse me.' Talantire reached across Beatrice to pause the tape. 'This whole case is a bit of a puzzle, isn't it, Mr Sutton?' she said, looking pointedly at the solicitor. He looked up, guiltily. 'So have you found the answer you were looking for? To help your client present his best case, paid for by public funds?' She pointed at his lap.

The man harrumphed and shuffled his papers, no doubt hiding the magazine. Talantire continued to stare at him for a few seconds afterwards and he could not meet her gaze.

Having made her point, she started the tape machine again.

'We'd like to look at your phone, Tyler,' she said.

'Tch.' His face contorted in adolescent outrage, as if she had requested a body cavity inspection. 'It's personal, innit?' He turned to the solicitor. 'Can she do that, mate?'

Sutton winced at the familiarity. 'She can request your co-operation, and if you refuse, which is your right, she can order it, so long as there is a genuine suspicion it is relevant to the investigation. Unfortunately,' he said with a shrug.

'This is bollocks,' Tyler said, scowling at no one in particular.

'No, it's the Police and Criminal Evidence Act 1984,' Talantire said. 'And the Regulation of Investigatory Powers Act 2000, which allows me to confiscate the item, access all the data stored within, and, if necessary, force you to divulge the pin code.'

'Tyler, if you've got nothing to hide, you've got nothing to fear, have you?' Beatrice said.

He scratched his hair ferociously. Talantire thought of the old joke of the millions made homeless by such manoeuvres.

'If you don't know Jade, there won't be any messages to her, will there?' Beatrice remarked.

Tyler quirked his lips. 'Maybe.'

Talantire jotted down the time on the tape of this ambiguous response: 10:35 a.m.

'I've got nothing to do with her disappearance, I promise.'

'We'd love to take your word for it, but we can't, can we? Come on, Tyler, give us your phone,' Talantire said, putting out a hand. 'We can get everything we need anyway by contacting your service provider, but if you really care about finding this missing girl, then you won't cause unnecessary delays to the investigation.'

He hesitated, then pulled a phone out of his back pocket and passed it across. It was an up-to-date Apple model, greasy and scratched.

'Am I under arrest?' he asked.

'No, you are free to go,' Talantire said. 'But remember the caution.'

As he stood, he poked a finger at them and said: 'You lot should be looking at Finlay Roscoe. He was the bastard who two-timed Jade. Then she dumped him, and he was right savage about it.'

A uniformed officer arrived to escort him up to the desk sergeant to sign him out.

As he left the interview room, with the brief in tow, he muttered, 'Bitches' under his breath.

'A charming individual,' Beatrice said. 'One of many from my patch.'

'Well, he's not wrong about Finlay Roscoe,' Talantire remarked. 'We've got Tyler's Fiesta on ANPR around Camborne on the Saturday night and Sunday morning, no further than that. That's an hour away from the crash. But Finlay's Vauxhall shows up three quarters of the way across to Bodmin Moor.'

'But we can't prove that either car was following the Merc, can we?'

'No, it could even be a third vehicle.'

Talantire's phone rang. It was Commander West.

'Jan, I need you up here, with the forensic team.'

'Whereabouts are you?'

'Eastern edge of the moor, between the abandoned Phoenix mine and the Hurlers Stone Circles. We've found a shoe, which is probably Jade's. I texted the photograph of it to her mother who confirmed her daughter has a similar pair.' He hung up.

Talantire emailed the news to the rest of her team, who were still in Liskeard, and, after scouring Crownhill for some forensic supplies, set off with Beatrice, blue-lighting it the whole way.

Chapter Ten

The Phoenix United Mine was a disused copper facility near the village of Minions, on the south-eastern edge of Bodmin Moor, and five miles due east of the accident. There was no direct road across the rough moorland between them, just some rough tracks, remnants of old tramways for moving ore. The ground rose steadily to the north-west, culminating in a rocky tor. The main building, built in the 1830s, had been turned into a mining museum, but the remains of numerous other stone-built outbuildings were still to be seen over a wide area.

Talantire parked in the museum car park at 11:15, to find the Liskeard team already there, loading up with forensic baggage. They headed uphill together along a track towards a knot of uniformed officers who were gathered around a small white crime-scene tent. They arrived to see Brent West, directing a fingertip search of the area.

'Jan, good to see you,' he said. 'Since we spoke, Jade's mother has confirmed that her daughter's identical pair is missing from the wardrobe. You'll find the shoe itself inside the tent.'

Talantire pulled a fresh Tyvek crime-scene suit from her kitbag. Normally, she would have just donned gloves and booties, but knowing that West was such a stickler, she didn't want to take any chances. He watched her, arms folded, as she wriggled into the crackly overalls, gloves and booties before unzipping the waist-high tent and clambering in. The canvas rippled and billowed in the wind as she crawled inside. She spotted the shoe right in the middle, resting on a patch of moss and liverworts. The spaceship-light quality and the natural soft feathery green cushioning made the solitary high-heeled silver strappy sandal look like a fashion exhibit, or perhaps a prop from a remake of *Cinderella*. Whose foot would fit within?

The thin ankle strap had been torn, but in the tiny buckle a tiny dark fibre could be seen. She had been told that nobody had moved or touched the item when the photographs had been taken. Using tweezers, she extracted it and put in an evidence bag. The shoe itself was a size five, and the heel was scuffed. Nudging the shoe with a gloved hand, she peered underneath. There was a price label bearing the retailer's name – New Look, £19.99 – still on the instep. On the leather sole was a small blackened patch, probably chewing gum, now hardened. She took a magnifying glass from her pocket and scrutin-ised the thumbnail-sized area. Chewing gum was fantastic for retaining the history of where someone had walked, though the lens revealed nothing.

Slipping the shoe carefully into an evidence bag, and pressing a yellow marker into the moss from where she had removed it, Talantire peered around the green damp vegetation. It was thick and spongy, and could conceal many things. She searched carefully by fingertip, delving into the damp beneath to see if anything else had been dropped. She found nothing.

After she had satisfied herself, she wriggled backwards out of the tent, bottom first, straight into the gaze of Brent West.

'An elegant exit, Jan,' he remarked, looking down at her. 'You might want to come and see this,' he said, indicating a group of men in overalls, harnesses and helmets, about fifty yards away.

'Have you got a caving team together?' she asked.

'Yes, but we are going to do this search a more modern way.' He led her over to them, and to a muddy depression with a rusting metal platform, and introduced Talantire to Sam Borrowdale, one of the men in the caving gear.

'This is my deputy,' West said to Borrowdale. 'Perhaps you could brief her?'

Borrowdale, a bearded Yorkshireman, said: 'Happily. There are dozens of old shafts down here, not just those from the Phoenix mine, but going back hundreds of years before, when tin was taken out by hand. The safest way to explore them is by drone.' He pointed to one of his colleagues who was kneeling down attending to a hand-sized quadcopter. 'That little fella is the safest way to explore the labyrinth of old shafts. It's got a very powerful light and a microphone. We'll get a good idea quite quickly if there's anybody down there, because it can get to places that even our skinniest of potholers would struggle with. This way, there is no need to risk rockfalls or the collapse of ancient woodwork that held up the tunnels.'

'Very good,' she said. 'How many tunnels and shafts are there around here?'

Borrowdale turned to a colleague, whom he described as a local man. 'There are thousands, probably most of them partially blocked by soil and vegetation.'

'So this could take a while, couldn't it?' she asked.

'The point is, Jan,' West interrupted, leading her away from the men, 'that we need to be seen to be doing something.'

'So you've invited the press?'

'Naturally.'

She nodded. 'All right, I've got other leads that I'm chasing down.'

'Yes, some forensic tests on the shoe for a start,' West said.

'You don't have to tell me how to do my job,' she replied.

'No indeed, I heard great things about you from the Ruth Lyle case. You took on the high and mighty and won. Play your cards right and there could be promotions for you.'

'My days of playing anything with you are over.'

He laughed, just as his assistant Samantha arrived, carrying what looked like a drone control unit. She shot Talantire a filthy look, and then turned her back, inserting herself into the conversation. 'Brent, I've done a sweep of the area north-west of here and turned up nothing.'

Talantire walked away, evidence bag in hand. The lack of personal space between Brent and Samantha, and her use of his Christian name, indicated he was playing fast and loose with his staff. She could feel her temper rising, all that bottled-up childhood anger. She took several deep breaths as she walked up to Nuttall, who was in conversation with Beatrice Dodds and Maddy Moran.

'More trouble with his lordship?' Maddy asked, seeing the expression on her boss's face.

'No, just the same trouble.'

'The word is that he is shaping up to be appointed as the new chief constable,' Nuttall said. 'It's been vacant for a while, and he's apparently got a manifesto to revolutionise the force, which is more than Noone ever had.' Assistant Chief Constable Jeremy Noone, desk-bound and old school, had been running the constabulary since the departure of the last chief constable a year ago. He was the opposite of hands-on, and was rarely seen outside Middlemoor.

Talantire sighed heavily, hands on her hips, and stared to the horizon. 'We've got work to do, Dave. A seventeen-year-old girl is missing.'

'I know,' he said, defensively.

'She didn't walk five miles across the moor wearing this, did she?' Talantire said, holding up the evidence bag. 'And we know she can't drive. If any of you can think of a reassuring explanation how this shoe got to be here, I'd very much like to hear it.'

Nuttall said nothing but exchanged a knowing boss-in-a-bad mood glance with Maddy.

'Maybe she was in the second car and got driven round here later,' Maddy suggested.

'Voluntarily?' Talantire asked. 'Her best friend, Leanne Moyle, was in the crashed car. We have Jade's fingerprints all over the back of that Mercedes where she banged on it, trying to get her out. Wouldn't she have stayed at the crash scene?'

'Maybe she was scared of being blamed for it, like we said,' Nuttall said. 'If the second car was racing, then whoever was driving was guilty of causing an accident.'

'I think you're on the right lines,' Talantire agreed. 'I think Jade was compelled to leave the scene of the crash. And the fact her phone was turned off from that moment makes me very concerned for her safety. Finding her shoe over here seems all wrong to me, wouldn't you say?'

'There would be no reason for her to want to come right over here,' Beatrice said.

'Exactly,' Talantire replied, then pointed across the landscape, a barren moorland, swathed in gorse. 'There are hundreds of old mineshafts here, perfect places to store a body. A car could have been driven to within a hundred yards of where we are standing and a body dragged at night, somewhere out there, and a shoe lost en route.'

'You think she's dead, don't you?' Beatrice asked.

'I've had that suspicion for a long time,' she replied. 'What I want you to do now is to check for any vehicle tracks between here and the car park.'

'Well, there's one lot for a start,' Nuttall indicated. 'Commander West's Ford Explorer was driven right up from the car park, over the tor and parked behind.'

'You're kidding,' Talantire said, following his gaze. Sure enough, she could now see the aerial from the cab, poking above the top of the rocks that marked the high point of the area.

Talantire made her way across to the two-tonne vehicle's distinctive tracks, which, as Nuttall had pointed, were carved into the landscape. After checking that none of the other vehicles belonging to West's entourage had made the same journey, she, Maddy, Nuttall and Beatrice spread out looking for other tracks.

It took just five minutes for Beatrice, who was working the car park end, to find a set of tyre prints where a vehicle had come off the moor and left a trail of mud on the tarmac. She took photographs and called the others over. They then traced back the marks on the moor, taking more images until they reached a place where they had largely been squelched by the later tracks of the Ford

Explorer. However, in some places they deviated just enough to be followed.

They stopped at a set of low rocks which the Ford Explorer, with its high ground clearance, had been able to mount and pass.

'It might well be somewhere around here that Jade's body was removed from the boot,' Beatrice said.

They all looked up as another vehicle drew into the car park. It was a blue van, which they recognised.

'That's the press, right on schedule,' Nuttall said.

'They're using a drone to explore some of the mineshafts,' Talantire told her team. She could see West's point. A focused rescue with brave explorers and a dash of technology was a made-for-TV event and again diverted the focus of the media away from the Camborne community where Talantire considered the answer to this riddle would be found.

A man in a leather jacket emerged from the van and waved good-naturedly towards them. Another went to the rear and began to unload a TV camera.

'No word about the shoe, all right?' Talantire warned her colleagues.

While they were talking, a drone took off, seemingly from the back of the Ford Explorer, and whizzed away further into the moor.

'I may be deputy SIO, but I'm not exactly being kept in the loop about this,' she said as she watched the tiny aerial vehicle disappear until it was a dot. 'Let's return to the incident room and have a quick meeting.'

They brushed past the reporters without answering any questions.

Back in the Liskerrett Community Centre, Talantire set up a midday meeting. With her were Maddy, Dave and Beatrice. On Zoom from Barnstaple, they had Primrose. Talantire had invited Commander West, assuming he would also be on Zoom, but had received a message back from his assistant that he was travelling to Exeter for urgent consultations. What that meant, Talantire didn't know, but she was happy to escape the micromanaging and have some measure of power over the course of the investigation.

She started by listing all the names of the youngsters, starting with Jade Kernow in the centre of the whiteboard. Then she ticked off the four they had originally found in the car: Aaron Darracombe, Scarlett and Lily Jago, and Jordan Bailey. Jordan was dead, the rest were in intensive care, along with Leanne Moyle, Jade's best friend, who was thrown from the car and found by Talantire on the moor.

She then listed the peripheral teenagers: Jade's ex, Finlay Roscoe; Tyler Darracombe, Aaron's older brother; and Holly Skewes, who had been in the car but exited before it left Camborne. On the edge of the board, she listed the various parents, friends, uncles, and so on. A couple of loose ends had been tied up by Beatrice. Maz, who had messaged Jade to ask if she was still angry with Scarlett, was Melanie Philpott, a school friend who claimed to have been nowhere near Camborne on the night in question. The frizzy hair spotted on a video taken in the car belonged to Carl Boateng, a fifteen-year-old from Truro, who claimed only to have been in the stolen car for half an hour, around one a.m. But, crucially, he said he saw Jade, who was in the car before he got in, and remained there after he got out.

'All right, everybody,' Talantire said. 'Here are the facts. At 2:17 on Sunday morning, a Mercedes E-Class crashed into the garden of Bodmin Rectory, at a speed of 107 mph. We have contradictory witness statements. One, from Lily Jago, suggests that Jade was in the car. It is perhaps unreliable. Another from Holly Skewes, says she wasn't. But Holly, by her own account, left the car at 11:45 p.m. before Jade was seen at 0:12 on Sunday morning by CCTV at a bus stop outside Truro getting into it. Carl Boateng left the car at 1:30 a.m. when Jade was still there, which may or may not be reliable. The last reliable sighting remains at 0:12 a.m. However, data from the car, analysed by Doug Blackstone, shows the vehicle was stationary from 1:47 a.m. to 1:52 a.m. at the A38 junction to East Taphouse. At 1:48 the rear driver-side door opened and was closed within a few seconds. This is possibly the moment when Jade left the vehicle, and cell mast data seems to confirm it, as by 1:54 a.m. her phone and those within the car were pinging different masts.' She pointed to the various timings on the whiteboard. 'This is where we believe she left one vehicle and soon afterwards entered another. Those two vehicles converged, with Jade's phone pinging the same tower as those in the Mercedes for the last few minutes before the accident. Jade's phone showed that it – if not she – was certainly very close to Bodmin Rectory at the time the accident took place.'

Talantire put up an image. 'Here we also have Jade's handprints, upside down on the Mercedes, indicating that she touched the vehicle after it turned over.' She drew an arrow from Jade's name to a little picture of a car. 'She was definitely there, at the time of the accident, and if her finger- and handprints tell any story it is that she tried desperately to get the car door open so that her friends could be extricated. She must have been unaware, at least at that time, that Leanne was thrown from the vehicle over the garden wall and onto the moor.'

'What about the footprints?' Nuttall asked.

'I was coming to that. At the scene of the accident, all footprints seem to have been obliterated by those of rescuers. However, impressions from Jade's distinctive high-heeled sandals were found not very far from the point where Leanne's body was found. We cannot at this stage be sure whether or not she found her friend's body. However, until this moment at least, the forensic and electronic evidence seem to indicate she was in control of her own actions, and that is a very important point.' She tapped the whiteboard for emphasis. 'The forensic trail tells the story of Jade trying to help a friend after an accident. However, the logical next stage would be for her to have rung the emergency services, yet no such call was made. Indeed, there's been no sign of her phone at all from 2:20 a.m. when its signal vanished from the nearest mast. Would she have turned it off herself? I don't think so. So my hypothesis is that somebody else was with her.'

'Someone who was in the second car, with her,' Maddy suggested.

'Very probably, yes. Thanks to Commander West's investigation of the smiley face speed camera in Trenewan, we do know that there was a vehicle in close pursuit at high speed. We have no clue which vehicle that was. Finlay Roscoe's Vauxhall Nova certainly left Truro to travel on the A30 at the right time but did not trip the second ANPR camera. This could mean that it went on the back roads, or somewhere else altogether. There is no record of Tyler Darracombe's Ford Fiesta in the area, either, so we're still in the dark.'

Beatrice raised her hand. 'What about the tyre marks at the Phoenix mine car park and up to the tor where the shoe was found?'

'We have got some clear tread marks. To a layman like me they look no different to the almost illegally shallow tread on Finlay's Vauxhall, and to Tyler Darracombe's Ford Fiesta. Thank you for getting those reference samples by the way, Beatrice. I have sent them off to specialists to see what else we can learn. It might take a few days.'

'The shoe seems to be an important clue,' Maddy said. 'It is definitely hers and matches the prints found near where Leanne was found. The fact that the ankle strap was torn might indicate that Jade was abducted.'

'Yeah, I think there is a good chance we'll find her body in one of those mineshafts,' Nuttall said. 'It seems pretty obvious.'

'Maybe it's too obvious, Dave,' Talantire said. 'First off, if somebody had already murdered Jade, why drive an extra fourteen miles on tiny roads to take her to a different bit of Bodmin Moor. There are mineshafts all over he could have used. And if she wasn't dead, there seems even less reason to drive all that way.'

'So you don't think she could have walked by herself?' Beatrice asked.

'Not on this terrain. If she had other shoes, maybe. But in our CCTV at the bus stop she didn't seem to have any luggage with her. Another thing about the shoe. It's a pretty big piece of evidence to sloppily leave behind, wouldn't you say, for someone who has been meticulous up to this point.'

'You mean an abductor?' Beatrice asked.

'Yes, I think that's where we are now,' Talantire said. 'Whoever was driving the second car, perhaps racing, would undoubtedly feel that if Jade attempted to call the emergency services and stay with the vehicle, he would be implicated in the killing. And if we discover that she is dead, that is my assumption for the motive.'

'Right,' Beatrice said, getting up, 'I've got to go back to Camborne now, to see how the community team are doing. I'll be back for this evening's news conference, with Meghan Kernow in tow. She's willing to make an appeal, in case anyone is holding her.'

'Okay,' Talantire said. 'Just make sure Uncle Gary is kept away.'

'Understood,' Beatrice replied.

After she left, Talantire said: 'We've got to find that second car. Ideally before the news conference.'

'How are we going to do that?' Maddy asked.

'Let's look at the map,' she said, extending an Ordnance Survey map of southern Bodmin Moor. She spread it right across the table. 'There are two possibilities: one is that the pursuing vehicle was Finlay Roscoe's Vauxhall. If so, it took a back route as we know it didn't trigger the ANPR camera on the A30 before the turn-off to St Trenewan. The second possibility is that it is another vehicle entirely. The best way to discover that is to download all the data from the ANPR cameras from Camborne, Truro and along the A30 along the southern edge of the Moor for the relevant hours.'

'That's gonna be thousands of cars,' Nuttall complained.

'It shouldn't be a problem,' Talantire said. 'We can start by picking the fastest ones, not just those breaking the limit measured at the camera site, but using an average speed checker across the network to find the fastest twenty per cent of vehicles that triggered the cameras between ten p.m. on the Saturday night and three a.m. on the Sunday morning. I think it's a reasonable assumption that whoever was following wanted to keep up with the Merc as best they could.'

'Yeah,' said Maddy. 'And we know from the smiley face camera, that the second vehicle was doing 82.8 mph. So it clearly wasn't a tractor, a quad bike, a lorry or a moped.'

'It could have been a motorcycle, car or van,' Talantire said. 'But my instinct is a car.'

'Was it stolen too?'

'Beatrice said the Merc was the only vehicle reported stolen in the Camborne and Truro area in the three days prior to the accident.'

'We should perhaps look for high-speed return journeys too,' Nuttall said. 'Someone fleeing after seeing the accident.'

'Good point,' Talantire conceded. 'All high-speed traffic at those times is potentially suspicious, so let's widen it to four a.m.'

Maddy was peering closely at the map. 'So going back to the idea that it was Roscoe's Vauxhall, there are three villages here across the back roads which could lead to St Trenewan. They are St Neot, Pengarth and Warleggan. The last two are tiny, but St Neot is big enough to have a pub. Maybe it will have a smiley face camera too.'

'It's the same parish council as St Trenewan,' Nuttall said. 'I'll get onto them to see if they can get me a download.'

'We'll need some uniformed resources too, for door-to-door. I want to see if there are any doorbell cameras, private CCTV – anything that might give a view of the road,' Talantire said. 'Even a glimpse of a passing vehicle may help. I need to ring his lordship, because none of his minions will do a thing without his permission.'

'Good luck with that,' Nuttall murmured.

Talantire rang West and left a message. 'Right,' she said. 'Let's get over to St Neot ourselves and take a look.'

The three detectives piled into her car, and they headed off on the twenty-minute drive.

Chapter Eleven

The village of St Neot was a straggly collection of a hundred homes dotted along narrow overgrown lanes in deeply wooded countryside. At its modest centre was a large car park opposite the St Neot Social Club.

'CCTV!' exclaimed Nuttall, pointing at the eaves of the club.

Talantire pulled into the car park, leaving Nuttall to negotiate the release of any footage, while she and Maddy walked in opposite directions along Tripp Hill looking for doorbell cameras. In Talantire's section, most of the stone-built terraced homes adjoining the street had nothing, while the larger and newer homes in the village were set too far back or obscured by bushes to be able to survey the road. They rendezvoused back at the car fifteen minutes later as arranged.

'How have we done?' Talantire asked, as they stood in the warm sunshine.

'Not exactly brilliantly,' Nuttall replied. 'The club's camera hasn't worked for years; it's just there to discourage break-ins. They had a few over the years, targeting spirits in the bar. The bloke I talked to did say that boy racers were a problem. There've been no end of accidents over the years – some of them fatal.'

'Did he remember anything from Saturday night?' Talantire asked.

'He wasn't on duty and, besides, they close at ten. He doesn't live in the village.'

Talantire turned to Maddy. 'Anything?'

'Nope,' she shrugged. 'Some old lady stopped me to whinge about people speeding through the village. They're trying to raise money for a smiley face camera. She pointed out an abandoned car on the verge opposite her house that had been there for a month.'

'Definitely not from Saturday night?' Talantire pressed.

Maddy smiled 'No, definitely not. She remembers the local bobbies coming to knock on her door after she'd reported it. It's got "police aware" tape all over it now, and it's just waiting to be collected. Someone has already nicked the alloy wheels.'

Talantire rolled her eyes. 'No doorbell cameras?'

'None that I could see. If you get a proper door-to-door from the uniforms, we might be able to get some dashcam footage from drivers out and about that night.'

'All right, everyone, let's just spend a few more minutes on the remaining roads, then head off to the next village.'

Ten minutes later, they were heading off to Pengarth.

'Ooh hold on,' Talantire said, braking the car sharply after they had just passed a farm entrance. 'There is CCTV on that building.' She reversed the car speedily back to the edge of a modern metal-framed barn, which overlooked the road. Sure enough, there was a CCTV camera which would appear to cover the farm entrance as well as the road. She pulled into the barnyard, emerging from the car to be greeted by the enthusiastic barking of a collie dog.

A man in wellingtons and blue overalls stood in the entrance. Talantire greeted him, and after showing him her warrant card, he led her into the farm office. Five minutes later she re-emerged, triumphantly holding a data stick.

'Right, that's twenty-four hours of footage, from midday on Saturday to midday on Sunday. We should be able to find something,' she said, as she clambered back into the car and drove off.

'While you were in there, I was looking through the latest social media that Primrose has dug up,' Maddy said. She leaned forward from the back seat and showed Talantire and Nuttall her iPad. 'This is from Leanne's phone, a TikTok video in selfie mode from the back seat of the Mercedes, showing Scarlett, Leanne and Lily, singing, right?'

She turned up the sound. The girls had taken laughing gas, a balloon was still visible in Leanne's hand, and their voices were high-pitched and silly.

'It's "Rolling in the Deep" by Adele,' Talantire confirmed.

'Suitably mangled, and very jerky too,' Nuttall remarked. 'I thought we'd seen this one before? It doesn't show anything, does it?'

'Ah,' said Maddy. 'We did see it, but you're understandably looking at pretty young girls enjoying themselves in a fast-moving car, which is not what you should be looking at.'

'So what should I be staring at?' Nuttall asked, peering more closely at the screen.

'Yes!' Talantire exclaimed. 'Car headlamps through the rear window.'

'Got it in one,' Maddy said. 'And the time on this recording is 2:13 a.m., which is just four minutes before the accident.'

'So we now have an image of the pursuing vehicle,' Nuttall said. 'But it will be hard to identify it just from the dazzle from a pair of lights.'

'Maybe,' Talantire conceded. 'And it's conceivable it's not the vehicle we are looking for. However, Doug Blackstone might be able to find out exactly where the Mercedes was at the time, using the data from the airbag module. If we can establish the precise speed of the Mercedes at the time, then we have a good chance of knowing whether there was a race taking place between the two cars.'

'How long is the video?' Nuttall asked Maddy.

'Just twenty-two seconds, before someone dropped the phone in a giggling fit.'

'I think Primrose has the tools to analyse this properly, get the vibration off the image, maybe even enhance the portion which shows the headlights,' Talantire said. She put the car into gear and headed off back to Barnstaple.

Slowly, but surely they were making progress. There was another press conference due at five o'clock, and at least they would have something to say. There was nothing worse in the hunt for a missing youngster than not having any investigatory progress to share.

–

Talantire, Nuttall and Maddy peered over Primrose's shoulder at the screen. The digital evidence officer applied a camera-shake removal algorithm to the video of the three girls singing in the back of the car, and then replayed it. It succeeded in removing the most high-frequency vibrations, but the image still lurched alarmingly.

'I'm going to try another tool, which centralises and fixes the image we're looking for,' Primrose said. Using her cursor, she defined the glare of the headlamps from the vehicle behind, an hourglass-shaped space between the heads of Lily and her sister Scarlett. She then ran the software for a couple of seconds before replaying the video.

'Ah, that's better,' Talantire said. 'If you can zoom in at all, we might even get an idea of the light layout.'

'I thought I saw a sidelight,' Nuttall said. 'If we can confirm that, we can find the make and marque of the car.'

Primrose managed to get a twenty per cent magnification. 'That's the maximum before pixelation obscures the image,' she confirmed. 'I'll screenshot them.'

'That's good,' Talantire said.

'Now, seeing that you are interested in what is behind the car,' Primrose said, 'there is an earlier video on Leanne's phone, in which the driver and front passenger talk to each other, and the passenger turns around to look behind.'

'What do they say?' Talantire asked.

'Good question,' Primrose replied. 'They're playing really loud rock music, and you can't hear a word.'

'Can you play it for us?'

'Sure.' Primrose clicked on her screen, and a video began with Lily and Scarlett pulling faces into the camera, while AC/DC's 'Highway to Hell' was playing at full volume. The view panned right to the front of the car. It caught driver Aaron Darracombe glancing up to the mirror, then turning to Jordan Bailey in the passenger seat. Jordan then turned round to look behind. It was clear from his emphatic jaw and facial movements that he was swearing.

'I reckon that's "fucking hell, it's Finlay",' Maddy surmised.

'Yeah, the bottom lip comes under the top teeth. That's definitely an F or two,' Nuttall agreed.

Talantire laughed. 'It's a Rorschach test, isn't it? You read into it what you want to. I don't think it proves anything, seeing as we can't hear them.'

'I could try to remove the music,' Primrose suggested.

'Do *what*?' Nuttall asked, incredulously.

Primrose turned to them. 'Okay, so you've seen spy films, where two people talk to each other with the shower running, to hide their voices from any bugs in the room.'

Talantire nodded.

'Well, by modelling the exact sound, echoes and all the other characteristics of a running shower at a particular water volume, it is possible using digital signal processing to filter out the shower sound and then determine from the residue what was being said. In the case I had, it also meant subtracting traffic noise, air conditioning, that kind of thing, to get back the conversation.'

'How on earth did you learn how to do that?' Talantire asked.

'When I was doing my masters at the University of South Carolina. Then, when I was at Langley, they had me reconstructing audio from crackly radio transmissions in Afghanistan.'

'Really? You worked for the CIA?' Maddy asked.

'No. I was an intern at a technical subcontractor, so I only had limited security clearance. Part of my master's was in forensic audio, with an emphasis on adaptive filtering.'

'Wow,' said Nuttall. 'I'm surprised you didn't need security clearance for that, overhearing spies.'

She laughed. 'The only conversations I worked on were in a local language. I didn't find out until afterwards, after everything had been turned over to the CIA, that the language was Pashto and it took place in Afghanistan. I don't speak a word of it.'

'So you can do something with this video?' Talantire asked, tapping the screen.

'Maybe. The audio output on the digital file is made up of three things. One is the song, and the great advantage we have is that it has a known electronic signature. Then we have the background noise of the car and the other people in it, and then we have the target signal, which is the conversation between the driver and front seat passenger. In theory, it's quite simple to remove the music, but separating out the two residuals from each other may well be difficult as they are such a small part of the overall signal.'

'How long will it take?'

'All night, maybe.'

'Not sure it's the best use of your time, Primrose,' Talantire said. 'It's gone two now, and we've still got so much data to examine. Let's put it on the backburner for now. Dave, let's look at the CCTV?'

Nuttall returned to his terminal, inserted the data stick and ran the footage from the farm building, while Talantire looked over his shoulder. The camera was monochrome but good and modern. However, because its main focus was the farm gate, it gave only a peripheral image of the road. Moving the timer up until midnight, the few vehicles that passed could be identified only by their silhouettes. A couple of vans, three cars and a motorcycle. Fast forwarding through, they had missed it at first: a brief flash at 1:55 a.m. Going back for a second look, a car shot past, from one side of the screen to the other in a little over a second.

'That is seriously fast for a tiny country road,' Nuttall muttered.

'Run it at half speed,' Talantire advised.

In slow motion, the car gave up some of its secrets. 'It's small, and certainly could be a Vauxhall Nova,' Nuttall said. 'Both headlamps are working, but you can't see both sidelights.'

'Right, I'll send it and the video screenshot to the car ID unit in Exeter,' Talantire said. 'I think we can arrest Finlay Roscoe on the strength of this.'

'What about his alibi?' Maddy asked.

'Family and girlfriends? Those are not reliable alibis. Look, he used to be Jade's boyfriend. It's either him or "uncle" Gary.'

They were interrupted by the noise of heavy feet mounting the stairs. The doors to CID burst open, and Police and Crime Commissioner Lionel Hall–Hartington lurched in, bringing a fog of alcohol with him.

'Ah, Jan. How's it going on the missing girl?'

Talantire straightened up and responded: 'We are working as hard as we can, and have got—'

'—Marvellous, hope she's found soon,' he said, and veered left towards the gents'. Talantire realised that there must've been a meeting at the George Hotel across the river. It wouldn't be the Rural Crime Committee, because that was a Wednesday. She heard the crashing of doors inside the gents' and shook her head towards the rest of CID.

The next minute, the lift doors opened and Mrs Helena Hall-Hartington reversed her wheelchair out.

'Where is the old bugger?' she asked.

'In the gents', Talantire responded, indicating its location with an inclination of her head.

'For God's sake,' she muttered, as she wheeled herself towards the door.

Mrs HH was a handsome woman in her late fifties with fine cheekbones, who, decades ago, had been a model in London. Now, with the onset of multiple sclerosis, her horizons had been dramatically curtailed. Everyone felt very sorry that she was married to the old soak.

She pulled out a telescopic walking stick and rapped sharply on the bathroom door. 'Come on, for Christ's sake, Bagpuss. It's my hair appointment in ten minutes. If you're not out in thirty seconds, you can get a bloody paid taxi.'

There was some answering shout from inside, which Talantire couldn't decipher.

Mrs HH wheeled herself back to the lift, used her stick to press the call button and when the doors opened pulled herself back inside.

The commissioner emerged just a few seconds after the lift had departed, tottering slightly as he tried to pull up his flies, and then waved a vague goodbye before crashing down the stairs.

The moment the double doors had closed behind him, everybody in CID had just one word to say: Bagpuss!

'He does look a little like him,' Maddy said.

'What's a Bagpuss?' Primrose asked.

'It's a cartoon character from kids' TV in the 1970s,' Maddy said. 'A cat with a florid face. Just like his.'

What a fabulous pet name. The Honourable Lionel Hall-Hartington was out and Bagpuss was in.

The doors reopened, and the commissioner put his head back in. 'By the way, a new chief constable is being appointed this afternoon. Thought you'd like to know. The post's been vacant for too long.'

'Who is it, sir?' Talantire asked. Surely not, surely not. It couldn't be.

'Mum's the word,' the commissioner said, tapping the side of his nose.

As he disappeared, a single female shout could be heard from downstairs: 'Come ON!'

The door banged shut, and everyone in the team laughed, bar Talantire.

'What's the matter, Jan?' Maddy asked.

'I cannot bear the idea of Brent bloody West as the chief constable,' she said. 'But he's been away in Exeter all day, and not returning calls. It's the only logical conclusion.'

'Never mind, he'll be more effective than Noone.'

'More controlling, certainly,' Jan said. 'It's just so *wrong*.' Her phone rang, and she picked it up angrily. 'Talantire.' She then noticed the number: her mother.

'Jan, dear. I was surprised you didn't ring me, after rushing away in the middle of the night like that. I've left two messages on your personal mobile. But no, you didn't reply.'

'I've been very busy, Mum. It was an emergency.'

'Like always. You're always too busy. Too busy to visit Bella, too busy to find yourself a man, too busy—'

'Mum, I'm at work!'

'Well, I think it's stress. I've seen all the symptoms in you. The insomnia, poor dietary habits—'

'There's nothing wrong with my diet—'

'And of course your temper—'

'Got to go, Mum, bye.' She killed the call, and steepled her hands over her face. Talantire's relationship with her mother had been fragile for decades. But yes, she was right. Bella. Her identical twin Bella, oxygen deprived at birth, and institutionalised since the age of three. She was only in Bristol. She'd not been to see her for years. Had avoided every entreaty, every hint from Estelle. The reason for her evasion she could never admit: she couldn't bear to stare at her own features, particularly her own big blue eyes, on Bella's now-bloated body. Bella, with a face somehow full of reproach: *I could have been you. And you could have been me.* The guilt was unbearable, and she'd been hiding it for years.

-

It was with some trepidation that Beatrice went back to the smallholding to interview Jelly Skewes. The man received her in the same rank caravan that she had sat in before, but at least this time the cat litter tray had been moved elsewhere. Holly's father was tall and skinny, and dressed as usual for the beach, with a stained vest, baggy faded shorts and on this occasion no shoes. His toenails showed green nail varnish.

'Mr Skewes, I just need to ask you a few more questions in connection with Jade Kernow.'

'Is this about the website and the Facebook page? I am talking to the others about tightening up the commenting, like you suggested.'

'No, it's not. I just wondered if you knew the Roscoe family at all?' Beatrice knew that one crucial piece of evidence she had of the connection was that Jelly's DNA had turned up in the stolen Mercedes, but none of the known passengers had mentioned him being part of the joyride at any stage.

'I know *of* them,' he said. 'Finlay used to work at the local garage, and his mother is head of the junior school. But I don't know them to talk to or anything.'

'When were you aware that their car had been stolen?'

'Not until I heard of the accident,' he said.

'Your DNA was in the car, Mr Skewes, can you explain that?'

His mouth hung open like a stranded fish. 'No, I cannot,' he said eventually.

Beatrice let him twist on the hook, just looking at him.

'You know there were drugs found in that car, don't you?'

'No, I didn't know that,' he replied. 'Look, my conviction was a long time ago, you can't come round trying to pin that on me.'

'I'm not trying to. But there is forensic evidence, and so far you haven't given me an explanation of how it could have been there.'

He shook his head, and his dreadlocks flicked over his shoulder. 'I can't think.'

'There were ecstasy tablets in that car, Mr Skewes. You've not been dabbling, have you?'

'No, I haven't.' He looked quite upset. 'Every time anything to do with drugs comes up, you always come round talking to me.'

'Well, you can see why we would.'

'I was at my shack at Newquay all day Saturday, loads of people saw me there.'

'Anyone in particular, someone we can check your alibi with?'

He looked up in the air, and stroked his beard. 'They were mainly tourists, but I took some sales. They would be recorded on the card machine.' He got up and went out of the room, returning a minute later with a cloth shoulder bag from which he took a portable retail device. He pressed a couple of buttons and it printed out a long point-of-sale tally. He tore it off and showed it to her. It did include three or four sales over the course of Saturday.

'May I keep this?' Beatrice asked.

'You may indeed. With my compliments.'

'That's helpful, thank you.'

'While we're at it. Look what else I've got for you.' He put his hand in the bag and pulled out a circular cork display board on which were pinned a dozen different enamelled lizard broaches. He unpinned a metallic green one, a well-made sinuous creature the length of a finger. 'This goes well with your lovely pale complexion,' he said, holding it up next to her face.

'No thank you, Mr Skewes,' Beatrice said, gathering her things together and standing up. 'I can't accept that.'

'What do you mean? I'm not giving it to you. Now, I could offer you a good price. But I've got to feed my family, so it wouldn't be free.' He held it again, next to her ear, and she backed away towards the caravan door. 'If you do want something free. We've got some nice earrings.'

'No, thank you.' She was now very anxious to leave.

Just as she reached the door, he said: 'I think I know why my DNA may be there. I mended Holly's handbag strap on Friday, and she had it with her in the car, didn't she? So if the tests are that sensitive, that may have picked it up, yeah?'

Beatrice shrugged. It was plausible.

Beatrice left just after three p.m. Jelly went straight to his shed, unlocked the door and made his way inside. He lifted up a plank in the floor and removed a small metal tobacco tin. He prised off the lid, and took out the polythene bag within. Taking a hammer, he gently tapped at the bag, until the mauve tablets within were a powder. He peered out of the door, to ensure that the cop had really driven away. Then he took the bag, walked out of the shed and over to the goat enclosure. He emptied the bag into a large plastic sack of goat food supplement, then, leaning over the pallet fence, topped up the food hopper, mixing in some water.

'You have a happy trip, girls. Courtesy of the nanny state,' he said. 'You'll be E'd out of your minds!' He laughed to himself, then in a brazier in the yard lit a small fire in which he burned the polythene bag.

Chapter Twelve

It was half three, and Talantire had heard nothing from West, despite leaving a second message. It could only mean he was still in meetings at Exeter. Typical that he put his own career before trying to find the missing girl. Without the resources that he could bring to bear, there was a real chance of a public relations disaster too. Beatrice Dodds had sent her a couple of links to the Find Jade website and Facebook group. With crowdfunding pages, conspiracy theories, traded accusations and insults, it only succeeded in raising the temperature. Long threads of comments were loaded with predictions that a member of the close family would eventually turn out to be her murderer, and furious denials from within the family. Camborne Community Policing had made several pleas both on Twitter and in posts on the group, urging users to refrain from hurtful or speculative posts, but it had no effect. Despite his promises, Jelly Skewes as administrator had resolutely kept the group open to all, rather than making it a closed membership as Beatrice had suggested.

'Basically, it's turning into a complete shitshow,' Beatrice said, when Talantire rang her. 'No one has discussed what's happening with the press conference, which is supposedly taking place in just ninety minutes.'

'I assumed it was taking place at the Liskerrett Community Centre,' Talantire said. 'I'm just about to head off myself. Is Jade's mother coming?' She stood up, the phone still pressed to her ear.

'Yes, she said she would.'

'Fine. If I don't hear from West, I will run it myself. Moira is making the arrangements.' She ended the call.

'One more thing, ma'am,' Primrose called out, as Talantire logged off her screen. 'I've been working my way backwards through Jade's calling records. There are a lot of calls to one number, which she has recorded under the name Simon. I'm not aware of anyone on our persons of interest list of that name. Do you want me to pursue it further?'

'Yes, particularly if there were any calls on the day she disappeared.'

'There were, but not in the last hour. There are also some text messages on the night, which look interesting.'

'Show me,' Talantire said, as she scooped up her briefcase and papers ready to leave.

The screen showed the times and caller.

23:56 Simon: Wait a mo. I'll ring you in two.

00:14 Simon: I couldn't hear a word. Who's driving?

00:15 Jade: Aaron

> **00:15 Simon:** Stay with it.

> **00:37 Simon:** Result?

> **00:37 Jade:** No. I'm in the back.

> **00:38 Simon:** Bale then, as agreed.

The final text from Jade was a heart emoji, the same minute as Simon's final message to her.

'It looks significant,' Talantire said. 'A close relationship, and something agreed beforehand. This was almost two hours before the accident. I want a trace on the Simon phone.'

'It's a burner,' Primrose said. 'I already found that out.'

'That makes it much more suspicious. I need to know exactly where it was from the twenty-four hours leading up to the accident to the twenty-four hours since; I want every tower that it pinged.' Talantire had already reached the door, when Primrose called to her.

'One I've got right here, ma'am. The Colliford Lake South cell tower on Bodmin Moor, the nearest one to the accident. And yes, it's on there at the right time.'

'Great work, Primrose, get me everything you can. I'll see if Camborne Community Police know of anything about this Simon.'

–

Talantire hurried to her car and roared out of Barnstaple police compound with the blues going. She knew she was cutting it fine to get to Liskeard by five p.m., but she could always put the press conference back by fifteen minutes if necessary. It's the kind of thing that happened all the time, though it looked best if paired with some kind of last-minute breakthrough. She couldn't count on that. All she had right now were some promising leads.

The unmarked Skoda whizzed through the industrial estate and out onto the A39. She left the urban congestion behind before she returned Moira Hallett's call. The PR chief for Devon and Cornwall Police was already at the community centre where the conference would take place. Talantire asked her if she had heard from Commander West, and she said not.

'The rumour is he is about to be appointed chief constable,' Moira said. 'He's been in with the ACC half of the day, and a planned announcement in Exeter for six o'clock has been postponed.'

'At least you're not trying to do two things at once,' Talantire said.

'Absolutely,' Moira replied. 'Though I hope he does get it.'

'That's not my view,' Talantire responded. She had been immensely cheered by the prospect of snags in West's hitherto meteoric ascent, but Moira was clearly of a different opinion. Talantire could certainly see why anyone would prefer having a man with the leadership panache of Brent West rather than see Jeremy Noone promoted. But surely there should be somebody else who could do the job as well as West without the dodgy personal history?

While she was on the hands-free to Moira, she saw West's mobile number flash up on her call waiting screen. Finally.

'I have to go now, Moira, the man himself is on the other line.'

'Good luck,' she replied, cutting the call.

'Jan, how are you?' West asked.

'I'm fine, thank you. Just hurrying down to Liskeard for the press conference. It seems you had a busy day.'

He chuckled. 'Yes, been stuck in meetings. It's all quite unfortunate really, given the urgency of this case.'

So you have *noticed that, then*, Talantire thought to herself.

'So are you going to be our next chief constable?' she asked.

West laughed softly, and she was now aware that he must be driving too, from the background noise. 'It's certainly impossible to keep a secret. Yes, it's just a question of dotting the i's and crossing the t's. I've spent more time with the headshrinkers than the appointment committee.'

'I can see why you might be nervous about that.'

Talantire was aware of the fearsome reputation of the human resources department, recently beefed up by the appointment of Fiona Hendricks from the Met, where she had reinvigorated the recruitment vetting process in the wake of the Wayne Couzens scandal. The headshrinkers' role, ultimately, was to ensure that no one like the killer of Sarah Everard could ever join the police, so if they were doing their job, they should also be able to stop someone like West from reaching the top.

'Funny you should say that, Jan. I was hoping we could have a little chat after the press conference.'

Talantire was stunned. 'You're coming to Liskeard?'

'Of course, I've got a press conference to run.'

'I assumed it would be down to me, as you were busy.'

'No, I'm sorry about the short notice but appreciate that you are backstopping me. Anyway, I thought we could have dinner afterwards.'

'Sorry, I'm washing my hair.'

He laughed again.

'Seriously, Brent, I have no desire to socialise with you at all. I thought you knew that. I've been fully vaccinated against your charms.'

There was a prolonged silence.

'All right, I'll see you at the conference hall. But we do need to talk.' He hung up.

–

Talantire arrived at the community centre just two minutes before the delayed start to the conference. She could see Brent West's Ford Explorer already there, dominating the car park like a tank at a tea party. There were a few broadcast vans as well, and as she parked her own car and hurried inside, she was buttonholed by a couple of reporters. She told them nothing.

Once inside, she saw West's team buzzing around getting everything set up. Moira Hallett was among them. The press was corralled behind tables on the left-hand side of the room, and the police on the right with a series of whiteboards displaying pictures of the missing girl and the site of the accident. Beatrice Dodds was there, seemingly arguing with a rather petulant-looking Meghan Kernow and her family liaison officer Tina Smith, but Talantire avoided them. She needed to speak to Moira, to know what angle West was going to go for.

'I think the fact that an arrest has been made shows progress,' Moira said. 'We're obviously not going to name Heaton at this stage, but at least the press can see we're being proactive.'

'But I understand he has a good alibi,' Talantire said quietly, careful to avoid being overheard by the press. Gary Heaton, despite his dodgy past, would have needed a time machine to have been anywhere near Jade at the point of her disappearance.

Moira shrugged. 'It's all we've got that West is willing to share.'

At that moment, the man himself emerged from the back, resplendent in his formal uniform, his cap tucked under his arm. Tall and well-built, he really did look the part, that was the damn problem with him. He called the meeting to order, and arranged for a still unhappy-looking Meghan Kernow to be sitting to his right, with Talantire and Moira to his left. He breezily summarised the situation, that the investigation of the missing girl was being separated from that of the tragic accident at Bodmin Moor.

'However, we are keeping an open mind about links between the two events. What I do have to tell you is that this afternoon we made an arrest in the Truro area, and a man in his forties is currently in custody—'

'He bloody shouldn't be,' Meghan Kernow interrupted, leaning towards the microphone. 'Gary's done nothing wrong, he was with me the whole time. I don't know what they're thinking. And while they're questioning an innocent man, the guilty man is out there somewhere and maybe targeting your child.' She pointed an accusing finger towards the press.

West looked horrified, but thanked the woman for her comments. 'I think at this stage it would be good for everybody to hold back from judgement. This is a fast-moving inquiry, with a great deal of electronic evidence still to be assessed. Rest assured that we have not in any way given up on pursuing other leads.'

'What other leads?' called someone from the back of the press conference.

'We are not at liberty to share the details,' he said.

'But isn't it true that Jade's phone showed her to be at the scene of the accident?' asked another reporter.

'Yes,' West conceded. 'But I would urge you not to speculate.'

Talantire peered sideways at him. Asking the press not to speculate was as pointless as asking a dog not to salivate before its dinner was served.

Moira then took charge, and asked for questions, all of which she wrote down and then said. 'We'll get back to you on these when we have enough information to share. However, I would continue to appeal to the public to send in any evidence of sightings of Jade, either now or on the evening she disappeared. Everything will be treated with complete confidentiality.'

Meghan Kernow started to speak again and Moira deftly switched off the microphone. For all that, everyone heard what she had to say.

'The police have made a complete mess of this. She was missing a *whole day* before they took it seriously, and we had to set up our own search.'

Several of the reporters rushed up to her, keen to find out more details, but Moira, Beatrice and liaison officer Tina Smith tried, with various levels of subtlety, to lead her away. Talantire had rarely seen such a PR disaster.

West's absence for most of the day, and the ill-advised decision to have Meghan sit with them when she was clearly unhappy, had not been thought through properly. Moira was a PR professional but had clearly taken on trust what she'd been told about the mother of the missing girl. Still, it gave Talantire a frisson of schadenfreude: anything that damaged Brent West's career couldn't be all bad.

—

Talantire had just emerged from the ladies' when Brent West steered her into a playroom at the community centre. 'I just need a quiet word, Jan,' he said, closing the door behind them.

'I've got lots to do,' she warned him. 'I'm heading off to Truro to interview Gary Heaton.'

'I shan't detain you long.' He swept his hand through his hair, and then made eye contact with her. 'As you know, I'm hoping to be the next chief constable.'

'I had heard,' she said, with a note of sarcasm.

'Look, I know we don't see eye to eye, but I just need to know that you're not going to start breaking crockery.'

She knew exactly what he meant but wanted him to spell it out. 'I've no idea what you're driving at,' she said.

'Come on, Jan.' He looked heavenward, and sighed. On the window ledge right behind him was a big cross-eyed gonk, and the floor was scattered with tricycles, a toddler's plastic swing and a box of Duplo Lego. The perfect place for some infantile powerplay.

'I better tell Beatrice I'll be a bit late,' she said. She slipped her iPhone from her pocket and checked her messages. She pretended to text her and then surreptitiously hit the voice note icon, before slipping the phone back in her pocket.

'You're still renting, aren't you?' he said.

'I've been too busy to look for somewhere to buy.'

'It's got awfully expensive down in the south-west, hasn't it?'

'Yes, but I get by.'

'Don't be obtuse, Jan. I'm offering you an opportunity.'

'Are you trying to pay me off?'

'Oh, no no no, you've got completely the wrong end of the stick,' he said, managing to look offended.

'After you secretly filmed us having sex, you now have the nerve to try to get me to shut up for a payment?'

'I didn't film you.'

'I saw the lens hidden in the headboard.'

'I never filmed you, I promise on my life.'

'I know what your promises are worth,' she said, folding her arms, a barrier between them. The affairs she had discovered, the wife who she'd been told he was separated from. The controlling behaviour. All lies upon lies.

He approached her and she unconsciously backed towards the wall.

'Stay back,' she warned him. Her head was now resting among crayoned pictures of fire engines and police cars scrawled by five-year-olds, perhaps the only remaining constituency for whom the law was a source of comfort and inspiration. How much they had to learn.

One of his arms was on the wall beside her, and in front a crocodile smile of perfectly whitened teeth. She seriously considered how easy it would be to knee him in the balls right now. But if even half of the recording worked that would be a more elegant revenge. After all, she had an expert on the team in Primrose to enhance the sound if necessary.

'Fifty grand says it never happened, Jan,' he crooned into her ear, his lips almost brushing her hair. 'Just sign an NDA, you get the cash and it'll all be over.'

She planted a hand in the middle of his chest and pushed him back. 'You think you can just buy your way out of any trouble, don't you?' She pressed harder and he backed away, the smile fading. There was anger in his eyes.

'If you damage me or my career, Jan, I promise I will destroy you,' he hissed.

She managed a tight smile. 'How pleasant you are, Brent.'

She walked away feeling powerful eyes burning holes in the back of her head.

The moment she got to her car, she checked her phone and listened to the recording. Much of it was crackly and hard to hear, not surprising as the phone was in her pocket. But his threat to destroy her was as clear as a bell, along with her careful phrasing of exactly what he was trying to do. It was dynamite, that was certain, but what was she to do with it? She had to consider that very carefully.

She watched as his black 4WD thundered out of the car park. Once he was gone, she then began to shake, and despite her best efforts, she rested her head on the steering wheel and hot tears of fury came into her eyes.

I will not let this happen to me. Never again. Never.

It took her back. Eight years old. Sitting with babysitting neighbour Mr Pye watching a James Bond film. She recalled it like yesterday. It was a day her brother was playing football after school, and she was on her own with him. He had hauled her onto his lap, and she had felt the growing lump beneath her bottom, his fat, liver-spotted old-man fingers sliding over her thighs. She had announced that she needed the toilet.

'No you don't,' he'd said. But she had wriggled out of his grasp anyway, and refused to share the sofa with him.

When her mother had arrived from work, she'd said: 'I don't like Uncle Lenny.' But she didn't have the words to say why. Instead, she was told she was being difficult, seeking attention while her mother was trying to look after her disabled sister. 'Mr Pye has his disabled wife to look after, it's very kind of him to babysit, and you should be appreciative. I don't want to hear any more of this nonsense about him.'

And the babysitting had continued, Mr Pye confining himself to stroking her hair as she sat by his side, the big smelly waxed jacket over his lap. Next time she was alone with him, he had given her a fine silver necklace with a tiny red gem like a drop of blood. He'd said it had once been owned by an Indian empress who ruled a land of spice and was carried around on an elephant. He'd called it 'our little secret'. She had accepted the pretty bright thing, and hid it at home.

His gambit was successful.

A few weeks later, when his hand was busy beneath the jacket on his lap, she had wriggled from his grasp and fled out of the door. He had looked for her, calling out, but didn't find her. She was hiding in the cold, rainy darkness, sheltering behind the communal dustbins, to wait shivering for an hour for her mother's arrival. But Uncle Lenny got their first. He had rung Estelle at work, saying Jan had stolen some of his wife's jewellery and run away when confronted. So when Jan ran sobbing to her mother, as she emerged from the car, she got a stinging rebuke not sympathy. Frogmarched indoors, the necklace was soon found. Jan's tearful insistent protest 'But he gave it to me!' earned her a slap and confinement to her bedroom. 'You're not just a thief, but a liar. A wicked little girl!' her mother had said.

From that moment, the shadow of maternal abandonment had never quite left her life.

When she was eighteen, she had brought up the subject again, only to be told that there was no way Mr Pye would do anything like that. 'Don't be ridiculous. You *stole* from him.'

A few years later, when she announced she was going to join the police, her mother had laughed, a hard bitter sound she could still hear. 'You?' she had asked, before looking away. *A thief*, the unspoken words.

Was it her destiny never to be believed? She gripped her phone and played the recording of Brent West again.

'...I promise I will destroy you.'

Chapter Thirteen

Talantire reached Gary Heaton's home at 6:30 p.m. It was easy to find, sitting atop a hillside crescent, because some enterprising individual had spray-painted 'pedo' and 'nonce' in fuzzy red right across the double garage doors. This had been achieved even though there was supposed to be a PC on the door day and night.

Talantire parked her Skoda between Beatrice Dodd's Nissan and a patrol car, ducked under the blue-and-white tape and walked past a gaggle of children who were staring at them. One child, a boy of about eight, had an oversized pair of binoculars that he was training on the windows of Heaton's three-bedroomed semi. How could Cornwall do so badly economically, given all the enterprising kids who lived here?

Beatrice emerged from her car to greet Talantire, and the two detectives signed in at the door with a very apologetic young PC who, unprompted, told them he had no idea how the graffiti came to be there. After they had returned the clipboard to him, the young officer let them inside.

The place was a gigantic man's shed, stuck in some perma-Christmas, with red, green and white festive carpet and a banister draped with flashing lights. There was a TV in every room, and shelves and workspaces cluttered with knick-knacks, tools, a display of aged cameras and more

165

wall-hung nets of Christmas lights flashing merrily. The main bedroom boasted a waterbed, and a heart-shaped mirror on the ceiling. Vases of pale pink plastic roses adorned the room. In a second bedroom, there was a large collection of country and western on vinyl, lots of Johnny Cash, and Day of the Dead Mexican memorabilia that matched his rings: a life-size skeleton in plastic, plus numerous decorated skulls.

'It's like he just went to a garden centre January sale and bought everything they had left after Christmas,' Beatrice said, resting her hand on the shoulder of a waist-high concrete nymph in the hallway, in whose hand there was a plate used to store dozens of different types of keys.

'How soon before we get the DNA results?' Talantire asked.

'An hour or two probably, now that we have the budget to use the express service.' She smiled. 'I don't think there will be anything conclusive forensically, because Jade was a regular visitor here, especially when she had fallen out with her mum.'

'A Christmas grotto, with the chance to sit on Santa's knee no doubt,' Talantire said.

'We've got three mobile phones, including one from the car,' Beatrice said. 'I've couriered them off to Primrose.'

'I think they will have to go on to Exeter, because she's flat out. I mean, the electronic evidence for this case is already huge.'

'I'm sorry, I wasn't sure. I was wondering whether there were any digital evidence officers in Commander West's entourage, but they seemed to disappear when he did. Chief Inspector Campbell has had a similar problem. No one seems to be in charge.'

'I gather there is no hole in Heaton's story for the night in question?' Talantire asked.

'Not that I can see,' Beatrice replied. 'Jade's mother says he was with her from when he finished his taxi shift at 11:30 p.m. until when she woke up again to try to get hold of Jade.'

'Although we tend to discount family alibis, I think we can assume that Meghan Kernow wouldn't vouch for Gary Heaton if she had any suspicions about him abusing Jade. They came over together to me at the site of the crash about three a.m.,' Talantire said. 'Which is a two-hour journey. So he couldn't have been anywhere near Jade at the moment when her phone was switched off, because he and Meghan would have been in the car together.'

'I checked his taxi against the ANPR records you sent me. The Renault was in and around Camborne during his shift and only on the journey on the A30 across to Bodmin after three a.m., so it completely checks out.'

'I think we had better release him, then. I'm surprised West didn't order it earlier.'

—

Talantire was standing outside Heaton's graffitied garage when she got a call from Primrose. 'Ma'am, I've made some progress on Simon's phone. The texts on the night were made from a moving vehicle around the town of Bodmin.'

'Definitely moving?'

'I would think so. Too many cell towers pinged in quick succession to be anything else. It's mostly been off since her disappearance, but it has consistently pinged masts close to Finlay Roscoe's home in Truro, much more often than it has been to Camborne. In fact, there are only two visits to the Penypul estate, both since the theft of the Mercedes on Thursday.'

'That's great work, Primrose,' Talantire said. 'But have you got anything on where it is now?'

'No. It was briefly on yesterday evening, about ten p.m., close to a mast in Truro for a few seconds. And it was on again this morning for a few seconds near Minions.'

'Minions? That's potentially dynamite,' Talantire said. 'You have to go through it to get to the Phoenix mine. And Jade's shoe was found there.' For the first time, she felt she was closing in on the truth. And one line of enquiry came right to the fore: Finlay's home was in Truro, he had connections in Camborne, including the garage where he'd worked, and he and Jade had history. His car had been most of the way to Bodmin on the night in question. It was a far better fit than Uncle Gary. Talantire continued: 'I've already asked Beatrice, who has confirmed to me that there are no Simons in the Penypul group of youngsters – at least none of those close to the group in the car. Likewise, by a process of elimination, we can be pretty sure that this phone doesn't belong to any of the joyriders, yet it was close to the Mercedes at the time of the accident.'

'I can do better than close,' Primrose said. 'I've looked at the mast handoff timings from Jade's phone and Simon's phone in the last ten minutes before the accident. There were no messages between them at this time, yet both phones moved from one cell mast to another at precisely the same time, and indeed crossed each cell boundary at a speed which indicated they were travelling rapidly and together.'

'So they were in the same vehicle?'

'That's the only conclusion I can come to. Being in a car together would also explain why they weren't messaging each other at that time, because they were able to talk.'

'That's brilliant, Primrose. In sum, it all points to Finlay Roscoe. His car was in the vicinity of the accident, he knew Jade, after all they had dated. By all accounts, they had fallen out months before and hated each other. But maybe they had reconciled?'

'Yes that's what I thought, ma'am, but then why would he use a pseudonym and a burner phone?'

'It's a good point, and I don't have an answer for it.'

'Maybe Jade didn't want her family or friends to know she was seeing him again.'

'That's possible, I suppose,' Talantire said. 'But a bit elaborate. Right, let's go and see if we can find where the Merc was being stored after it was stolen.'

–

Gary Heaton put the key in the lock and opened his front door. Released from police custody after thirty-six hours, he was hugely relieved. The first thing he did was to put the TV on, for some background chatter. He texted Meghan again, and looked in vain for a reply. She had supported him publicly, even at the press conference, but then she had discovered the *Daily Mail* article about him: 'The creepy taxi driver who insinuated himself into Jade's life', as the subheading described him. Meghan had asked about Operation Ore and whether it was true. He had tried to explain, about the terrible time in his life when his marriage had broken up, that it was just a distraction, nothing else. But she had stormed out, and now wasn't returning his calls.

The police had been all over his home, that was clear from the odd way things had been tidied up. They had left a form in case anything was misplaced or lost. He was pretty confident they wouldn't have found his treasure. It was so well concealed that he doubted anyone would ever find it. But he had to check anyway. It was a hot-water bottle in a fleecy owl cosy in the linen cupboard. He slid the rubber bottle from the cover, and inverted it so he could see the slit at the bottom, held closed by a press stud. Stuffed inside were dozens of pairs of women's knickers, stolen from washing lines, and even one set of Jade's. Each was coded in biro, so he could conjure up an image of the owner.

It took less than two minutes to reassure himself. He returned to the kitchen and made himself a cup of coffee while examining the post. There was a hand-delivered letter from 123 Aardvark Minicabs. With a rising sense of foreboding, he pulled open the formal-looking letter and saw that his services were no longer required 'due to a change in business patterns'. He knew what that would be. The school's business, 123's daytime mainstay, had probably evaporated once news of his arrest got out. The kids from outlying villages, the children with special needs, they would all be taken to school by somebody else.

He sighed, and put the letter back on the kitchen table. Squatting down under the sink, he pulled open the cupboard and brought out a bottle of acetone and a cloth. He sighed again and headed out through the front door to tackle the graffiti on his garage.

–

Detective Sergeant Maddy Moran arrived at Plymouth hospital, where, in the crowded entrance hall, she met PC Naga Krishna, the family liaison officer who'd been allocated to the Moyle and Jago families. Naga had been at the hospital almost continuously since the accident, dispensing advice, a comfortable shoulder and an endless supply of hankies to the two extended families. But now, news of Scarlett Jago briefly regaining consciousness offered a glimmer of hope to an inquiry that had become bogged down in electronic evidence. Sometimes all that was required was some first-person testimony to make sense of what had happened.

'How is she doing?' Maddy asked Naga.

'She's been in an induced coma since yesterday, and last night they operated to drain some fluid and reduce the cranial pressure. The surgeon says he is optimistic about her eventual recovery, but she's certainly not in a condition to be interviewed.'

'Has she said anything?'

'Nothing really coherent,' Naga replied, leading Maddy along the corridor towards the intensive care unit.

Naga ordered four coffees from the refectory, and offered one to Maddy, which she accepted. On arrival at the ICU, Naga introduced her to the head staff nurse, who emphasised that Scarlett was in the very early stages of recovery.

'Please don't try asking her any questions, and no drinks or food inside.'

Maddy agreed and after leaving her coffee at ICU reception was led through to the private room where Scarlett's mother, Joyce, and stepdad, Pete, were gathered closely around her bed. Scarlett's younger brother, Noah, ten, sat in a chair in the corner on his Xbox, silently slaying what seemed to be an endless army of zombies.

Pete looked up, and placed a warning finger in front of his lips. Joyce was stroking her daughter's hand and murmuring something to her. The girl herself was barely visible. Her head swathed in bandages, and her face bearing yellow traces of antibacterial ointment and mauve and purple bruising. She was rigged up to various machines, and to Maddy's untrained eye, the traces looked regular and rhythmic.

Noah raised a pale fist, and hissed 'Yes' as he progressed to a higher level in the game.

Naga gestured for Pete to step outside with them. He was wearing stained tracksuit bottoms, knock-off Crocs and a white UCLA sweatshirt. He had clearly abandoned all attempts at shaving in recent days. His neck was a ruff of grey hairs and there was a vague waft of BO about him.

'How are you doing, Pete?' Naga asked, handing him one of the coffees.

He blew a sigh and ran his hand through his grey stubble. 'I don't know.'

'Has she asked you anything?' Maddy asked.

'Not really. She's mentioned Jordan's name, but we haven't broken the news to her yet.'

Maddy nodded. The death of her boyfriend would be a blow for her to take when she was stronger. Especially because it was, in all likelihood, the impact of her own head, when she was thrown forward from her unrestrained position in the back of the Mercedes, that had killed him, the only person in the car to be wearing a seat belt.

'How's Joyce? There's a coffee for her.'

'Thank you,' Pete said. 'She's not stopped talking to Scarlett since the moment we were allowed in. Not a single trip to the toilet, not a mouthful of food or drink.'

Maddy had seen it many times before, particularly when she was in uniform. The umbilical between mother and child was so strong, willing the life force from her own body into that of her child. She had even witnessed one mum reading childhood bedtime stories to her twenty-eight-year-old son who lay brain-dead after a motorcycle accident, all six foot four of him, just postponing, with the tiniest sliver of maternal hope, that dreadful moment when the machine would be turned off.

Here, at least, there was hope. Not only for the recovery of a girl from the most horrific of injuries, but some insight into Scarlett's feelings about her supposed and now-missing enemy – Jade.

–

Talantire drove behind Beatrice's patrol car into Camborne. It was still light, and on this summer Monday evening the Penypul estate looked at its best. It certainly didn't fit the stereotype of a run-down crime-infested ghetto. There were no burned-out cars to be seen, no boarded-up homes and only the occasional three-piece suite abandoned in a front garden. But looks can be deceptive. In Birmingham, Croydon and Newcastle, opportunity was rarely more than half a mile away. Jobs, even if they were warehouse or delivery gigs, were available. Camborne had few such chances. Most youngsters settled for casual seasonal work on the coast. Those with drive for a career often needed to go at least as far as Exeter, if not Bristol. Those left behind in grey pebble-dashed semis were bypassed by opportunity and eventually hope. Those in their fifties seemed to settle for the disabilities that a workless life often brought. If not diabetes, then at least depression. That way lay the less onerous regime of unfit for work, rather than fruitlessly seeking it. When Talantire had done her stint in uniform here, the closure of the last nearby factories almost thirty years before was still a raw wound.

They arrived outside a row of lock-up garages behind Cleet Hill Avenue. They were the usual type of arrangement for council houses and flats built in the 1970s, before an individual garage became the norm for new homes. A patrol car from Camborne Community Police was already parked there, along with numerous vehicles of residents in various states of repair.

PC Rob Parker was standing there waiting for them.

'So these two are both rented to Tyler Darracombe,' Beatrice asked Parker, pointing to adjacent garages.

'Yes. He's refused us permission to look inside,' Parker said.

Beatrice displayed her iPad to him and clicked on a PDF. 'I think a search here is covered in the wording given on the earlier warrant for his home. It says any premises owned, rented, leased or otherwise occupied by the aforementioned individual.'

The male officer nodded. 'The locksmith is due any moment. I'm not sure we really needed him; these locks are easy, you can break in with a penknife.'

'Yes, but you might damage the lock and if it can't be relocked, then we would be liable for having to secure it afterwards,' Talantire said. 'It's best done by the book.'

While they waited, Talantire checked again the GPS map on the Mercedes tracing app, using the log-in supplied by Finlay's father. The car had certainly vanished somewhere between Cleet Hill Avenue and Cleet Hill Close in the early hours of Friday morning, only to reappear at the same spot about twelve hours later on Saturday afternoon. This seemed the exact location, certainly the only one where a car could be concealed from a GPS signal.

She looked up as the locksmith's van arrived. She and Beatrice donned booties and gloves while the locksmith got to work. As predicted, it took just a few seconds to open the up-and-over doors on both garages. One was empty but for a couple of plastic carrier bags, and the other packed with car components and tools neatly stacked on metal shelving units around the room. You could say one thing for Tyler Darracombe, he was organised.

They concentrated on the full one to begin with, turning on the strip light and finding numerous sets of alloy wheels, half a dozen exhaust replacement kits and car stereo units.

'Pound to a penny this lot has been nicked,' Beatrice said. 'Either from Yelland's Garage or fenced for somebody else.'

They took plenty of photographs, but found no evidence of anything other than some minor theft.

Talantire looked again at an anonymous tip-off from the Crimestoppers helpline. 'It says Jade was held hostage in a lock-up garage. But I can't see any sign of it.'

'There is not even a chair, let alone a sleeping bag,' Beatrice said.

'I was sceptical right from the start,' Talantire said. 'Anonymous tips are perfect for settling scores. And who would know, except a close associate of the hostage taker?' She went back to her car and took her forensics bag from the boot. 'I'll do some gel lifts for dabs and hair here. If you want to take a peek in the empty one. There might be some fresh oil stains, though probably not as it was a Merc.'

Beatrice exited the garage while Talantire worked away, taking fingerprints from the edges of the metal shelving. Half a minute later, she heard a celebratory shout, and stepped out to see what was going on. Beatrice was standing with Rob Parker, holding a plastic bag and a mobile phone in her gloved hands.

'What's in the bag?'

'According to Rob, it's a relay device,' Beatrice said, opening the neck of the carrier bag.

Talantire could see two devices that looked like Wi-Fi routers, with stubby aerials, and on one of them an encircling loop of cable. 'So this is what Darracombe stole the car with?' she asked.

'Could be,' Parker said. 'A keyless car is designed to register when its keys are in close proximity and will automatically unlock. The relay device foxes the car into believing the keys are closer than they are. One thief presses the device with the loop on the outside wall of a house close to where the keys are kept, say in a kitchen, and the other holds the second device near the vehicle. Once the two devices are connected, the car doors will unlock and the vehicle can be started with a push button.'

'He's a mine of useful information, is Rob,' Beatrice said.

He gave a mock bow in acknowledgement.

'This is a bit more interesting,' he said, plucking from the bag an electronic console the size of a packet of cigarettes. 'Darracombe is a bit more up to date than we thought.'

'Why?'

'It's an RFID copier, and it solves something that was puzzling me. You see, the relay device is fine for pinching the motor to begin with, but when you've finished your joyride or whatever, and park it up, you can't restart it later.'

'Because the key's not in range?' Talantire suggested.

'Exactly. But this device creates a new key, by copying the unique radio signal from the fob onto a blank. You can buy a copier and the blanks on Amazon for less than twenty quid.'

'That's crazy,' Beatrice said. 'Any idiot can steal a car then.'

'Well, the newest vehicles have some extra security features, so it won't always work. But yes, in principle it puts professional theft tools into the hands of every toerag and ne'er-do-well,' Rob said.

Talantire dug out separate evidence bags for the phone, relay devices and RFID copier. 'I'll get this lot to Primrose, and see what she can find.'

She beckoned the locksmith out of his vehicle. He did his best to lock the two garages again, fiddling with the flimsy locks, while Talantire messaged West to tell him what they had found. She suggested that they arrest and charge Tyler Darracombe for car theft, which would give an opportunity to hold him for long enough to ask him about many more important things.

Good idea, Jan, came a quick reply from West. *Do it.*

It took a few minutes to establish where Tyler was; not at home, but with his parents at the bedside of his brother in Plymouth. Good, DS Maddy Moran was already there. She could guide the uniforms who came to make the arrest, ideally in a low-key manner away from the rest of his family.

—

It was 7:30 p.m. when Maddy took Talantire's call. She was standing in the hospital corridor, where, as luck would have it, she could see several members of the Darracombe family. But not Tyler. Their own family liaison officer, PC Cathy Kirby, was being berated by Roky Darracombe, the matriarch of the family, and grandmother to Tyler and Aaron. She was a sizeable woman, a good four inches taller than the FLO, with a tired face, dyed blonde hair and a dozen rings in each ear.

PC Kirby spotted Maddy, and introduced her.

Roky looked at her through narrowed eyes. 'What do you want?'

'I was hoping to speak to Tyler,' Maddy said.

'What, *again*? He's upset. We're here because our poor lad Aaron has lost a leg, and all you can do is harass his brother.'

'I just want a quick word.'

'What about?'

'Where is he, Mrs Darracombe?'

She shrugged her massive shoulders. 'Having a fag, I should think.' The woman turned her back and started working her phone.

Maddy thanked her and made her way back towards the lift. Fortunately, as the police already had Tyler's phone, he couldn't be tipped off by his grandmother. Maddy rang the two uniforms who were going to make the arrest and relayed the information that their quarry was supposedly having a cigarette outside the hospital. She urged them to carefully check his ID. Arresting the wrong person would be very embarrassing.

Maddy peered out of the corridor window, hoping to see the front of the hospital, but the view was obscured. In fact, there were numerous entrances and exits where Darracombe could be filling his lungs with toxins. Maybe a hospital wasn't the best place for an arrest.

Maddy took the lift and as the doors opened at the bottom, she found herself face to face with the two uniforms she had been speaking to.

'No sign of him?' she asked.

'No.'

'Okay, wait with me here, let's see if he comes back.'

Maddy then rang the control room to put out an alert for Tyler Darracombe. She passed across the details of his vehicle and told the operator that a mugshot was available to upload from the Plymouth police local database, where he had been interviewed earlier in the day.

–

Talantire was driving back from Plymouth to Barnstaple with Maddy sitting next to her. They were both exhausted, but the working day wasn't over. Not even close. They had a pile of evidence bags with them on the back seat, including the phone that had been recovered from Tyler Darracombe's garage, for Primrose to examine on the Aceso Kiosk on their arrival. The gel lifts from the fingerprints taken in Camborne had already been sent on to Exeter in a separate vehicle, but the phone had become a priority. The moment they had examined it at the lock-up it had seemed out of place. A very clean and unscratched white iPhone in a rather fashionable dark green OtterBox case. Not the kind of thing that Tyler Darracombe would own, and besides, they already had his phone.

While they drove, Maddy used her iPad to look through the descriptions of what the missing girl had with her. There was mention of a green phone case, but the device colour had not been given. Maddy had already rung Tina Smith, the family liaison officer, to ask Jade's mother to describe the daughter's phone. If the descriptions matched, she would then show her a photograph which Talantire had sent her.

They were waiting for the call back.

It was nearly nine by the time they arrived at Okehampton at the northern edge of Dartmoor, and halfway back to Barnstaple. They hadn't eaten anything more than a quick sandwich for hours, so when they saw a convenience store, Maddy suggested they stop. Talantire pulled in on a double yellow, and the detective sergeant jumped out of the car and ran across the road into the shop. Tied up outside the store was a dog, a youngish creature. It was scanning the street in both directions, pulling on the lead. It was an appealing animal, and a couple of passers-by stopped to stroke it, which temporarily suppressed its anxiety. On its own again, it began to yelp. It was a distinctive sound which Talantire had heard before.

Yes, one black ear and one white. Could this be Adam's puppy, Scamp, three months older?

The door of the convenience store opened and a woman emerged: heels, short skirt, expensive jacket, lots of make-up. Eyelashes like paintbrushes. The dog went berserk, straining at the lead, then jumping up, which she clearly didn't relish.

Talantire buzzed the window down. She heard the woman shout, 'Calm down, Scamp, for God's sake.'

It was Adam's dog! The delightful creature he had brought along on their first meeting, one of only a handful of dates they had before it all fizzled out back in April.

The woman began to untie the dog as Maddy emerged from the shop with a carrier bag. She crossed the road and climbed into the car. 'They didn't have any sandwiches left, but I got a Cornish pasty, a plain chocolate Bounty and... What's the matter?'

'Maddy, take a look. Her with the dog.'

She leaned across. 'Someone you know?'

'I know the dog. Scamp, Adam's dog.'

'Been stolen then?'

'No, it's not that. I think that's the ex.'

Suddenly, Maddy was a lot more interested. 'Ahh, the love rival. What's her name?'

'Pepsy.'

'Got a bit of fizz about her, I suppose. Maybe that's why he put your relationship on ice?'

Talantire turned to her and made a face.

'Sorry, that fell flat, didn't it?' Maddy chuckled at her own supposed wit, and looked at the woman again as she led the animal away. 'Looks very high maintenance to me, Jan. Plenty of bling.'

'Yeah.' A twinge of jealousy needled her unexpectedly, along with a pang of something else. Loneliness perhaps? She wasn't sure.

'Plenty more fish in the sea, eh?' Maddy said.

Talantire watched as a hot pink jeep, a Suzuki, stopped at the kerb next to the woman. It carried the logo of some beauty salon. Adam was driving. He didn't glance in her direction, but she recognised his profile. He leaned across to open the front passenger door, the dog jumped in and the woman followed.

'Look at that,' Maddy muttered. 'If she is what he goes for, you two were never suited.'

'My thoughts exactly.' Talantire put the car into gear and drove off. She hit the accelerator, leaving the image in the past.

'Still better him than Brent West, eh?'

Talantire could detect the fishing expedition a mile off.

'So do you really want to know the story of me and Commander West?'

'Well, the qualities of the man seem relevant, seeing as we are all likely to be serving under him as chief constable.'

'He's an abuser, a serial philanderer and a liar.'

'Yeah, but what about his bad side?' Maddy said, laughing.

Talantire chuckled. 'Brent was utterly charming at first, but ended up being very controlling. I was an idiot to fall for him, that's what still annoys me. In hindsight, I'm sure he had lots of other women officers on the go, as well as still being married when he claimed to be divorced. He seemed to be a good listener, but I suspect there was some spreadsheet with all of our details, likes and dislikes and backstory on there.'

'Dodgy.'

'He used to hang-glide over the three-storey flats where I lived in Exeter, and land in the communal gardens.'

'With a box of chocolates, presumably?'

'Something like that. One summer Sunday, when I was sunbathing on my top-floor balcony, I heard this engine noise, and it was a cherry picker, and he was in the cradle wearing a DJ and bow tie, carrying a bottle of champagne and a tray of sushi, right up to me.'

'It's very romantic,' Maddy said. 'What's not to like?'

'It would have been romantic if he'd just knocked at the door, but no, he had to get a bloody cherry picker so everyone could see him doing it. When we went out, he liked to tell me what to wear and how to have my hair cut. He bought me a beautiful Versace dress, size six. He knows I'm a ten, but said I could slim into it. I thought I loved him, so I did try.'

'That's classic. Neville once bought me a small tent, for the same reason...'

'It's not bloody funny, Maddy!'

'You've got to get past it, Jan.'

'I thought I had, until now.'

'So what was the final straw?'

'He secretly filmed us having sex.'

'Bloody hell!' Maddy exclaimed.

'I still don't know what happened to the recording. It's probably circulating on some male officers' WhatsApp group.'

For a few minutes, nothing more was said, but Talantire caught her concentration lapsing. She was driving a little faster than before, something she only noticed because Maddy had tensed up and was holding the passenger door handle again.

'Sorry, Maddy,' she said, slowing down.

'That's all right. Who wants to live forever, anyway.'

Maddy's phone rang and she answered it.

'Hello, Tina... Yes, right... Okay thanks.'

Talantire couldn't catch what was being said on the other end, but it was clearly written on Maddy's face.

After she hung up, she reached into the bag and picked up the plastic evidence bag. 'This is definitely Jade's phone.'

'Right,' said Talantire, putting on the blues and twos. 'Let's just hope they can track down Tyler Darracombe quickly.'

'You think he might do something stupid?'

'Well, he's got quite a track record of stupidity, so we can't rule it out.'

Maddy tuned into the patrol car radio system, so they could hear the messages going out to uniformed officers. It was clear that Tyler wasn't yet in custody. Camborne Community Police was in charge of co-ordinating the search, but seeing as the fugitive had last been seen at a hospital in Plymouth, he clearly could be anywhere by now.

Chapter Fourteen

Once they arrived at the Barnstaple police HQ, Maddy went home while Talantire rushed upstairs to CID with the pile of evidence bags. It was gone ten in the evening, and Primrose was the only officer there, sitting at the Aceso Kiosk machine. Nuttall was off duty until six a.m. and DI Lockhart was out on call.

'So how's it going?' Talantire asked her.

The digital evidence officer's hands flicked across the keys, as she hacked into the various categories of data. 'It's definitely Jade's phone,' Primrose said. 'She's the registered owner. What do you want me to go for first?'

'All the contacts with Simon,' Talantire said. 'And any pictures.'

'All image data has been deleted,' she said. 'Videos, photographs, you name it. And the trash can was emptied too, so they can't be restored from there. But they may still be on the cloud, and even if not, we should still be able to get copies from the service provider.'

Talantire steepled her hands over her face. This was an ominous development. 'It's not the fact of what's on the photographs that concerns me so much as the decision to get rid of them. I can't think of a reason why Jade herself would delete all her precious photographic data, so this shows she wasn't in control of the phone at the time it happened.'

'I agree,' Primrose said.

'It's looking less and less likely that she's alive. Can you get a date and time for the deletions?'

'Very recent. Starting at five a.m. this morning. In fact, there was a lot of activity on the device at that time.'

'So let's get this right,' Talantire said. 'We're talking about the first new use of Jade's phone since the accident?'

'That's right. The last ping we were aware of was just a few minutes after the accident. I last checked for usage yesterday evening. I put a real-time tag on the phone with the service provider for just this eventuality, so I can immediately download an updated map to find out where it was when it was used.'

Talantire watched Primrose as she displayed an updated Google map. It showed a single dot, on a rural lane just off the A30. The phone did not move at all during the ten minutes when the data was deleted.

'This isn't going to help us, is it?' Primrose asked.

'Well, it is certainly evidence of electronic forensic awareness. Or maybe it's just coincidence. Either way, if this is Tyler Darracombe, and he is smart enough to delete data on Jade's phone which might identify him, why was he stupid enough to keep the phone in his garage?'

'Are his fingerprints on the phone?' Primrose asked.

'I sent the dabs off to Exeter. We should know by first thing tomorrow morning.'

She watched as Primrose suppressed a yawn. The woman was looking very tired but not surprising considering she had slept in the office last night. All credit to her, she hadn't asked to leave earlier today. She pretty much seemed to have been working thirty-six hours straight. The trouble was Primrose was such an important resource, and would be needed quite early the next morning too.

'Primrose, is your mother okay to be left on her own overnight?'

'Yes, she's quite resourceful.'

'I was just wondering if you wanted to crash at my place tonight to save that two-hour journey each way?'

'That's very kind, ma'am.'

'Please, no need to call me ma'am.'

Talantire started to shut up the office, leaving a message for the Prince of Darkness, who was out on a shout in Okehampton. She watched as Primrose removed a small neat overnight bag from the floor beneath her desk.

–

The beep of the phone broke into her dreams. Talantire flailed out to the bedside table to answer the device. It was four a.m. The call was from a duty officer at Exeter, who reported to her that Tyler Darracombe had been arrested at the house of a friend in Camborne a few minutes ago and was being taken to the cells in Plymouth.

'That's great news,' she said.

'He put up quite a struggle by all accounts and kept protesting his innocence.'

'I'm not surprised. I'll interview him in the morning.' She thanked the officer and then hung up.

She could hear a noise in the house. She slid out of bed and wrapped a bathrobe around her pyjamas. Primrose was in the spare room along the landing, and it sounded like she was mumbling. There was a light from underneath the door. Talantire crept along in bare feet until she was next to it. Then she realised it was the sound of prayer. She recalled that Muslims pray several times a day at prescribed intervals, but that only the most devout wake up to pray in the small hours.

She listened a little while longer until the sound ceased, and the light went off. She slipped back silently to her own room, making her own brief thanks to whatever deity was out there that she had managed to secure the services of this most outstanding and talented officer.

–

Talantire awoke, covered in sweat. She had just had a dream – a truly disturbing one. She was on a station plat-form running for a train, and sprinting side-by-side with her was a young woman, who she knew without looking was Jade Kernow. They were overtaking other passengers, pushing past, hair flying, going fast, presumably to get to a particular carriage before the train left. There was an exuberance about this moment, a joy, which seemed to embody a shared past, as if Jade was her daughter, or perhaps a younger sister, certainly someone she cared deeply for. As the station attendant's whistle sounded, Talantire sped up further, and the modern train became a more old-fashioned type, a steam train, with the piercing shriek of the whistle and the rhythmic rumble of pistons as it pulled away. They were missing the train!

She was now aware that Jade was not with her, but through the window of one carriage ahead, she could see her, already on the train. She looked fearful and desperate, staring through the window, bloodied hands pressed against the glass. But it wasn't Jade, it was her own twin sister, Bella. She was being taken away in this train, and there was nothing that Talantire could do to stop it. With a superhuman spurt of speed, she got level with the window and called out to her sister repeatedly, hammering her hands against the glass. But as she surveyed the escaping carriage, she realised that it had no doors, only windows, and the shriek of the engine turned into her own screams. Because the face at the carriage window was no longer her identical twin sister.

It was her own.

She turned around and fell on the platform, her face hitting the concrete. As she slowly got to her feet, she saw the place was empty of people, no longer the busy modern station but an abandoned halt at an obscure branch line, with a boarded-up waiting room, peeling maroon and cream paint, long-dead flowers dangling from hanging baskets that squeaked in the wind under the metal canopy. The rails nearby were rusty. As she made her way reluctantly to the exit, Talantire felt an overwhelming guilt drench her, and that feeling of neglect and betrayal stayed with her as she awoke. Even her face felt sore, where she had banged it on the platform in the dream.

Bella.

There was no excuse for not going to see her. She knew that. It was the biggest source of friction with her mother, who had dedicated so much of her life to trying to improve Bella's life chances.

During her childhood, when Jan had been having a tantrum, her mother often said: 'Bella wouldn't behave like you do. Sometimes I wish I could go back to 1985 and make it the other way round.' Once, in temper, her mother had even said it was Jan's fault. And, in a way, it was, a crime committed before birth.

Estelle had been working for VSO in Uganda, and had been planning to return home for the birth of what she thought would be one child. She'd missed ultrasound scans because a bout of malaria had made her too sick to travel, and then her waters had burst five weeks early in a *matutu*, a shared taxi on the way to Kampala. Medics at the small regional hospital where they pulled in did their best, but with Jan, the tinier and concealed twin, nestling behind her sister, a loop of Jan's umbilical cord had tangled around Bella's own. It constricted Bella's blood flow and oxygen supply, causing her life-long brain damage.

There was a knock at the bedroom door, and Primrose's voice could be heard through it. 'Are you all right, ma'am? You were screaming.'

'God, I'm sorry. Bad dream, that's all.' It seemed bizarre that Primrose should call her ma'am, in her own house.

Talantire checked the clock. It was just before six. She shook her head to clear the shadows of the night. Poor Bella. In the shadow of the nightmare, Talantire now made a promise to herself. Her first free weekend, she'd head off to Bristol to see her twin. Not with guilt, she vowed, but with celebration. She must live to the full the precious life she had been given and that Bella had forfeited. For both their sakes.

—

First thing on Tuesday morning, Talantire was making coffee at home when she got a text from Maddy, who had just got into the office. No prints from Tyler Darracombe had been found on Jade's phone. That was unhelpful, though clearly he could have wiped down the phone after deleting the images and videos.

As she laid the table, she could hear that Primrose was still in the shower. She hadn't prepared for her guest and could only offer a couple of different types of cereal and some wholemeal bread with either honey or marmalade.

She put on the TV local news to see the latest coverage. Just a brief report saying that Devon and Cornwall Police had arrested a nineteen-year-old in connection with Jade's disappearance and that a forty-six-year-old man had been released on police bail. However, the newsreader did mention an exclusive interview with the mother of the missing girl for the six o'clock bulletin in the evening. It sounded like Meghan Kernow was going freelance again. She didn't envy Moira Hallett's job as media relations chief in trying to rein in the family.

Talantire felt a presence and turned to see Primrose in bra and pants, her hair in a towel, watching the news behind her. She seemed quite unembarrassed, and Talantire was a little surprised to see that instead of some dowdy beige underwear, Primrose's were, if not quite racy, then at least expensive and fashionable, and she had a slim but curvy figure. Of course, it now occurred to her that the woman's modesty was particularly focused on avoiding the male gaze, and that she might be no more shy in front of a woman than anyone else. Well, good for her.

Later, Talantire updated her now fully dressed colleague over toast and marmalade. She would drop Primrose at the Barnstaple HQ and then head down to Plymouth to interview Tyler Darracombe.

–

While Talantire was having coffee, Cornwall County Council contractor Eric Robinson reversed his tow truck up to the verge where the abandoned Volkswagen Polo sat. The council contractors had mowed round it, but the grass close by was knee-high and needed strimming. The recovery job had been on the list for a while, but they were down two members of staff because of long Covid, and they'd been told to concentrate first on clearing the fly tipping blocking some of the local farm gateways. Well, this one was five weeks, so still within the legal threshold. The legal department had received no reply from the owner to its letters, so the paperwork was all in order, all the boxes ticked.

He looked out of the window at the car, which had an open window driver-side, and from the height of the cab could clearly see the abandoned takeaway containers on the back seat, covered in flies. He had been warned it was a stinker, but when he got out of the vehicle, the horrific stench hit him. Holding his gloved hands over his nose and mouth, he peered through the window. It had been warm, but this was disgusting. Rotting takeaway, spilled on the back seat, covered in maggots and flies. The car was due down the depot, but the duty manager would not thank him for bringing in something like this.

He opened the rear door. He grabbed a shovel out of his hopper and a big bin bag. Using the shovel, he scooped up two aluminium food containers and dumped them and their wriggling contents into the bag, which he then knotted and set on the verge. Sure, the food smelt bad enough, but there was something worse, something horrible. The split rear seat was partially folded forward, leaving a narrow gap into the boot, and flies were crawling from it. He stood in front of the boot, braced himself, then opened it. A cloud of flies poured out. The stench was so gut-wrenching that he ran over to the ditch dry heaving.

He'd never forget that sight, as long as he lived.

He called 999.

Chapter Fifteen

It was the worst start to a Tuesday morning that Talantire could recall. Despite her growing suspicions, she had hoped and prayed that Jade would be found safe and well. But as she arrived at the village of St Neot at nine a.m., she could see the crime-scene tent at the rear of the abandoned car, along with two CSI vans, and a host of figures in their characteristic white suits. The road was closed off with plastic barriers and crime-scene tape. She nosed her work Skoda right up to the barrier.

Hurriedly wriggling into a fresh white overall, she put on a hairnet, facemask, booties and gloves. She signed in with the uniformed cop at the edge of the tape. Even at thirty yards distance, and with all the gear, she could still detect the unmistakable sweet-but-rank odour of a rotting body.

Inside the CSI tent were a few officers she knew, including Barnstaple-based Pavel Kaminski, who worked in the next office to CID. 'It's very bad, Jan,' he said. 'Very bad.'

'Is the forensic pathologist here yet?' she asked.

'No, he's on his way.'

Pavel led her over to the rear of the car, which protruded inside the tent. A tunnel of plastic sheeting had been taped to the edge of the car boot to minimise the number of flies, and an air extractor was running from a noisy generator. A table inside the tent showed a limited array of evidence that had been found at the scene, and Pavel explained that fingerprint lifts and DNA samples had already been taken.

Talantire decided to see the images first, to inoculate herself as much as possible against the horror of the body itself. The CSI officers had been working from an iPad, which was in the middle of the table, and she flicked through to see the photographs that had been taken so far, and the evidence markers. The victim, crawling with flies and maggots, had been folded into a foetal position, on her side, arms in front. Telling exactly who the deceased was wasn't straightforward, because quite apart from the insects, the body had begun to bloat, and bloody fluids from internal decomposition were spilling liberally from the nose and mouth. The body was fully clothed, but seams had begun to split, and one of the two brass zips on her skirt had broken open. This item of clothing was the giveaway, along with earrings that matched those that were on the evidence file.

It was Jade.

Talantire felt bile rising up her throat, and tears squeeze into her eyes. She blinked them away, but couldn't fight the surge of emotion: sadness, and a growing spark of rage at whoever could do this. Although the rational part of her had long feared that Jade would be found dead, she had hoped to be wrong. This outcome was not how it was meant to be.

She texted Beatrice Dodds to let her know. She dreaded to think of how Jade's mother would react when Camborne Community Police broke the news.

She got an immediate reply from Sergeant Dodds, just three letters: OMG.

There would still be a tiny sliver of hope; yes, possibly it could be somebody else in a similar skirt. But this car was only a few minutes' drive from where Jade was last seen at two in the morning, by the crashed Mercedes. The deterioration in the body was about right for two and a half days in warm summer weather since Jade had last been seen alive.

Two officers were busy taking swabs around the boot, and Talantire peered around to get a glimpse of the body itself. Spotting the wriggling mass of fly larvae, reclaiming Jade for food, was appalling. This was a small car, and the body had bloated to fill most of the storage space. For that reason, Talantire guessed she must have been put in there soon after death. Being close enough to touch a festering corpse was a gut punch that you never get over. The smell and the sight stayed with you. It came back in your dreams, you could taste it in the small hours when your mouth was dry, and you could smell it just for a second or two as an imposter in your own laundry basket, in the bathroom or the garden shed. Every domestic fly, buzzing on a window at home, reminded you.

She stepped away and exited the tent to get some fresh air. One of the technicians was bent double at the side of the road, heaving. Talantire sympathised; she didn't feel great herself. But there was work to be done.

She found a convenient root under a mature beech tree to sit on fifty yards away upwind. It was going to be a pleasant warm day, but, being early, the humidity hadn't yet begun. She closed her eyes for a moment to let the sunshine caress her face and listened to the gentle susurrus of the leaves above, which dappled light across her clothing. After a two-minute breather, she flicked through her own iPad, and logged into the evidence file for the abandoned car.

The vehicle had first been reported here on the verge in St Neot on 9 June. Whoever had dumped the body around a month later had been very clever, stowing it inside a vehicle which was already in the bureaucratic reporting process. Taking advantage of the 'police aware' tape that was already across the windscreen ensured that the authorities would be unresponsive to new complaints about it from residents. In fact, during the winter, it may have been a week or two before the stench of the body would have led to its discovery.

The DVLA records were copied onto the file. The registered keeper of the vehicle was one Geoffrey Tolland, seventy-eight, who lived in Redruth, the next town to Camborne. He had reported his VW stolen from a car park in the town on 7 June. A few weeks later, well after the car had been found, he had been written to about the abandoned vehicle, with no reply received. Copies of the documents were on file, along with a brief summary of the latest information. This morning, uniforms had gone to visit the address, and found no one there. One neighbour said Mr Tolland had gone into a care home, and offered the address and phone number of a daughter who lived in Wolverhampton. This was the constabulary doing what they did best, chasing down the myriad bureaucratic pathways and closing off possibilities. This all helped CID enormously. In this case, it pretty much shut down any idea that Mr Tolland had anything to do with the stowing of the body.

Whoever had originally stolen the car had probably thought they had got away with it. No arrest at the scene, no witness sightings. But this particular joyrider, whoever he was – and almost all were male – would almost certainly be tracked down if he had any kind of criminal or forensic record on file. Stealing and dumping a car was such a common and minor crime that the forensic checks needed to catch the culprit were rarely deployed, much to the frustration of the victim of the theft. But now, with a murder to investigate, Talantire was pretty sure the thief would be in an interview room inside a day. For all that, she felt, there was only a slim chance that he had anything to do with the body.

There was already a fair amount of message traffic among officers on the case. Moira Hallett had circulated her media plan for the day: firstly, a brief statement to say that a body had been discovered in the search for Jade Kernow. That would be released only after the family liaison teams had broken the news to the nearest and dearest. Then, with DNA results due by around midday, a second statement would run, either confirming the victim was Jade or, possibly, not. Moira suggested that today's press conference should be held at six p.m.; firstly, because that coincided with the evening news bulletins, and live coverage was always better than edited, but secondly, it gave them a crucial window of opportunity to try to catch the killer.

'It's always a lot better in a tragic case like this to have some answers when you're facing questions from the press,' Hallett had written.

Talantire quirked her lips in agreement. Moira's approach was totally professional and at least gave the chance for the police to stay ahead of the media.

What hadn't been seen as yet was anything from Brent West, who was supposedly SIO. She had copied him in on most of her messages, and so had Moira. Talantire hadn't seen anything of West's personal team either, not since yesterday. All that youthful glamour and drone technology. All that adulation. No, they wouldn't like it out here. They wouldn't like to see the vile stinking purge fluids streaming out of the victim's nostrils as she had just done; they wouldn't like the stench. They'd be throwing up in the ditch. Useless.

Talantire shook her head and realised she had been gritting her teeth. Best to clear out any thoughts of Brent bloody West. And those green-eyed musings about his acolytes. That could only mean one thing. If she was jealous, then at some level she must still want him. Despite everything. That it might be true only made her angrier. Still, maybe if he was made chief constable it wouldn't be so bad. There would be virtually no chance of dealing with him directly, as she was now. He'd be so high above her, so stratospheric. But this made her seethe too. Why should a man like that get to the top? An abuser, a manipulator. Why couldn't they see what he was like? If she wasn't so busy, she could send an audio file of his threats to the headshrinkers at Exeter. Human resources needed this stuff. Let him come after her if he dare. She wasn't afraid of any man. The trouble was, she needed Primrose or someone else, to help her enhance the quality of the recording and that would take time. And, in the meantime, there was much more urgent work to do.

No, she was being self-indulgent. Poor dead Jade Kernow needed her skills and experience right now. That was the justice she had signed up to the police to dispense. Catching killers. Putting them behind bars. Her own private quarrels could wait.

Talantire looked up again at the dappled leaves and exhaled quietly.

Time to go off to Liskeard for a quick incident-room meeting, and then interview Tyler Darracombe at Crownhill Police Station in Plymouth. Hopefully, by the time she got there, the DNA tests might be in. They had gone off from the scene by police dispatch rider an hour ago and would already be at the lab in Exeter. For a high-profile case like this, an hour's turnaround was possible. The results would be dispatched by email.

–

By ten a.m., the Liskerrett Community Centre was a hive of activity. Talantire's team of Dave Nuttall and Maddy Moran were brainstorming the new evidence in front of a series of whiteboards.

'So let's assume the body is Jade—' Nuttall said.

'—It definitely must be, in that distinctive skirt,' Maddy interjected.

'—we are working on the idea that whoever killed her did so on the night of the accident, sometime after she was seen in the grounds of Bodmin Rectory.'

'That's right,' Talantire said. 'We are assuming she was in the pursuing car with the killer. The motive being that she probably wanted to stay around until paramedics arrived to help her friends, but whoever murdered her thought that her presence would be incriminating for him.'

'So, given our prime suspect is Tyler Darracombe,' Maddy said, 'AKA Simon… what would be incriminating enough for him to kill her?'

'Drugs, found in the Merc,' Talantire said. 'Probably a couple of hundred MDMA tablets, maybe more.'

'Why would he have left them there?' Nuttall asked. 'He admits to having been in the vehicle earlier in the day, but why on earth would he leave his stash behind?'

'Because he's an idiot,' Maddy replied. 'Considering her phone was found in his garage.'

'Yes, but clever enough to have a burner phone in the name of Simon,' Nuttall remarked.

'Drug dealers have burner phones,' Talantire said. 'It makes sense for them.'

'There was nothing on this phone that indicated dealing,' Nuttall said, looking through the activity report prepared by Primrose on his iPad.

'Come on, Dave,' Talantire said. 'Some dealers have a dozen phones. Or they take advantage of the encryption of WhatsApp. If he's a professional, we wouldn't expect to see an electronic record, at least not one that isn't in code.'

Nuttall shrugged. 'You're describing someone a bit more sophisticated than Tyler Darracombe.'

Talantire inclined her head in acknowledgement. It was bugging her too. Tyler was a tearaway, but could he be a murderer? There was no history of violence. No history of dealing, for that matter.

'Let's set that aside,' she said. 'Look at some of the other stuff we've got. The body was stowed in an abandoned vehicle, and there might be plenty of DNA and dabs around that site. Once we've filtered out that of the owner, we should be left with the original car thief, and that of the murderer.'

'Assuming they are not one and the same,' Maddy said.

'What about Finlay Roscoe?' Nuttall asked. 'How does his alibi check out? His is the only vehicle that we have a record of close to Bodmin Moor at the same time as the accident.'

Talantire looked through the notes that Beatrice Dodds had sent her. 'It's pretty solid. He was heard going into and out of his girlfriend's home on the night of the accident, by her parents, and the girlfriend's brother. Still, there's nothing to preclude him having slipped out for a few hours to take part in a chase. Roscoe's Vauxhall Nova was definitely out and about, even though he claims not to have been.'

'Maybe Tyler Darracombe stole it,' Maddy said. 'Considering they were enemies.'

'Just like he stole the Roscoe family car,' Nuttall said. 'It could be a pattern.'

'All right,' Talantire said. 'Here's something else to consider. Jade's shoe was found near the Phoenix mine, which is several miles from where her body has been found. Was she taken there while in captivity? Or did someone deliberately plant the shoe to draw us away from the hunt?'

'I think it's a clumsy plant,' Nuttall said.

'Would that be a triffid?' Maddy asked, with a smile.

Having reached no firm conclusions, and with no DNA results yet in, they wrapped up the meeting and headed off to Plymouth, where a nineteen-year-old suspect was awaiting them in a cell.

–

Tyler Darracombe sprawled across his chair in the interview room, a squirming, nervous six-foot-one lad, running his hands through his tight mullet of curly hair. From the observation window above, Talantire, Nuttall and Maddy watched and waited. It was eleven a.m. and the long-expected DNA email still hadn't arrived, and they wanted to interview him fully armed with every piece of evidence.

Fifteen minutes passed, and good takeaway coffees were offered by the desk sergeant to the visiting detectives. It was a much-appreciated gesture, seeing as the Plymouth station's own coffee machine seemed to be a relative of Barnstaple's Doctor Crippen.

'He was crying in the night,' said the sergeant, as he carefully placed the coffees on the table. 'Quite upset he was.'

'It's nothing compared to what he'll do when we hit him with the full weight of the evidence,' Maddy said.

Talantire stroked her chin. In her experience, it was the innocent who cried and wailed. On arrest, it was the guilty who lay back and went to sleep, the tension relieved, the uncertainty of whether they would be caught finally over. So Tyler Darracombe's upset was not a good omen.

Three phones pinged simultaneously on the table, the email alerts set up for the DNA lab. Three hands grabbed, the emails scrutinised. First up, DNA found on Jade's phone recovered from Tyler's garage: her own, that of Leanne Moyle, her best friend, and two other traces: one known and one not.

'Shit, Tyler is not on there,' Maddy said.

'But Uncle Gary is,' Nuttall stated.

They both looked up at Talantire, but she was on the next email, the results of tests that had been biked at high speed to Exeter that very morning.

'The body *is* Jade,' she said, pausing to blow a sigh and exchange a glance with her colleagues. 'And there are both fingerprints and DNA from Tyler and three others in the abandoned car. He's on the steering wheel, gearstick, glove compartment, driver-side door, inside driver-side door catch and on a plastic fork in the takeaway.'

'Fantastic,' Maddy said. 'Bang to rights. He's bloody everywhere.'

'Not so fast,' Talantire warned. 'There's another email.'

The three detectives speed-read the final email. Nuttall then folded his arms and looked up at the ceiling, his face crinkled up as if the answer was written somewhere around the dingy flickering strip light.

'No trace of Tyler on the body,' Talantire said. 'Not surprising, we didn't get much from her skin, given the decomposition. But they tested her belt, the zips on her skirt, her earrings and fight-back scrapings from under the fingernails. There are traces, but they're not Tyler Darracombe.'

'Finlay Roscoe,' Maddy read out. 'A partial match under one fingernail.'

'And Uncle Gary on the zip of her skirt.'

'I'm confused,' Maddy said. 'There's still loads more of Tyler there than anyone else.'

'All it proves is that he was the original car thief,' Talantire said. 'He nicked the car from Geoffrey Tolland in June and dumped it. If he came back a second time with Jade's body, then he was forensically very clean, which just doesn't sound like him. If he's that smart, why didn't he wipe down the steering wheel and the gear change, and all the other bits where he left his marks first time?' She glanced back at the emails. '"It seems significant that there are no traces of his DNA inside or outside the boot." And look at this: "There is evidence of sodium hypochlorite on some of the swabs – bleach in other words. Many of them show nothing else".' She swiped on her iPad to access the full set of photos from the scene. There were hundreds to flick through. 'Yes, we've got some images here of the boot after the body was removed.' The others crowded round to look. The grey textile base of the boot was stained by a horrid greenish-grey goop from the corpse, but higher, on the walls and grey plastic, it was spattered white.

'Yes, that does looks like bleach,' Nuttall said.

Maddy turned to him. 'I didn't have you down as the type to have ever cleaned a toilet.'

He gave her a sarcastic smile. 'Maddy, I have been divorced for a number of years, so yes, I have.'

'This is more evidence of forensic sophistication,' Talantire said.

'By Dave?' Maddy asked.

Talantire smiled. 'If the killer was Tyler, would he have had the nous to swill the body in Domestos?'

'He might well, it's a fairly obvious precaution,' Nuttall replied.

'And it implies pre-meditation, too,' Talantire said. 'And that's not what we were assuming, is it?'

'So, overall, you don't think Tyler killed her?' Maddy asked.

Talantire smiled. 'No, but he may well have been involved. He could still have been driving the second vehicle, with a third person in as well as Jade. I mean, the second vehicle could have been as full as the first one.'

Nuttall looked through the window at the fidgeting prisoner. 'Well, we've got lots to ask him about.'

–

The interview room was crowded. Talantire sat with Nuttall on one side of the table, while Darracombe sprawled at the other next to his solicitor, a very well-dressed and presumably expensive brief who had come down from Bristol at the request of the Darracombe family. Maybe they had more money than she imagined.

After prepping the ancient recording machine, as big as a 1970s boombox, Talantire looked at her watch. It was noon; they had six hours before today's press conference to get some answers.

'Tyler, perhaps you could begin by telling us where you were on the evening of Saturday the seventh of July?'

'I was watching *Strictly*, with me grandma at her house.'

'It wasn't on, Tyler,' Talantire said. 'It's an autumn show.'

'Must have been repeats then, or catch-up.' He shrugged.

'And you say you left your grandma's house at half-past midnight?'

'Yeah, that's right.'

Talantire had seen the supporting statement from Roky Darracombe, an alibi which stretched from eight p.m. to half past midnight. Beatrice and her team had half a dozen contradictory statements from youngsters in the area, who had seen Tyler out and about with his brother Aaron and the now deceased Jordon Bailey. She had no intention of confronting him with those as yet.

'Where did you go then?' Talantire asked.

'I went round to Colin's, to play computer games.'

Colin Moyle was Leanne's older brother. Beatrice had a statement from him too, which extended the alibi until 4:30 a.m. on Sunday morning when the baton was passed back to Mrs Darracombe, who said she had heard Tyler using his key to come in. Talantire had no statements to contradict this. The best Beatrice had found was a doorbell camera which covered the pedestrian route that Tyler would have taken from the Moyle household back to his grandmother's. It showed no sign of him passing.

'So who did you see on *Strictly* that night?' Nuttall asked.

Darracombe smiled and trotted out half a dozen celebrity names. Talantire exchanged a glance with Nuttall. She had seen that episode, but as an alibi it was rubbish as he could have seen it any time. Besides, although in theory there was no reason why a garage mechanic couldn't be an enthusiast for a show about ballroom dancing, it didn't convince her. She suspected he'd been coached, and given the details needed to support the alibi. Roky Darracombe was clearly giving her grandson a spirited defence.

Unfortunately, Talantire didn't have anything on Darracombe's car on the evening Jade died. His souped-up Ford Fiesta had not been along the A30 towards Bodmin, according to the ANPR data. Yes, it had been around Camborne in the early evening, caught on traffic light and road safety cameras, but there was no evidence that it had gone beyond the town. There were always other routes to Bodmin, of course, but none could match the fastest hour-long journey of the main road. If Tyler had been joyriding with his brother, there would have been no point in a second vehicle taking slower rural roads. Which left the question: did Tyler have access to another car?

'In a previous statement, you've admitted having been in the stolen Mercedes belonging to the Roscoe family, but deny being involved in the theft of it.'

'That's right.'

'And, as we mentioned, your DNA has been found extensively in the Mercedes.'

'That isn't a question,' the brief said.

'I'm reminding him,' Talantire said. 'But the question is this: do you still deny stealing this car?'

'Yes.'

'But you have stolen cars in the past?'

'Not for years.' He turned to his brief. 'I was fifteen. I got a suspended sentence.'

'Is this really relevant?' the brief asked.

'We determine the relevancy of the questions,' Talantire said. 'This isn't a court and you're not the judge.'

The solicitor's eyes widened at this retort.

'So, Tyler,' she continued, 'you've not stolen any cars since you were fifteen, is that correct?'

'Yes.'

Talantire handed across a photo of the abandoned VW Polo on the verge at St Neot, taken that morning. The image did not include the rear of the vehicle. 'Do you recognise this car?'

He shook his head.

'Speak up for the tape.'

'No,' he said.

'I'm surprised,' Talantire said. 'It's been on a verge in St Neot for weeks after being stolen on June the ninth from a car park in Redruth. Your DNA and fingerprints are all over it, inside and out: steering wheel, gearstick, glove compartment, driver's door handle inside. Shall I continue?'

He shrugged.

'In the boot of this vehicle, earlier this morning, we discovered the decomposing body of Jade Kernow. And we found her phone in one of your lock-up garages in Camborne.'

'No way!' Tyler Darracombe slumped back in the chair, his eyes wide. 'Ain't nothing to do with me.'

'All the evidence is there, Tyler,' Nuttall said. 'Her body, your DNA, her phone at your property. We've got you bang to rights, mate. For murder. You're looking at life in prison.'

Darracombe was now making whooshing sounds, his stained hands steepled over his face. He groped into his pocket and brought out his inhaler. He sucked greedily on the blue device and gasped, then began to cough violently. There seemed nothing fake about this. Talantire had seen stress- induced asthma before, and it wasn't pretty. She immediately stopped the tape and offered to suspend the interview. The solicitor then asked for a recovery room elsewhere, to talk to his client in private. 'Once his attack has ceased,' Talantire said. 'I want an officer in there with him who can call an ambulance if necessary. We'll get him a strong coffee, that usually helps. We'll resume in half an hour.'

The brief and Darracombe were escorted to another interview room by the desk sergeant, while Maddy joined Talantire and Nuttall.

'It certainly sounds pretty devastating evidence,' Maddy said.

'He hadn't heard about Jade's body being found,' Nuttall said.

Talantire shook her head. 'It's all bullshit though, isn't it? Okay, he stole the Polo, but someone else put the body in. And that same someone else put the phone in his garage to incriminate him. And whoever did that was almost certainly Jade's killer.'

The other two detectives nodded.

'Who do we know who hates Tyler Darracombe enough to do that?' Talantire asked.

'Finlay Roscoe,' they chorused.

'It's a good motive,' Talantire said. 'They hate each other. And it could be vengeance for Tyler stealing the family car.'

'We don't have much forensic on Finlay, though, do we?' Nuttall said.

'A tiny scrap of his blood under one fingernail of Jade's,' Maddy replied. 'Clear evidence of fightback, don't you think?'

'Not necessarily on the night of her death,' Talantire said. 'Finlay and Jade broke up, a few months ago, right? After Finlay's one-night stand with Scarlett. It's quite conceivable the two former lovers met up again recently, perhaps a reconciliation attempt, but then had an argument. And perhaps in this row Jade slapped him or scratched him. She had quite long nails, and DNA in blood could survive weeks or months on the underside of those nails.'

'You're right,' Maddy said. 'I hadn't thought of that.'

'We should bring Finlay in anyway. But what this is about,' Talantire said, indicating the tape machine with her chin, 'is scaring Tyler enough that he names names. I want to know who was with him in the Merc, at every stage from when it was stolen to when he left it. I want to know who he thinks might want to frame him, and most of all I want to know about the second car, and who he reckons might have been in it with Jade.'

Chapter Sixteen

Aaron Darracombe had been dreaming, flying over the Bodmin Moor, chasing the beast, its black tail disappearing through a hedge. Someone was whispering to him, calling his name. He felt a soft warm cloth on his face, and opened his eyes. A dark-haired nurse in a blue uniform was wiping him. Behind her, he recognised his grandmother, Roky.

'What's happened?' he croaked, through a throat as rough as sandpaper. He realised that stuff was attached to him: tubes, bandages. And he had a particularly annoying pain in his left foot.

'You were in an accident,' the nurse said softly. 'Do you remember?'

'What accident?'

His grandmother made her way over. Roky was a tough woman, drawn from a long line of tinners from the mines. Aaron had never seen her cry, or heard her sob. Her big rough hands grasped his, and squeezed, her many rings almost painful against his fingers. 'Aaron,' she said, and stroked some of the little wisps of hair that escaped from the bandages on his head. 'My little darling,' she cooed. 'We thought we'd lost you.'

'What happened?' Aaron said. He had a huge crushing headache which came from nowhere.

'You crashed a car,' Roky said, tears flowing down her face. 'It wasn't yours.'

'I don't remember. When can I get up?' he asked.

Roky looked at the nurse, who was shaking her head. Something was going on, and he didn't know what it was.

'Do you remember anything?' the nurse asked.

He tried to think, but his head was exploding with pain. He couldn't think of anything.

'The duty doctor is due in a few minutes. He will explain to you in detail, but you have head injuries, and have spent two days in an induced coma.'

This only confused him more.

'Gran, can you scratch my left foot for me? I can't reach.'

And for some reason that he couldn't fathom, she burst into tears.

–

The interview lasted two more hours, until two p.m. Tyler was incoherent half the time, initially with anger, shouting and swearing, but later with upset, recriminations and bouts of sobbing, interspersed with the occasional use of his inhaler. Talantire took it as far as she dared, tiring him out with repeated questions, and accusations of guilt, but she certainly didn't want to provoke a full-blown medical emergency. The Crown Prosecution Service would take a very dim view of anything that seemed coercive, so she asked him repeatedly if he felt all right to continue, and fighter that he was, he said he did.

Nuttall added descriptions of what it was like to be fresh meat in a prison with murderers and rapists, who would certainly have a welcome committee for him. They went back and forth over his statements, tripping him up as much as possible until they were close to the line that separated interrogation from psychological abuse. She didn't have a lot of time to get the answers she needed, and knew she was taking a risk.

The results so far were mixed. Tyler had insisted that he hadn't been in a second car, and had no idea who might have been in it. He listed his brother's friends, and the girls that he knew hung around with Jordan. 'I don't know Jade, I really *don't*.' He angrily wiped away a tear track from his face. Not so tough now.

Talantire called a five-minute break, and then arranged for the chicken tikka masala, chips and poppadums which the desk sergeant had heated up in the microwave, to be served to the prisoner. Talantire happened to know, thanks to Camborne Community Police, that this was the dish that Roky Darracombe used to serve at least once a week to her grandkids. She got Maddy to bring it in on a tray to him, with a bottle of zero-alcohol beer. The lawyer had taken the opportunity to go and ring the family, now the formal interview was suspended and the tape machine off.

'You've had a bit of a rough session, haven't you, Tyler?' Maddy said, as she set down the food.

He sniffed and blew his nose.

She remained there, not so much the good cop as an angelic one, while he gobbled down the food with a plastic spoon. 'All this can end if you confess to stealing the Merc, and just whisper to me who really was involved in this,' she said.

And it was at that point that he opened up, between mouthfuls of food. Unsurprisingly, Finlay Roscoe was top of the list. 'He's such a stuck-up twat. We fell out big time at the garage. He was such a lazy arse, swanning around talking to customers like he was the know-it-all but not doing any of the work. Typical son of a headmistress. The boy who can do no wrong. Mr Yelland got rid of him eventually, but he still drives round Camborne in his Nova.'

'Did you steal the Merc?'

'Yeah, me and Aaron nicked the car. It was a piece of piss honestly; they had the keys by the kitchen window, and with the relay it was within range of the RFID copier, so we cloned it onto a new fob. After riding around for a while that night, I stuck it in the garage for a few hours in the morning so the GPS was blocked, just in case there was a tracker or something. I meant to leave it on the waste ground somewhere, maybe burn it. But Aaron had this big idea to look for the Beast of Bodmin, which he'd seen with Dad years ago.' He chewed thoughtfully for a moment. 'Should have set it on fire. Bound to get caught hanging onto it. But Aaron was insistent, he'd been telling Jordan all about it, and some of the local girls were up for it too.'

'So are you telling me you were never in the car after it set out on the journey?'

'No, never. And all this stuff about Jade Kernow. It's total bollocks. Finlay's set me up.'

'How?'

'Planting the phone. It's not that hard. There's a bit of free play on the lock-up door, and you could easily get your hand under, slide the phone in.'

'What about the other car, the VW Polo?'

Tyler sighed heavily as he mopped up the last of the masala sauce with his chips. 'Yeah, okay. I did nick it. Me and Scarlett went out for a ride while my own wheels were being repaired.'

'Your Fiesta was off the road?' Maddy asked.

'Yeah, I'd smacked it into a bollard, and the tracking was fucked. So I took this VW from the car park, we got a takeaway and went out into the country, but it was almost out of fuel. We rang her stepdad, said we'd missed the last bus, and he came and drove us home. I left the car where it was.'

Maddy now realised that the unknown trace on the other plastic fork must be Scarlett's. It seemed no elimination sample had been taken from this sociable young girl. That was certainly an oversight, seeing as she was a girlfriend of the deceased Jordan Bailey, one-time lover of Finlay Roscoe and a friend of Tyler Darracombe's. What testimony she could offer, were she not now lying in intensive care in hospital.

–

Talantire and Nuttall watched through the one-way glass as Maddy gradually reeled in the truth from Tyler Darracombe.

'I believe him,' Talantire said, as they listened over the intercom. 'He doesn't seem to know Jade, and the evidence plant theory does seem plausible.'

'I agree,' Nuttall said. 'Even though his alibi is weak, we can't place him close to the scene of the accident. There is no forensic.'

Talantire looked at her iPad. 'I've been badgering Primrose to get onto this, but she's got so much on, poor thing. She has spent the last hour looking through Tyler's phone, and there's nothing incriminating. She said it was only a quick look, and obviously we will need to get the full records and see if anything has been deleted. For example, I would have expected to see a selfie of him by the Merc at some stage, seeing as he nicked it. If there was one, it's been deleted. But you can't falsify the tower data. Tyler's phone was nowhere near Bodmin Moor on the night in question, and it was on the whole time. It was in and around Camborne, and there were messages which appeared to have come from him around that time, including one to his grandmother, and another to Colin.'

'Is that the lad who supposedly played computer games with him?'

'Yes, a main part of his alibi.'

'So Tyler definitely isn't our man,' Nuttall said.

'No. It's got to be Finlay. He's got a motive for planting evidence against his enemy, Tyler, and we can put his car pretty close to where the accident occurred.'

'Are we going to arrest him?'

'The matter is already in hand,' Talantire said, holding up her phone. 'I asked Beatrice a couple of hours ago to bring him in. Okay, let's release Tyler on police bail. But first let's charge him for the car thefts. I think he'll be happy to admit to those, knowing he's not in the frame for killing Jade.'

Chapter Seventeen

Two hours earlier

Shona Roscoe was in her Peugeot, driving home from school at lunchtime. Whitcombe Primary was, as many schools were, short of staff. It was still suffering the occasional bout of Covid among both staff and pupils. She generally did playground duty or supervised lunch on Tuesdays and Thursdays, but this particular Tuesday, she had left the assistant head in charge. Besides, she had been on the verge of tears ever since she'd heard. A member of staff had told her that she'd seen on Facebook that a girl's body had been found that morning, in an abandoned car in the village of St Neot, and she'd confirmed that horrible rumour by looking on the BBC news website. Social media was rife with speculation that it was Jade, but it hadn't been confirmed. Then, a few minutes later, she'd received a phone message from Sergeant Beatrice Dodds that the police were urgently looking for Finlay. This woman had suggested they would arrest him at work, but Shona had pleaded with them not to do that. He was a trainee manager at the local Wetherspoon's pub, and a public arrest would destroy his career before it had even begun.

'I'll get him to come home, then you can talk to him here,' she had said.

Dodds had reluctantly agreed, so long as he was there within fifteen minutes. Otherwise it would be an arrest at the pub.

The moment she had got off the phone, Shona had texted Finlay, but got no reply, then tried to ring him, but he hadn't answered. She left a message for him to call her urgently. He would be busy. But surely he would call her when he saw the news? Wouldn't they let him come home, knowing that it was probably his ex-girlfriend they had found? He'd only been in the job for eight weeks, so surely he couldn't be that essential. It was only a pub after all not a school, although having visited the place during the day once, the resemblance to a crèche was quite remarkable, most notably in the noise level in the family dining section. She fervently hoped he would find a better job, one with some proper prospects. But then he had been a perennial disappointment to them both for—

Oh good grief! She slammed on the brakes at a pedestrian crossing, not having seen the young mother who began to cross with her pushchair. The woman scowled at her, and Shona mouthed her apologies through the windscreen. Oh, that would have been terrible. To be so distracted about Jade and Finlay that she knocked down some poor innocent woman and her child on the local zebra crossing.

Shona felt tears pricking her eyes. She was just about holding it together, but she needed Finlay to come home so she could speak to him before the police did. She had trusted him utterly, but news that the police were now looking for him had shaken her to the core. Especially after the discovery she had made yesterday evening in their own home. That, above all, had suddenly made her question everything that Finlay had told her. She and David had discussed it. David had decided to give him the benefit of the doubt, but she could not. Especially now. Some things were too important to be brushed under the carpet. Finlay had been lying to the police, and that reflected on them as parents. But, most of all, it was Finlay himself who was careering towards destruction.

She turned into her own street, but there was no sign of Finlay's car. It could be that it had broken down, because she desperately hoped he had come home, or maybe someone had given him a lift. David's hire car, an Audi provided by the insurers since the theft, was in the drive, so maybe he had picked Finlay up. She fervently hoped so. God, she needed David's support now. They had to be tough, they had to stick together, just as they had when Finlay was found in possession of cannabis at fifteen. It was a good marriage, strong, and David had always accepted Finlay as if he was his own. Men like that are hard to find.

Shona half mounted the pavement and parked outside the house, just behind a grey saloon. She put the hand-brake on and fumbled to remove her keys from the ignition. She saw Sergeant Dodds emerge from the car in front, together with a male uniformed officer. Shakily, she extracted herself from the car, as the detective walked over to her, grim-faced.

'Is he not here yet?' Shona asked, already fearing the answer.

'No. And he is not at the Wetherspoon's either. A plain-clothes officer slipped in there to check a few minutes ago.'

'Oh, I'm so sorry,' Shona said. 'He is a good boy.'

'That remains to be seen,' Sergeant Dodds responded. 'At nineteen, you are a man, and have your own decisions to make.'

To Shona, that felt like an affront. Finlay had always been her little boy – naughty yes, but lovable.

'Have you been in contact with him today, Mrs Roscoe?'

'Once I heard the news – you know, *that* news – I messaged him, but he didn't reply and I tried to ring.'

The sergeant looked unconvinced. 'If you've warned him, there will be consequences,' she said. 'It is an extremely serious matter, perverting the course of justice.'

Shona's heart was hammering like it was trying to burst its way out of her ribcage. 'Oh, I do understand. Would you like to come in for a cup of coffee?'

'We need to come in, but we'll skip the coffee, thanks all the same. I want you to show us Finlay's bedroom.'

Shona looked at the other officer, who was donning a pair of blue plastic-looking gloves. He had with him a black fabric bag, labelled 'forensics'. Her home a crime scene? She looked back at Sergeant Dodds, and felt the blood draining away from her head. She felt dizzy and toppled back against the car door. The last she heard was a buzzing in her ears and she saw a white arc of sky above as protective arms reached out to stop her falling.

–

Shona came round on the sofa, with David sitting with his arm around her. He was smiling gently into her face, his reading glasses dangling on the lace around his neck. 'Are you feeling better, love?'

'I'm fine,' she said. 'Has Finlay come back?'

'No, and he hasn't responded to my messages,' David said.

She could hear the sound of activity upstairs, footsteps and the moving of furniture.

'The police are in his room, and they've gone into the Symmonds' house too,' David confirmed, indicating with his head the house of Finlay's latest girlfriend Ellie, at the end of the road.

'I'm so terrified,' Shona said, as she sat up. 'He wouldn't do anything like this. He just wouldn't.'

David smiled. He hugged her and cooed gently into her ear. 'Everything is going to be all right, love.'

'But what about, you know…?' Her eyes strayed to the ceiling as if she could be overheard.

'Taken care of,' David said.

'Do you think…?'

'I don't think he killed her. Honestly, you and I both know it's not in his nature.'

His arms squeezed her more tightly and she began to cry. He shushed her and rocked her gently. He only released her when they heard heavy boots on the stairs, and the uniformed officer came past with two big polythene carrier bags, containing what appeared to be Finlay's laptop and some other electronic gear.

David stood up and gazed out of the lounge window. 'Oh well, it's entertaining the neighbours at least. There must be ten of them standing out there, now that a patrol car's arrived.'

'I'll have to leave my job, David,' Shona sighed. 'It'll be the end of me.'

'Not if he's innocent, and he *is* innocent.'

'But no one will look at me and think first about my educational achievements.' She had turned round three successive failing schools, all of them now 'outstanding', and played a major role in national literacy campaigns, which had led to an appearance on TV. Shona's one-minute interview on *Good Morning Britain* five years ago had been a highlight of her life.

'They won't forget about any of that,' David said, smiling.

'They will! I'll just be the head teacher whose child was accused of murder.'

The doorbell rang, and David went. He came in with another two uniformed officers, one male, the other a small slim woman in uniform. She was very smiley and introduced herself in an Irish accent as Nuala Cary. 'I'm a special constable with the community police, and I'd like to stay with you in case Finlay comes back, or calls in.'

After a few stilted pleasantries were exchanged, Nuala said: 'I'll just go off and make some tea, shall I? I think we could all do with a cuppa.'

Eventually, Beatrice Dodds came down. 'We're finished upstairs, now. Does Finlay have his own shed, lock-up garage or any other property that is exclusively used by him?'

'No,' David said. 'The shed is mine, and the garage is just used by us. Do you want to look around?'

'Yes, please,' Beatrice said. 'The staff at Wetherspoon's say that Finlay disappeared around eleven without saying anything to anyone. His car is no longer in the car park.'

'Oh,' the two parents said, simultaneously.

'If he contacts you, in any way, it is your legal duty to inform us.'

'Yes, of course,' Shona said.

'We've heard nothing,' David added.

'Do you still have a landline?'

'No,' David said.

'Would you permit me to examine both of your mobiles?'

The parents looked at each other.

'Yes, why not?' Shona said. She unlocked, then handed across her phone and David did likewise with his.

Sergeant Dodds quickly checked recent messages and texts.

'That appears to be fine,' she said. 'I would ask that you both stay here and leave your phones with Nuala.'

'Ah, the tiny tea lady,' David muttered.

'She won't answer any incoming messages, but we need to see immediately if Finlay makes contact.'

'But I *have* to go back to school,' Shona said. 'I'm the head. I can't just take time off.'

'All right, but I'd really prefer if your mobile stays here.'

'Do I have any choice?' Shona asked.

'Yes, we can't force you,' Beatrice said. 'It's probably just for a few hours, until we find him. Look, if you are contacted on any other matter, Nuala will ring the school and pass on the message.'

Shona and David stared at each other with widened eyes. The turnaround to formality in Sergeant Dodds' behaviour was chilling. Shona knew that neither of them could even contemplate the idea that Finlay had been involved in killing Jade. It just wasn't in his nature, as David had said. But the behaviour of the police, the search of their home, the DNA swabs and the fingerprints were concrete contradictions of her faith in her son.

It was a few minutes later when David agreed to drive Shona back to school and pick her up again at the end of the day. He would work from his office up the road in Truro town centre, instead of from home, happy to leave the special constable in charge of the house. He complained that he had orders to go out that he hadn't processed that day and was behind on lots of paperwork.

Still, not having to answer well-wishers on the phone would mean he'd get some work done. If Finlay was found, someone could email him. Shona barely listened, concerned more about the reaction she would get on her return to school.

As they parked just before the yellow zig-zags outside the gates, two facts hit her like a brick wall. One, Jade Kernow, that lovely girl with a big heart and a warm smile, was dead. Murdered. Two, her only child, Finlay, just nineteen, was being sought in connection with her murder.

And this afternoon she had to chair a staff meeting to prepare for the next Ofsted visit.

She reached into her bag and pulled out a silver blister pack. David noticed and said: 'You shouldn't really take another one today, love.'

'How else am I going to get through the day?' she asked.

—

News of the difficulties in finding Finlay Roscoe reached Talantire as soon as she and Maddy had set off from Plymouth to go to Camborne.

'He won't get far,' Maddy said.

'Hopefully not,' Talantire replied. The plan had been to interview him at home, then bring him back to Plymouth Crownhill. She had decided that was now where all future incident-room meetings and press conferences on the case would be held. She had rung Brent West earlier, just as a courtesy, to let him know what she had in mind. She had planned to tell him that it would save a great deal of time to have meetings at the same place where you were holding suspects rather than ferrying the team backwards and forwards between Liskeard and Plymouth Crownhill. It was also a lot closer to police HQ at Exeter. No reply, so she'd left her proposal in a voicemail. This was getting beyond a joke.

'Let's head over now to Camborne,' Maddy suggested. 'See if we can help in the hunt.'

'All right,' Talantire said, pulling into a side road. 'But I've just got a couple of things to do first.'

On the hands-free, she rang her own line manager, Detective Superintendent Wells in Exeter, and pulled him out of a meeting.

'Sorry to disturb you, sir,' she said. 'I think I need your approval in the absence of Commander West.' She outlined her plans, which included getting him to host the six p.m. press conference at Plymouth Crownhill, freeing her up to go to Camborne, ninety minutes' drive away.

Wells listened carefully. 'That sounds fine to me, I'll get onto Moira Hallett. I just need you to get us a credible suspect under arrest before I face the press.'

'I'm doing my best,' she replied.

'So is it the older Darracombe brother? I heard the car where the body was found was minging with his DNA.'

'No.' She explained about the difference between the theft of the car and the later stowing of the corpse by a different person. 'We are looking for a lad using the pseudonym Simon, seemingly Jade's latest boyfriend, who might well be Finlay Roscoe.'

'Well, whoever it is, just make sure the evidence stacks up. I don't want any more dithering.'

Talantire was a little taken aback. 'With all due respect, sir, I've been left in the lurch with no contact from the SIO.'

'Well, Jan, his absence from the case looks to be the least of our problems.' He hung up without saying goodbye.

'A bit rude! Quite unlike him,' Maddy said.

'He's stressed,' Talantire said. 'I've seen him like this before.'

'And still there's radio silence about who's going to be our new chief constable. Doesn't sound like it's going smoothly, does it?' She said, rubbing her hands with glee.

Talantire smiled to herself in quiet agreement, then started up the car and pulled out onto the A38, heading for Camborne, while Maddy worked her phone.

'Ah, another useful forensic result, from the tyre tracks we found at the Phoenix mine,' she said.

'And?'

'Let me see.' She speed-read the document from the specialist forensic tyre unit. 'Yes, the tyre imprint from the Vauxhall Nova that Camborne sent in matches exactly the treads found at the mine. The tyres were apparently quite worn, which gives them an individual character, so it's not simply the same size and make.'

'Now *that* is a breakthrough,' Talantire said. 'We can place Finlay Roscoe's Vauxhall Nova at the Phoenix mine, which means he, or whoever else was driving it, could have placed the shoe there.'

'Great. All we need to do now is find him.'

'Okay, let's head over to Camborne ASAP. If we can catch tricky young Finlay in time for the press conference, Wells will be pleased.'

–

Finlay Roscoe was sitting in his Nova in the National Trust car park at Trelissick Gardens. The house and tearoom were closed for renovations, and there were fewer than usual visitors. He hid the car in the emptiest parking section, furthest from the footpaths and gardens, and shielded from view by a long wheelbase Transit van which looked like it had been there for weeks. He needed peace, and time to think. He had his phone in his hand, but he didn't dare turn it on because the police would be able to track him.

Ever since he'd seen the news about Jade on Facebook when he was at work, he'd been trapped in a nightmare. He really needed to ring Ellie, not only to hear a friendly voice, but to see if she could bring him a sleeping bag and a tent. They could sleep rough together for a while, until it all blew over. It would be wild. Just him and her against the world. But how could he contact her without giving his location away? He'd seen enough crime dramas to realise the cops might be tapping her phone too, just as they were bound to be waiting for him at home.

The moment he'd left Wetherspoon's, he'd rushed to the pound shop round the corner and bought several cans of green spray paint that were on special offer, a 99p multipack of gaffer, parcel and insulation tapes, a fleecy winter cap with ear flaps that he could use as a disguise and a multi-pack of crisps that were past the sell-by date. It was little more than a deranged trolley dash, something he realised when he was at the till, being given a strange look by the cashier. Had she recognised him? Paranoia hadn't taken long to get a hold.

Now, sitting in the car panicking, he realised what he should have bought: scissors and a razor to cut off his beard, and a burner phone. He hadn't seen one in the pound shop, but now guessed that Argos would have them, at Treliske Retail Park. Still, he just didn't have the bottle to go there, with all the CCTV they had.

He ransacked his Vauxhall for what limited resources were there. It was better than he expected. Part of his dad's toolkit, left from when he'd installed the spotlights for him, plus some of his mum's stuff. Normally he'd whinge at his mother for her borrowing his car and leaving her shit there. She had done it twice since the Merc had been stolen, but now the glove compartment yielded a pair of red-framed reading glasses that could help with the disguise and a pair of scissors, to trim his beard. He couldn't think of a use for the lipstick, but the moisturiser might help him have a wet shave if he could find a razor. In the boot, he found a plastic carrier bag with Shona's polka dot rain jacket with a hood, and a woman's white woolly hat with a pom-pom.

The car had darkened rear windows and Finlay sat in the back unobserved while he cut off his beard, catching the trimmings in a plastic bag. He returned to the front passenger seat to look at the results in the mirror on the sun visor. It looked awful and tatty, and offended his sharp self-image, but it would have to do. He put on the rain jacket, and then using the gaffer tape masked off the headlamps and windscreen while he resprayed the car. It was an awful glossy bottle green, but it would have to do. He then peeled off all the stickers, which made the car so distinctive. Finally, he removed the rear-window tint films. He couldn't get it all off and some of it split. It was messy, but it didn't look like his car any more. He unscrewed the spots, and yanked out the wires, before dumping them in the boot. The final touch, one he thought was particularly inspiring, was trimming some of the black insulation tape to alter the registration plates.

That way, he wouldn't be caught on automatic number plate recognition. He smiled to himself at his ingenuity, and his natural optimism and self-regard reasserted itself. Once it all blew over, everything would be fine.

But still he needed to ring Ellie.

He put on the reading glasses, zipped up the now paint-spattered rain jacket and decided to risk going into the gardens. Maybe he could borrow a phone from one of the old codgers here, saying his car had broken down or something like that. And then he saw something that amazed him. A public phone box, just a hundred yards away. Brilliant, just when you need it something turns up.

He decided to risk calling her. He sauntered across to the red phone box. He'd never used one, and was amazed to see that you couldn't use contactless. It smelled like his grandad's bedroom, a kind of retro 1950s taint. He had a couple of pound coins in his pocket that he kept for the old parking machine near the Wetherspoon's.

When he got through to Ellie's number, it was answered by someone else.

A copper.

He hung up immediately. This was bad news.

But then he had another idea.

—

Shona was an hour into the Ofsted committee meeting in the staffroom when the call came. It had been a harrowing afternoon, and she had barely been able to concentrate. Now the school receptionist, Linda Priestley, interrupted the meeting, and called her out into the corridor on an urgent matter. Once the door behind was closed, she said: 'It's a Detective Constable Smith from Devon and Cornwall Police. From a phone box. Says it's urgent.'

'Put it through to my office please, and make sure I'm not disturbed.'

Shona made her way shakily into her room, with its view over the school buildings, the children playing outside on their break. She lifted the receiver when it rang.

'This is Shona,' she answered, and was delighted to hear the voice of her son.

'Mum, this is the only way I can get hold of you. Can you ring me back on this number? I've only got a few coins.'

She scrawled down on her jotter the number he gave her, and then rang back.

'The police are looking for you,' she whispered. 'You've got to come home.'

'I know they are, and it's rubbish. The whole case is crap, I promise you. I didn't do it, I swear on my life I didn't do it.'

'Then come in and tell them so. If you're innocent, you have nothing to fear.'

'That's bollocks, Mum. You've been watching too many TV dramas. There's too many miscarriages of justice, and I ain't going to be one of them. I'll be camping out for a while, but I need you to get me my tent and sleeping bag from home, and meet me.'

'Finlay, this isn't the right way to do it. You'll get caught, this isn't *Hunted*. You aren't going to get away.' She knew that Finlay had enjoyed the TV show where teams of ordinary people attempted to evade the police, who were equipped with all the apparatus of the modern surveillance state.

'I've given it a lot of thought, Mum. I really have. They think that because I was her boyfriend, it must have been me. It's motive, innit? They'll fit me up. Stitched up like a kipper.'

Shona had never heard her son use that kind of phrase and assumed he must have picked it up from TV, along with that awful hip-hop and drill music he listened to, with its horrible misogynistic lyrics.

'Don't be like this, Finlay.' Her voice cracked. 'You're killing us, your dad and I, you are destroying us.' She sobbed.

'I ain't *done* anything, don't you understand?' he shouted. 'I'm the wanted man, and there ain't no justice. I'm only asking *you* because there's no one left. I tried ringing Ellie and the cops picked up her phone.'

She tried to ignore the slight, along with the provocative bad grammar. 'We just have to prove your innocence that's all,' she said. 'And you have to come back for us to do that. Don't you understand how bad it looks that you are a fugitive? They are after your car, there are all these cameras. You can't escape.'

'Mum, just drive over to see me. Sleeping bag, torch, tent, disposable razors. And some cash, a couple of hundred would do. And don't tell Dad.'

'Finlay, I can't. If I help you, it's perverting the course of justice, the police told me. I could go to prison just for not telling them that you rang me, let alone for delivering you all this stuff.'

'You are my last hope. Meet me at the old recreation ground at Mylor Bridge at five. If you don't show, or if the cops come, then I'm throwing myself off a cliff, because no one cares!'

'No, Finlay, no,' she sobbed.

He hung up, but she rang back immediately. No answer. Tears were flowing down her face and she blew her nose. She realised she was shaking.

There was a tap on the door, and Linda Priestley's head poked around. 'Are you all right, Shona? Anything I can do?'

Shona managed a watery smile. 'It's about Jade, the body they found. The details are quite horrifying.'

'I'll get you a coffee,' Linda said. 'Strange that the police would ring from a phone box, don't you think?'

'Yes, some technical glitch on the police network today, he claimed.'

'Right.' She didn't sound wholly convinced.

Shona slumped into her chair. She realised she was already well down the path of criminality. The lies had begun to flow, but that was only the start of her moral disintegration. Everything that she had ever told the children, broadcast to her hundreds of pupils, about honesty, about owning up, about integrity, was being corroded. She realised that in the end she would do anything, literally anything, to save her son.

But what if he had killed her? What then?

–

Shona Roscoe sat in silence as David drove her home. The confirmation that the body was that of Jade had deadened their mood, and she had told him nothing about her conversation with Finlay. She knew he would not approve her helping him evade the law.

As soon as they got in, David headed to his home office upstairs, and Shona began surreptitiously assembling the various items that Finlay had asked for. Sneaking the tent out from the garage would be the tricky bit, but luckily David had an errand to run, and the little policewoman was busy watching the phones. Shona waited for him to depart in the Audi, then stowed the tent, the sleeping bag and the other items Finlay had requested in the boot of her blue Peugeot. She told the policewoman she was going to pick up some groceries, but would be back soon.

It took fifteen minutes to reach the recreation ground car park. She remembered the place well, having brought Finlay here to play on the swings and slides when he was four years old, when she was a single mum and he was all she had. How that had turned out. She pulled to a halt when she saw Finlay by a car, looking like some homeless person, but wearing her rain jacket. Was *that* his Vauxhall? If so, he had been busy. It had been spray-painted some awful dark green, and the tinting on the rear windows was gone, along with all the stickers.

She emerged from the car, and headed towards him, arms wide. She thought she might cry and she could see in his face alarm that this might happen. He gave her a brief hug and then held her away as he asked: 'Have you got the stuff?'

'Yes.' She immediately handed him a wodge of cash, which he rapidly counted as if he might suspect her of short-changing him. 'It's two hundred, like you asked for.'

He nodded and pushed it into the back pocket of his jeans. 'Couldn't you get anything smaller than twenties?'

'That's what the cash machine dispensed. Sorry.'

'Mixed notes would have been more useful. Some fivers. They can trace card payments, see.'

She waited in vain for a thank you and then walked back to the boot of the car. He walked behind her, and she loaded his arms with the stuff he asked for. 'I brought your rucksack as well in case you have to move on foot, and some walking boots. It's supposed to rain tonight.'

'Thanks,' he said.

'You've sprayed the car,' she said.

'Yeah. And removed the spot lamps, the window tints and the stickers.'

'They'll still get you on the number plate,' she said.

'Nope,' he said. 'Bit of insulation tape, changed the numbers. Six to an eight, and the L to a U.'

She was appalled. 'Finlay, you are turning us both into criminals. And you've lied to me.' She told him about what she had discovered in the house. 'You said you hadn't seen her. But you have been with her, haven't you?'

'Yeah, but not like that.' He looked puzzled for a moment. 'We did meet up again, the week before she disappeared, but not at home. Thought we might get back together again, but we had an argument and she went for me.'

'What do you mean "went for you"?'

'Slapped and scratched me.' He indicated a tiny blemish on his cheek.

'What was the argument about?'

'She had a new boyfriend. She told me to hurt me.'

'Because you hurt her with your fling with Scarlett.'

'Probably. Anyway, she said this guy, he's everything I'm not. Caring, listening, considerate. But I reckon that's the bastard who killed her.'

'What's his name?'

'Simon. I never heard of him, but find out who he is and then I can come home.'

—

While Talantire and Maddy were driving to Camborne, Nuttall had parked himself at a borrowed screen in Plymouth CID and got on with attempts to find out if any other car, apart from Roscoe's Vauxhall Nova, could fit the bill for the second car in which Jade was travelling at the time of the accident. He pulled up a long spreadsheet packed with car number plates, all 1,870 lines of them. This was the download from all the ANPR cameras along the A30 on the night of the accident, sorted by highest average speed over the whole journey from Camborne to Bodmin, but excluding those flagged as emergency vehicles. He then sorted the remainder by time, from half an hour before and after when the Mercedes shot through. Only two other vehicles closely matched the excessive speed of the stolen car, but they were almost half an hour earlier. That was too big a gap. If they had been only a minute or two earlier, they could reasonably have been candidates for an accompanying vehicle. Although they had assumed that the Merc would be the lead joyriding vehicle, it being the fastest, there was no guarantee that it would be this way round.

DVLA checks on the owners for the two speeding vehicles in question showed one was a commercial delivery van, the other a BMW owned by a middle-aged man from Bristol, and registered to his business. Neither had been reported stolen, and the owners seemed unlikely joyriders. Speeding tickets were already on their way to them.

This left just one car. Finlay's Vauxhall Nova. ANPR data from Camborne to Bodmin showed it was fifteen minutes behind the Mercedes, rarely travelling at more than the 70 mph speed limit. It certainly didn't look like part of the joyride, more like a doomed effort to catch up.

All this would make sense if Finlay had claimed that his car had been stolen, given the enmity between him and Tyler Darracombe. But Finlay had never claimed that.

There was another conundrum. Tyler's DNA had turned up in the Vauxhall, yet at the time of the accident, his phone was nowhere near the car. Nuttall looked up where the sample had been taken from, and it was on the driver's seat, and the floor. Hair follicles. They could have been there for months, possibly even longer. It wasn't clear how long they had been enemies, but this could predate it.

The only other evidence they had was vague: first, the CCTV image of a small car passing a farm at speed, less than twenty minutes before the accident, second the smiley-face speed sign in the village of St Trenewan which showed two cars racing just before the accident, and finally the video taken inside the Mercedes which showed the headlights of the pursuing car in the background.

Overall, it seemed that Finlay's car was the only viable candidate vehicle. If for some reason Finlay wasn't driving, but Jade, his ex-girlfriend, was in it, there must be a limited number of people that she would trust enough to travel that far with. Simon. It had to be Simon. But was Simon Finlay?

Nuttall looked again at the messages exchanged on the night between Simon and Jade.

23:56 Simon: Wait a mo. I'll ring you in two.

00:14 Simon: I couldn't hear a word.
Who's driving?

00:15 Jade: Aaron

00:15 Simon: Stay with it.

00:37 Simon: Result?

00:37 Jade: No. I'm in the back.

00:38 Simon: Bale then, as agreed.

Then the final emoji heart, from her to him.

Nuttall steepled his hands over his face. Something was nagging at him about the exchange of messages, that they were about as far from the character of someone out to have fun as you can imagine. Something arranged in advance, something possibly serious, even before the tragedy of the accident. Was this someone trying to get even? Was this a spying expedition? What was it that Simon wanted? What was it that Jade couldn't get because she was in the back? The most obvious thing would be a phone, perhaps a glimpse of who Jordan Bailey or Aaron Darracombe had messaged. What else could you only get in the front of the car? To fiddle with the controls or the radio, the front-seat door pockets or the glove compartment. If Simon wanted something, for a 'result' as he put it, it either had to be information or an item Jade could not reach in the back.

Then it came to him. It was obvious really, the tablets. The little purple MDMA stash which was shattered by the impact and spread all over the car. Someone who had been in that vehicle earlier in the day had left their stash there. Probably in the glove compartment or possibly a front door pocket. The ecstasy wasn't from the joyriders that evening, but earlier in the day, hence the serious nature of the conversation with Jade.

He rang Talantire.

–

She answered on the hands-free and listened while he gave her his theory. 'It's pretty much what I was thinking,' she said. 'Maybe Finlay had got in deeper than we imagine. Dealing ecstasy, it's certainly something I'd considered.'

'Or somebody else,' Nuttall said. 'Someone we don't know about.'

'But do we have another car to put them in?' she asked him. 'If he's in Finlay's car, there's a limited number of people who it could be: his parents, who are each other's alibi, or a friend who he trusted. If it was nicked, he would have someone to blame, wouldn't he?'

'That's the blank wall I keep running into,' Nuttall said.

'So you've run the numbers, do we really have no other vehicles?'

Nuttall told her about the two earlier vehicles.

Something was nagging at the edge of her memory. 'Didn't the raw data mention something clocked just two minutes behind, also speeding? I only got a quick look, but I do seem to recall that at least a couple of the cameras on the A38 registered someone breaking the limit just a couple of minutes after the Merc?'

'Hold on a minute,' Nuttall said, turning back to the first tab on the spreadsheet. 'Ah yes, there was one. The plate is registered as emergency services.'

'Indulge me, Dave. There are dashcams on most emergency service vehicles these days, so let's see which one we've got.'

He hung up to get the data and rang back in two minutes.

'It's one of ours,' Nuttall said. 'And, bloody hell! I think we've found Simon.'

Chapter Eighteen

Talantire had been stunned when Nuttall had told her. Maddy had heard too.

'What on earth was he doing driving like a lunatic along the bottom edge of Bodmin Moor at that time of night?' Maddy asked.

'I have no idea,' Talantire said, but a small smile began to creep up her face. The police vehicle that Nuttall had found was the black Ford Explorer belonging to none other than Brent West. Or, to put it more accurately, the full name of the Devon and Cornwall police officer allocated the vehicle: Commander Brent Simon West.

'Well, well, our senior commander dealing ecstasy,' Maddy said. 'Who would have thought it?'

'That's a bit of a leap,' Talantire said. 'Okay he may have been only a minute or two behind the Merc and driving at a similar speed, but we've got a lot more dots to join before we can accuse him of killing Jade, or dealing ecstasy. Even if his middle name is Simon.'

'Simple Simon says put your hand in the glove compartment,' Maddy said, and giggled.

'Yes, of course I'd love it to be true,' Talantire replied. 'But we need a whole lot more.'

'It just makes so much sense,' Maddy said.

Talantire didn't respond. It was certainly an alluring idea, but she had to be led by the facts, not by her own prejudice. Just wishing something to be true doesn't make it so.

–

Inspired by the discovery that Brent West was close behind the Merc in the half hour before the accident, Nuttall re-examined the ANPR data series in detail. The Ford Explorer clocked each of the traffic cameras at almost identical speed: 74 mph. He would have known that Devon and Cornwall Police policy was to give ten per cent leeway above the legal limit before issuing a ticket. But if he was going at that speed, and was only two minutes behind the Merc, which had been clocked at ninety-six on that particular camera, then almost certainly the joyriders had overtaken him a mile or two before. Nuttall presumed that West had a dashcam, but, of course, at night it would give no real clue who was in the overtaking vehicle. West's Explorer had shown up on the system before Camborne. Laying out the route and speed that they knew for the joyrider's car and West's further under-mined any idea that Commander West was pursuing or in any other way involved with the joyriders. Indeed, he clocked a further camera after the Bodmin Moor turn, which showed he would have had no time to have tailed the Merc up through the villages towards the moor itself. It was your standard just-over-the-legal-limit journey and went right through to Exeter, where he arrived shortly after three a.m., according to cameras in the city.

Clearly there was a story behind his speedy late-night journey on that fateful night, possibly an interesting one, but it didn't look relevant to the carnage on the edge of Bodmin Moor.

Nuttall relayed his findings to Talantire, who picked up on the hands-free. She heard him out, then only hesitated briefly before ringing Brent West's mobile. It was ten to four. Surprisingly, he answered on the first ring.

'How's it going, Jan?'

'We've been working hard on trying to put Finlay Roscoe at the scene, but he has rather a stubbornly effective alibi.'

'We need to nail this down, Jan, the press conference is at six, and I want a watertight case.'

'The press release now talks about you being present, not Wells. Did you want me there?'

'I don't need you to drive ninety minutes back here to Plymouth to back me up, and Wells was frankly relieved when I said I'd handle it,' West said. 'And I can, so long as the case is rock solid by then.'

'Well, sir, I've been trying to get more resources to make it solid. But you haven't replied.'

'I do apologise for that,' he said. 'I've been tied up in meetings. Tell me what you need.'

'I need more uniforms in the Camborne and Truro area, for searches.'

'Okay. I'll get a minibus load from Exeter, but it might take two hours to reach you.'

'And there is one thing you can tell me straight away,' she said, exchanging a glance with Maddy. 'Your Ford Explorer was caught on ANPR just over the speed limit south of Bodmin Moor very close to the time of the accident on Sunday morning.'

'Yes, and?'

'Can I ask what you were doing driving so fast in the small hours of Sunday morning? Just to eliminate you from enquiries.'

'You've got a bloody nerve, Jan, if you don't mind me saying. Are you insinuating that I was in some way involved in this?'

'Not at all, sir. But there's a good chance that you would have been overtaken by the Mercedes, just before it turned off north towards Bodmin Rectory on the evening in question and I wonder why you didn't mention it.'

'I was overtaken by quite a few vehicles at various stages in that journey. I can certainly let you have dashcam footage, if it's any help. But you're barking up the wrong tree here, if at this stage of the inquiry you are chasing down tiny bits of information that only confirm something that we already know: that a Mercedes packed full of young joyriders broke the speed limit on the way over from Camborne and ended up in a horrific crash on the edges of the moor.'

'As you know, the crucial phone in the whole investigation is a burner, which communicated with Jade. She stored that phone under the name Simon, which is your middle name.'

'I think you've taken leave of your senses, woman. Get me a solid suspect by half past five so that I can go on national TV without looking an idiot. God knows what the CPS would make of any of your hare-brained theories.' He hung up.

–

Talantire and Maddy were approaching Camborne when Beatrice Dodds rang her. 'Bad news, I'm afraid. We still don't have Finlay Roscoe. After the news emerged of the body being found, he left work, didn't come home, and hasn't been seen.'

'It's a shame we couldn't nab him beforehand,' Talantire said. 'It was fairly predictable that news of the discovery would startle anyone who considered themselves a suspect.' Clearly co-ordination with the media department hadn't worked perfectly.

'I wasn't expecting the news to come so soon,' Beatrice responded. 'It's quite possible his mother tipped him off. I wouldn't put it past her. Thinks the sun shines out of him.'

'All right, we are where we are. Have you searched the house?'

'Yes.'

'Girlfriend's house too?'

'Not yet. Ellie Symmonds claims he didn't stay there last night. I'm a bit short of bodies to check that.'

'Not to worry. We've got a dozen or so uniforms en route from Exeter, courtesy of West, probably arriving by six. In the meantime, Maddy and I can go to the Symmonds' house for you, just brief us on all we know about them.'

'The interview notes are on the system, with both parents and a brother who back-up Finlay's alibi. None of them have any previous, that's all I can remember.'

No sooner had she hung up, when Moira Hallett from the press office rang.

'Busy day, Moira?' Talantire asked.

'Frantic, honestly, but I thought you'd appreciate the heads-up on something which I understand is close to your heart, or used to be.'

Talantire exchanged a glance with Maddy, who was clearly appreciating being in on what promised to be another snippet of gossip. 'Go-ahead then,' she said.

'There's a press release going out this evening about the appointment of a new chief constable. And it's not Commander West.'

Knowing that Moira had been a fan of West, Talantire wanted to play her cards carefully. 'Interesting. Who is it then?'

'The deputy chief constable of Nottinghamshire, the most senior ethnic minority policeman in the East Midlands, a guy called Hamid Sharif.'

Maddy burst out laughing, clapped a hand over her mouth but continued to shake with mirth.

'Oh, have you got someone there with you?' Moira asked.

'Only Detective Sergeant Maddy Moran. Don't worry, she's on medication,' Talantire said. 'So why didn't West cut it?'

'Well, that's the thing,' Moira said conspiratorially. 'The headshrinkers have received an allegation, and I quote, of "sexual abuse of a junior colleague".'

Maddy stopped laughing, and eyed her boss apprehensively.

'Do we know who?' Talantire asked.

'Well, after a bit of research, I had assumed it was you,' Moira said. 'Was it?'

'No, it wasn't,' Talantire replied.

'Ah, apologies, maybe I've been misinformed,' Moira said.

Talantire was aware that the media relations chief had been a business reporter on a national newspaper before taking the job at Exeter, but this was the first time that her investigative nose had made itself felt. She wondered who had told Moira about her affair with Commander West. Talantire had kept quiet about it, but a few female colleagues seemed to know, so presumably West himself had boasted about it at some stage. Typical male behaviour.

'So you don't have a name?' Talantire asked, enjoying turning the tables on her inquisitive colleague.

'No. It's been kept entirely confidential, and the head headshrinker, Fiona Hendricks, is apparently the only person who knows.'

'And who suggested my name?' Talantire asked.

'I'm afraid I can't divulge my sources,' Moira said carefully. 'But if I'm wrong, I'm happy to apologise.'

Talantire waited a moment too long considering whether to deny the affair, because Moira said: 'Ah! So I'm not wrong. You *did* have an affair with him.'

'I'm neither confirming nor denying, Moira.' She sighed, then said: 'Can we leave gossip aside and go back to the jobs that we're actually paid for?'

'Absolutely,' Moira replied.

'We could have done with a better heads-up on the news release about the discovery of the body, and naming the bloody suspect. Finlay's gone to ground before we had a chance to arrest him.'

'My hand was forced, I'm afraid,' Moira said. 'I'd planned to wait until noon, but started getting calls from the tabloids, who already knew from about 9:45 a.m. So it's clear that someone down at your end has been leaking information. So not my bad, Jan, sorry.' She hung up without saying goodbye.

'That went well,' Maddy said, staring out of the window.

'But who the hell leaked Finlay Roscoe's name?' Talantire slapped the steering wheel.

'Probably some bobby mentioned it to his mates. It's a small community.' Maddy looked at her boss. 'But it's not just that, is it?'

'I don't like people speculating about my private life,' Talantire said. 'It annoys me in principle, now it particularly irritates me that my name is linked to a pretty bad judgement call that I made several years ago.'

'Ah, the Rolf Harris defence.'

Talantire rounded on her. 'It's *not* the same, Maddy!'

'People will gossip, Jan, it's just human nature,' Maddy said with a shrug. 'You know as well as I do that Devon and Cornwall Police is just one vast multi-tentacled dating swamp, which makes Tinder look like a vicarage tea party. All those male WhatsApp groups, the firearms unit, the road patrol guys, the motorcycle fellas; they trade lists of conquests like boys swap Pokémon cards.'

'I know,' Talantire said with a long sigh, then turned to the sergeant, finding room for a smile. 'But you can fill me in on why you were laughing so much when we heard the name of the new chief constable.'

'Oh come on, Jan. Our new boss is the Sharif of Nottingham. All set up to lead Jeremy Noone and his band of merry men.'

Talantire smiled, and looked at her. 'Okay, that is funny and I think it might stick. In the meantime, I have a decision to make. If someone has made a complaint about Brent bloody West, perhaps I should do so too. I don't want some other woman having to take him on all on her own.'

'It could get nasty,' Maddy said. 'A wounded lion is very dangerous.'

'I think you've got the wrong animal there. A snake, or a rat maybe.'

'Or a weasel, or a skunk. Maybe a toad.'

'A wounded toad?' Talantire began to laugh.

They had just turned into the street where both Ellie Symmonds and Finlay Roscoe lived, and seeing the two patrol cars parked there brought them back to reality. After parking, the two detectives made their way into the Roscoe home to speak to the special constable, Nuala Cary. They were surprised to hear that neither of Finlay's parents were present. Talantire looked over the messages that had come in to the two phones that Nuala was babysitting, and could see nothing out of the ordinary; just a lot of worried friends and relatives. The absolute natural reaction to the horrific events of the last few days. But something was wrong. Very wrong. Talantire could feel that she had missed something, something vital. She began to re-evaluate some of her assumptions.

–

Talantire and Maddy were invited into the Symmonds' house. Daughter Ellie, eighteen, and son Dean, fourteen, were sitting between their parents Phil and Tina on a large sofa in the comfortable lounge. Ellie looked like a frightened rabbit. She was slim, blonde and pretty, and held her mother's hand. Dean was a classic bored teenager, his eye rarely straying from his phone for long. It was clear that they had no conception that allowing the girl to have a boyfriend stay over would end up in a major police operation, with forensic tests taking place in the girl's bedroom and the family bathroom.

'Your statements are very clear and consistent,' Talantire said. 'But I would like to stress that this is a very serious investigation. If you think there is any chance that Finlay was not present between midnight and three a.m. last Sunday morning, I want to give you the opportunity to correct your version of events.' Her eyes rested on Ellie's face, but she noticed her mother's fingers gripping hard on the girl's hand. Talantire felt she might make more progress by separating the girl from her family, so asked her to come through to the dining room with her and closed the door.

For the next fifteen minutes, she went over the girl's account line by line, right up to the point when her brother banged on the wall because of the noises they were making when having sex, at about one a.m.

'Did you fall asleep afterwards?' Talantire asked.

'He did, immediately. I was awake for a while, and texted a couple of friends, like I said before.'

Talantire nodded. She had copies of those messages, keeping friends up to date with the relationship with Finlay, the so-called great catch, lying snoring in her bed.

'It's just like we said,' Ellie said, in a tearful voice. 'Why don't you believe me?'

'I do,' Talantire replied. 'But we just have to check everything. To be sure.'

Talantire left the Symmonds family to their hurt and confusion. She had a growing feeling that she knew who the killer might be, someone who they hadn't even considered but should have.

While Maddy finished up answering questions from the family, Talantire returned to the car and used her iPad to do some googling to back-up her hunch. The answers she found were inconclusive but plausible. She had an hour to firm them up and get some real evidence before the press conference. It was a tall order. Fortunately, their investigations could start very close by, at an address she had noted on the web search.

When Maddy emerged, Talantire told her what she intended to do, and they headed off on the short drive into the centre of Truro. It was five p.m. If she was lucky, she might avoid having to get a search warrant. If the duty magistrate was an awkward or pernickety one, the press conference would be long over before the search had begun.

Chapter Nineteen

Special constable Nuala Cary sat at the kitchen table in the Roscoe household feeling a rising sense of anxiety. She wasn't sure where Shona Roscoe now was. She had come home briefly after school, while Talantire was interviewing the Symmonds, and then disappeared again in the Peugeot, shouting out something about collecting groceries. David Roscoe had also left to go to his office, and said he would be back within forty minutes. Nuala was used to babysitting distraught people and acting as a go-between between them and the investigative officers. But as Finlay's parents weren't there, she was instead babysitting two mobile phones and had filled two sides of A4 with notes. She had answered a dozen calls for Shona Roscoe, and noted a couple of dozen more texts, all of which were the kind of messages she would have expected in the circumstances. The husband's phone had been quieter, two or three work calls, plus a number of others from Shona's friends wondering why she wasn't answering her own phone.

When Shona hadn't come back after thirty minutes, Nuala let Beatrice Dodds know. The Camborne community police sergeant expressed grave misgivings, and felt that one or possibly both of the parents were conspiring to hide Finlay from justice. But it would be a major step to arrest them in order to prevent that. Beatrice was firmly of the opinion that Finlay would be caught within twenty-four hours, especially once they formally released photographs and a description. Beatrice told Nuala to text messages from her police phone in answer to the messages received by the Roscoe parents, explaining that they were holding the Roscoe family mobiles. 'You should pass on messages too, when you see the parents.'

'Okay, I'll happily do that,' Nuala said, then heard the sound of an engine. 'Hold on a minute, I think Shona may be back.'

'Good.'

Nuala walked to the window and watched Shona Roscoe emerge from the Peugeot. 'She's in tears, so I think my services may be required. No sign of shopping either.'

'Is Talantire still there?'

'No. She and DS Moran headed off into Truro fifteen minutes ago.'

'Okay. Try to find out Mrs Roscoe's story and call me back when you have a moment,' Beatrice said and hung up.

Nuala had the kettle on by the time she heard Shona's key in the front door. The woman looked haggard, her face grey and streaked with tears.

'Are you okay?' Nuala asked, her professional smile in place. 'Would you like a tea or coffee?'

'Can I have my phone please? I want to send a message.'

'Let me send it for you,' Nuala said brightly, picking up the device. She guessed Shona must have gone to see her son, or know where he was. That could be the only explanation for her failure to ask immediately whether there had been a message from him.

'It's private.' Shona's eyes briefly focused on Nuala's and in them was utter doom. The woman looked destroyed. Nuala sympathised. A son accused of murder must be an impossible burden.

'Sorry,' Nuala said, with a helpless shrug. 'Just following orders.'

'Like the guards at Auschwitz,' Shona muttered, and turned away. 'I'm just going upstairs for a lie-down. I'm taking a sleeping tablet, so please don't disturb me.'

Nuala watched her wearily ascend the stairs, as if going to the scaffold. Part of her wanted to stop the woman going to sleep, to ask her questions. Perhaps the husband would do it on his return. He'd told her he had no office landline any more, so she had no way to reach him.

She rang Beatrice back and told her that Shona had retreated to her bedroom.

'It's probably just as well,' Beatrice said. 'The press conference starts in half an hour, and her son is being announced as a suspect, so I'm sure she'd like to stay out of it for now.'

'Any news on where Finlay is?'

'Yes, we've had a sighting at a park just off the A39, heading towards Falmouth. I'm on my way there now. The ANPR doesn't show anything, so it could be a false alarm. But once we ask the public to help, I'm sure we'll reel him in pretty quickly.'

After the call finished, Nuala did as she was told, and began returning the messages she had noted earlier. Both Shona's and David's mobiles were ringing incessantly now, which she presumed were press calls. She'd never keep up with them, and didn't intend trying. They'd eventually give up and call the Exeter press office. Then her own mobile rang. It was Talantire and she seemed in quite a hurry.

'No he's not,' Nuala said. 'And Mrs Roscoe is upstairs, having a lie-down. Yes, I'll let you know. Goodbye.' The call was cut before she'd got the last word out.

–

'Damn,' said Talantire, as she hung up. 'There's still no sign of him.'

'It's half five, we don't have any time left,' Maddy said. They were both standing outside a small warehouse unit on the outskirts of Truro. The trading name on the aged sign said Felmar Petfood, but Talantire had already discovered that the firm went into liquidation years ago. The roller door was firmly padlocked to the ground, and no one was there.

'No one at the office and no one here,' Talantire said. 'And not much time to get a warrant.'

'Can we try ANPR to find him?'

'Yes, but it is too slow. He could be anywhere.'

'What about the landlord? They would have a key.'

'We need a warrant first and, besides, the property firm is on voicemail, probably closed for the day, seeing as it's half five. And the press conference starts in half an hour.'

'Well, we're stuffed then, aren't we?' Maddy said.

'I'll ring the duty magistrate anyway, and pray we get a co-operative one.'

'And I'll get a locksmith,' Maddy said. 'There's a local one Beatrice uses.'

–

Talantire stood in the middle of a small industrial unit, about the size of a treble garage, lined by metal shelves on which were neatly stacked a series of cardboard boxes. The locksmith had made short work of the padlock on the roller shutter once the warrant had come through just two minutes ago.

The place was surprisingly tidy, with the floor clean enough to eat your dinner from, but Talantire was really missing the promised busload of uniforms, last reported held stuck at roadworks half an hour away. There were an awful lot of boxes to open, and just her one Swiss army knife. She could see immediately that they weren't going to get a result before the press conference.

Before she could ring West to let him know, he rang her.

'It's ten to fucking six! Do you have *nothing* for me?' he barked.

'Not yet, I'm afraid, sir. I have a promising line of enquiry, but it's nowhere near ready. Is it possible to defer the press conference for two hours?'

'Are you a complete moron? At this notice, it will make me look a total idiot. The press are already here, dozens of them.'

'Then you can just go with the Finlay Roscoe angle, can't you? Along the lines of "the police are asking for the public's help to search for a young man in connection with the abduction and murder of Jade Kernow"—'

'Don't tell me how to do my job, detective inspector! Especially when you're clearly incapable of doing your own. So what is your fresh angle? It had better be good.'

She told him, and he said: 'What solid evidence do you have?'

'Now, very little. It's mainly a hunch, but I'm working to prop it up with some evidence. Mrs Roscoe could be very useful, if we can re-interview her, once the son is found.'

He swore and slammed down the phone at his end.

'What was his reaction?' Maddy asked.

'What do you think?' she replied, slitting open the first cardboard box with a particularly emphatic slash of her knife.

–

Nuala Carey clicked on the TV at six, and lowered the volume so it wouldn't carry upstairs. She had to wait ten minutes through other news for coverage of the press conference to start. Commander West was just addressing the cameras, looking gorgeous in his full uniform. Behind her, Nuala heard a key in the front door. David Roscoe stood there, glowering, clenching and unclenching his fists.

'There's TV vans in the street. I've just been asked loads of questions by reporters, and there's not even a uniformed officer to stop them.'

Nuala got up to look out of the window. There were two satellite vans and four reporters, probably nothing compared to what there would be later in the evening. Mr Roscoe had a point. They would need a uniformed presence now that the whole world knew that his son was the main suspect.

'Have you heard from Finlay?' she asked.

'Of course not. How can I, when you have my sodding phone? Has he messaged?'

'No, not that I'm aware of,' she replied.

'Is Shona back?'

'She's upstairs. Says she doesn't want to be disturbed,' Nuala replied.

Roscoe grunted. 'Yes, we all wish we could take a sleeping pill when things get a bit too much for us.' He thundered upstairs, clearly not respecting his wife's request not to be disturbed. Nuala rolled her eyes to herself.

She tried to ring Talantire, but the line was busy. The BBC coverage of the press conference had finished and she hadn't heard a word, so she switched channels, hoping to catch it on another channel. She redialled Talantire. Still busy. She thought she should text her instead, but the volume of calls on the two mobiles was a huge distraction. She had taken to photographing the numbers as they came up, which was quicker than jotting them down. She was busy taking a couple of such photographs when her own phone rang. Talantire. She picked it up.

'Is he there now?' Talantire asked.

'Finlay? No.'

'I don't mean *Finlay*, I mean David.'

'Yes. He's just upstairs, he's been here about ten minutes.'

'Ten minutes! For God's sake, I asked you to ring me, Nuala!'

'I did, but the line was busy. I'm sorry, all the phones were going, the press is outside, it's crazy here.'

'Is there a uniform outside?'

'No.'

'Right, don't let him leave, whatever you do. I don't care how you do it. Offer to sleep with him if necessary, or pepper spray him.'

'I don't have—'

'I'll be there in ten minutes.'

'Got it,' she said. 'But why—'

'He is the murderer, Nuala! This is the man we want.'

Chapter Twenty

Nuala Cary stared at her phone after the call was cut. She had been a special constable for eight months and had never had to arrest anybody. It was ridiculous for Talantire to ask whether she had pepper spray. She thought there might be handcuffs in the car, if she could remember how to use them. But she couldn't risk going out there to fetch them. Her most frequently used police tool was a box of tissues, and the occasional friendly hand on a sobbing shoulder. The idea of her arresting a tall solidly built man like David Roscoe was horrifying. She only weighed eight stone two, little more than a hundred pounds. It would be like trying to stop a tank with a feather duster. So she would have to use her wiles. Luckily, she could still hear David moving around upstairs, and as long as he kept busy for another few minutes, she might not have to do anything. She looked at her hands. They had already begun to tremble, but she told herself that she could only do the best she could do.

She had often imagined herself doing something heroic, years ago, when she had first applied to join the Police Service of Northern Ireland. Her fantasy was of chasing an armed mugger down the street and, despite a stab wound to her arm, painful but not debilitating, bringing him down with a flying rugby tackle. However, during training, her best attempts to immobilise a fellow officer during role play had brought only howls of laughter from the rest of the team. She had managed to clamp herself around the suspect's leg, and he had simply walked her out of the room like an ill-fitting sock. The trainer, once he had recovered his poise, had suggested that a role in either data analysis or family liaison might be the best for her. And she hated computers, so here she was, a part-time volunteer constable, unpaid, with an application for a full-time family liaison job in the post.

She saw a set of car keys on the table where David had left them and had a brilliant idea. She slipped them into her jacket pocket. At least he couldn't drive away. Then she looked at her watch, ignoring the trilling of phones, it was only a few minutes since Talantire had rung. How time drags! And now David Roscoe was coming downstairs. *Oh God.*

'How is Shona?' she asked brightly.

'Dunno, didn't go in. She'll be groggy as hell, so best leave her.' He seemed to be casting about looking for something.

'I'm not sure about that, I think we are planning to interview her again,' she lied. Or maybe it wasn't a lie. She wasn't sure.

'Have you seen my car keys? I left them there.' He pointed to the exact spot.

'No, I haven't. Perhaps, you left them upstairs?'

He looked at her, as if just noticing who she was. 'Nuala, I left them exactly there.'

'Are you sure, because, after all, it's very easy to lose things. I know with my own I never know where they are. I mean, I'm such an eejit sometimes.' She realised she was babbling.

'Look. We've been enormously co-operative, right? You've got my phone and my wife's phone, you've now swiped my car keys, my son, who is wholly innocent, has been accused of murder. Does it occur to you that we might be getting a little impatient with this whole charade?'

'Shall I make you a cup of tea?' she asked, wheeling out her best smile.

'All right, go on then,' he said, responding with his own grin. He was a surprisingly handsome and charming man.

She walked into the kitchen, feeling she'd really done a good job. It was hard to believe this man was a murderer, but that was a decision for others.

'So how long have you been with the police then?' he called from the doorway, as she rinsed the cups they had used earlier.

'Well, I was born in the Republic, but my late father was from Derry, so actually I started in Northern Ireland and then transferred over here when my fiancé began his training, and I'm just filling in as a special until I can get on the family liaison course—' She turned and he wasn't there.

For feck's sake! He'd vanished, silently and completely.

She checked her own pocket. Yes, his car keys were still there. She looked on the table, wondering why it was so quiet. Both phones had been taken. She rushed over to the front window, and saw that both Shona's and David's cars, the Peugeot and the rental Audi, were still present. So where was he?

Upstairs! She could hear him.

As she listened, she heard him tap on Shona's bedroom door and softly call her name. He hadn't disappeared. Thank God!

She went to the foot of the stairs and saw him enter the room.

'Shona! Shona!' he called, from inside, then: 'Oh for Christ's sake. Help!'

'What's the matter?' Nuala said, rushing up the stairs.

'I think she's taken an overdose. She's been sick, and she's unconscious.'

Nuala looked into the room. Shona was lying fully dressed, on her side on the bed, in a pool of vomit. 'Do you have any first-aid training?' she asked him.

'Not really, do you?'

'Yes. So, you ring the emergency services and I'll put her in the recovery position and keep her airways clear,' Nuala said.

'Thank you so much,' he said, with a sob. 'Ah, poor Shona! It's all just too much.'

Nuala pressed three nines on her own phone, and handed it to him. 'There you go, it's ringing.' It was 6:30 p.m.

–

'It was so obvious, Maddy,' Talantire said as she drove at speed back towards the Roscoe family home. 'One, that of course David Roscoe had a motive to try to track down his own stolen car. He had an app on his phone that gave its location.'

'Yes, but he already told us that and was dissuaded by the duty officer when he reported it.'

'So he said. While Finlay was sleeping with his girl-friend Ellie, David took Finlay's Vauxhall Nova and went off in pursuit.'

'I know, but we discussed that before and it just didn't seem likely. Besides, Shona's own statement said they were both there all night. A head teacher's alibi, after all,' Maddy said.

'But, as Nuala mentioned, Shona takes sleeping pills. She probably wouldn't have noticed her husband slip out in the small hours. Besides, we didn't know how strong a motive David had. That's where we come to point two. David Roscoe's business is distributing Dutch health food supplements across Devon and Cornwall. I looked it up on Companies House, and although it's profitable, it just doesn't seem a big enough money-spinner to justify such an expensive car.'

'Isn't he like a lot of people who just buy a pricey car to set it off against tax?' Maddy asked.

'Maybe. But look at his CV, which I found when we searched the house. A degree in biochemistry, a summer placement at a forensic laboratory in Maiden-head, and ten years in pharmaceutical distribution for Alliance Unichem. This gave him all the tools and contacts he needed for getting supplies. I have a strong suspicion David Roscoe was making and selling ecstasy tablets using the Dutch supplement business as a cover. The Camborne area, Redruth and Truro were known to be hotspots for MDMA seizures. If we had the time to check it out, there are probably a dozen burner phones linked to him, as Simon, county-lines style, with drop-off points and schoolboy intermediaries. Beyond that, there's a huge market: Newquay is only half an hour away.'

'That's true,' Maddy said. They were both aware that the buzzing North Cornwall surf resort, a year-round party magnet for youngsters, had spawned a sizeable drug scene. Seizures seemed to rise every year.

'So David inadvertently left a package of the tablets in the glove compartment at the time the car was stolen. He *had* to get them back, because he was aware they were in a jiffy bag that had been used to supply health supplements to him.'

Maddy's face crinkled up. 'So while his wife is teaching her pupils to be upstanding members of society, the husband is hard at work corrupting them.'

'Yes, probably via intermediaries, like Jelly Skewes.'

'All right, assuming you are correct, he had to get the drugs back, but how does this involve Jade?'

'It's the third point, and I have to admit it's guesswork. When Finlay slept with Scarlett, and his relationship with Jade broke up, she may well have confided in David. Shona certainly admitted that both of them really liked the girl and were close to her, so it's not too much of a stretch to imagine that if David met up with her to console her, they might have begun an affair.'

'He's old enough to be her father!' Maddy said.

'Yes, but he's good-looking, successful and has a bit of charm about him. There's many more unlikely relationships than that,' Talantire said. 'Jade had no father figure in her own life, just a couple of dodgy uncles who she didn't trust. It's not too much of a stretch to believe that David seduced her in her weakness and vulnerability. It would certainly explain all those messages between her and Simon, and his insistence that she only message him on the burner. He asked her to get into the Merc on the night of the accident, even though Scarlett was there too, in order to retrieve the package. She failed, then bailed out, as Simon's message suggested. She was then picked up by David in the Vauxhall. I'm going to ask Primrose to correlate the locations of Jade's phone and David's Mercedes over the last six months. My guess is that we will find dozens of occasions when they were in the same place.'

'That doesn't prove an affair,' Maddy said.

'I know it doesn't. And that's my big worry. It's plausible but not anything more than circumstantial. I'm sure the CPS will throw it back at me.'

'He's had plenty of time to destroy incriminating evidence,' Maddy said.

'Too right, and having worked at a testing lab, he'll be forensically very aware.'

–

Talantire snatched up the phone the moment she saw who was calling.

'It's Nuala,' Nuala said.

'Yes I know, it comes up with your name. So what's happened?'

'Mrs Roscoe has taken an overdose. I've called an ambulance.'

'Where is Mr Roscoe?'

'He's here, looking after her.'

'Okay, make sure he stays. We'll be there in two minutes. How is she?'

'I couldn't detect a pulse.'

'Oh God. This is terrible.'

'I've freed her airways, because she'd been sick, but I can't detect any breathing.'

'Shit. Do you have an ETA for the ambulance?'

'Two minutes.'

She thanked Nuala and hung up. It was awful news for a hundred reasons, but one was that Shona would be a vital witness to her husband's movements. They needed to talk to her.

Blue-lighting it, Talantire and Maddy arrived outside the Roscoe family home to see an ambulance already there, along with a gaggle of reporters. The two detectives rushed past them and, seeing the front door was ajar, made their way inside. There was no one in the lounge, but they could hear voices. Then looked up the stairs to see Nuala and David Roscoe crowding by a bedroom doorway, with the voices of at least two male paramedics coming from inside.

'How is she?' Talantire asked, as she arrived in the bedroom.

'Not good,' said one paramedic, looking up. 'We've given her epinephrine to gee her up, but there's no pulse and the ECG just shows an organised rhythm.'

'Does anyone know what else she might have taken apart from the zolpidem?' asked the other, holding up a plastic pill bottle.

'I'll get everything from the bathroom,' David said. 'There's three or four types of medication, including Prozac.'

'I think she's gone,' said the first paramedic.

Maddy looked at Talantire, her jaw hanging open. 'She can't die!' she said.

Talantire was grim-faced. This was a total disaster.

Chapter Twenty-one

'Why couldn't I go in the ambulance with her?' David Roscoe asked, as he sat in the back seat of Talantire's Skoda, on the way to Royal Cornwall Hospital in Truro.

'Because you are under arrest. We want to question you urgently in regard to the disappearance and murder of Jade Kernow.'

DS Maddy Moran, sitting next to him, clipped a handcuff onto his wrist and then onto her own.

'What! Are you out of your mind? My wife's just taken an overdose, and might be dead, and not content with persecuting my son over this case, you now seem to be accusing me.' His eyes were full of tears. 'I just can't believe it.'

'We'll take you to the hospital first and then you will be coming with us into custody,' she said. 'You are not obliged to say anything, but it may harm your defence if you do not mention when questioned something which you later rely on in court.'

'Right now, Mr Roscoe, we have a team of officers going through your lock-up warehouse,' Maddy said.

Talantire continued: 'That is where we believe you make and store ecstasy tablets, which are then sold and distributed throughout Cornwall.'

He laughed. It was a confident and derisive reaction. 'That is ridiculous. I distribute health supplements from the Netherlands. I'm not involved in anything else.'

'We realise you probably had the opportunity to dispose of many of your supplies; forensic officers are able to test for residues and we have every confidence that we will find them,' she said.

He shook his head and looked out of the window with his arms folded. 'You know what? I'm going to sue Devon and Cornwall Police for wrongful arrest,' he said. 'I'm going to get you both fired.'

'Knock yourself out,' Maddy said, but Talantire caught her expression in the driving mirror, which was along the lines of: *I really hope we haven't screwed up here.*

So do I, Talantire thought. *So do I.*

–

Shona Roscoe was confirmed dead on arrival at the hospital. The news cast a pall of gloom over investigative team. A hastily arranged eight p.m. virtual incident-room meeting had Maddy, Dave Nuttall and Talantire at Plymouth Crownhill Police Station, where David Roscoe was now being held in a cell, awaiting a duty solicitor. On Zoom were Commander Brent West and Moira Hallett from Exeter, Primrose Chen from Barnstaple and Beatrice Dodds from her parked car by mobile phone.

'This all seems to have come from nowhere,' West said. 'I hope you've got some solid evidence now.'

'Some, and more to come,' Talantire said. 'David Roscoe's DNA is all over this case, but, of course, we ignored it because it had a legitimate reason to be there: he was the owner of the stolen vehicle. We now believe that he was a main supplier of MDMA across Cornwall, manufacturing it at his lock-up facility in Truro, and distributing it via people like Jelly Skewes. We're awaiting the results of forensic and chemical analysis at the lock-up. David was communicating with Jade, as Simon, on a burner phone, as he desperately attempted to retrieve a package of ecstasy tablets that he had left in the glove compartment by mistake. It was clear that he had a close enough connection to Jade to persuade her to join her old friends for part of the joyride, even though she had fallen out with Scarlett. So it was David that was pursuing his own Mercedes, having borrowed his son's Vauxhall Nova in the small hours of Sunday morning, while Finlay was across the road with his girlfriend.'

'But what was his motivation for killing her?' Beatrice asked.

'Something like this: they were following the Mercedes when it crashed, Jade was with him in the Vauxhall Nova. They stopped outside the rectory and Jade rushed in and was desperate to try to help her friends escape from the car. But David only needed one glance at the wreckage to know that there was no chance of getting the drugs back. She was almost certainly hysterical, and knowing that somebody was living at the rectory, he probably felt he had to shut her up. My guess is that he put his hands around her throat, initially just to keep her quiet. While Jade would have wanted to call the emergency services and wait for them, he knew they couldn't risk that. First, the drugs might be associated with him if he was seen to be there; second, he was probably even more scared that his affair with Jade would be unmasked; and third, he knew he would be blamed for chasing the car to a fatal crash. So we think he killed her, probably reluctantly, because she refused to leave the scene. The murder will have taken place very close to the rectory. He put her body in the Nova and drove back the way he had come through the village and then dumped her in the abandoned VW.'

'This is all very imaginative and plausible conjecture,' West said. 'But so far, unless I am seriously mistaken, there is zero evidence. I can just imagine what the CPS would say.'

'And what the Great British public would think,' Moira said. 'Arresting a man just a few minutes after his wife is rushed to hospital with an overdose. It doesn't look great.'

'We only need a few hours,' Talantire said, with a hint of exasperation.

'Even if you get him for the drugs, there really isn't anything to tie him to the killing of Jade, is there?' Beatrice asked.

'I hope we will get something from the post-mortem,' Talantire replied. 'Besides, I haven't done an initial formal interview yet. He may co-operate.'

'Fat chance, Jan,' West scoffed. 'He'll see that you don't have anything.'

Talantire suspected he was right. She had very little except a hunch and a determination to prove that an innocent young woman was murdered by a calculating older man.

West cut the Zoom call, but she still heard his exasperated mutter, as he stood up from the screen: 'Why am I surrounded by fucking idiots?'

Talantire cursed, and banged her fist on the desk, making her keyboard bounce, and the mouse fling itself off. She took a deep breath, turned to Nuttall and said, as calmly as she could manage: 'Okay, Dave, let's see where David Roscoe went in his Audi in the last couple of days.

We might well discover he's dumped a lot of his drug equipment. I want to let him stew for a while before we interview him.'

Nuttall sucked his teeth in sympathy before replying. 'Jan, actually there is no satnav device in the Audi, and it being a hire car, the myAudi app wasn't activated, so tracing it isn't going to be straightforward. With luck, Primrose can get something from the history file of Google Maps on his phone, otherwise it will have to be ANPR first, and possibly CCTV. If we'd known earlier, we could have put a tracker on his car.'

'Well, we are where we are,' Talantire said. 'Fortunately, the warrant gives us broad powers over all the family property. We've got the post-mortem this evening and I really hope we can find something. I'll be going along myself. David Roscoe is obviously very forensically aware, but nobody is perfect. If he's left any kind of trace, we shall catch him.'

Ten minutes later, Primrose rang to say she'd made progress on a different car. Talantire put her on speakerphone.

'I've correlated the movements of the Mercedes with Jade's phone for the last two months, and there are at least half a dozen occasions where the car and the phone are in the same place. On three separate occasions, she was in the car at coastal beauty spots Portloe and Portscatho, for extended periods.'

'So they were parked up together,' Maddy said. 'For a kiss and a cuddle.'

'Seeing as she couldn't drive, someone else was in the car. It could be Finlay, if they had a reconciliation, but it could also be David,' Talantire said. 'It's something, but it's not enough. If it was David Roscoe, he still might claim he was helping her with her emotional difficulties over Finlay or even her homework. It's hardly a smoking gun.'

'It's a tricky one,' Maddy agreed.

'Roscoe might even claim that she wasn't with him but had left her phone behind in the car,' Nuttall said.

'He won't be able to claim that,' Primrose countered. 'There are messages to and from Jade's friends during some of those journeys.'

'You know something, we may get help from an unexpected quarter,' Talantire said. 'Finlay probably has no idea what was going on behind his back. His own father having an affair with his ex-girlfriend. He might be able to tell us a lot more about the circumstances at home.'

'When we finally track him down,' Maddy added.

'It really shouldn't take long,' Talantire said. 'In the meantime, let's go and have a word with our prisoner.'

–

'Mr Roscoe, where were you at two o'clock last Sunday morning.'

'In bed with my late wife, as she had already confirmed in her statement and as I had already said in mine.'

If the prisoner was nervous, he certainly didn't look it. The arrival of a polished-looking London-based solicitor to represent him had buoyed his confidence even more.

Talantire and Nuttall were doing the interviewing, and as Commander West had predicted, Roscoe wasn't having any of it. He looked relaxed in an open-necked white shirt and well-fitting jeans. Talantire noted that his designer belt which he'd been wearing at the time of his arrest was missing, and his expensive soft leather shoes were minus their laces. The custody staff at Crownhill had done their job. After the suicide of his wife, they weren't taking any chances.

Nuttall took up the questioning. 'While you claim you were asleep in bed at home, your son's car, a Vauxhall Nova, was caught on traffic cameras heading along the A30 and A38 towards Bodmin,' Nuttall said, passing across several photographs which caught the registration number. 'Were you driving this vehicle?'

'No. As I've said several times before, I was asleep at home in bed with my wife.'

The solicitor, a man with highlights in his hair, and what looked like threaded eyebrows, leaned forward, his hands steepled in front of him. 'Detectives, please, it was less than an hour ago when my client had the death by suicide of his wife confirmed to him. He is clearly in no position to be answering your questions, especially as it seems you have no evidence. I ask you again, please, release him on police bail so that he can go home and await the return of his son.'

'We can't allow him to interfere with potential evidence,' Talantire said. 'Mr Roscoe. Were you having an affair with your son's ex-girlfriend, Jade Kernow?'

'No, of course I wasn't! That's an outrageous thing to suggest.'

'Did you not have a burner phone, which she registered in the name Simon on her calling records, on which you contacted her on at least thirty occasions in the months before her death?' Nuttall asked.

'No.'

'The location of this phone was very close to your house on a number of occasions.'

'It's not my phone.' He gave an exasperated look towards the solicitor, then turned back. 'Look, I'd really like to help you, but I can't I'm afraid.'

Nuttall continued: 'Her phone records show she was in your Mercedes for three hours on Wednesday the third of July, and for over half that time your own tracing app shows the vehicle was parked in a secluded layby near Portloe. She was there again the next Wednesday, when she should have been at school.'

'I know nothing about that,' Roscoe said. 'Finlay must have borrowed the car. I suspected he was seeing her again.'

Talantire briefly closed her eyes. As predicted, he blamed his son. That was certainly every bit as plausible as the idea he was having an affair with her. More so, probably. 'All right,' she said. 'You are going to remain in police custody overnight, while a thorough search takes place at your home, place of work and the warehouse that you rent. I will reconsider the situation first thing tomorrow morning.'

Talantire terminated the interview and exchanged a worried glance with Nuttall. They were out on a limb here, and Roscoe and his brief both knew it. They desperately needed something from the post-mortem. If they could find just a trace of David Roscoe's DNA or fingerprints on Jade's body, they would have something.

Chapter Twenty-two

Talantire arrived at the Royal Cornwall Hospital in Truro and was shown into the mortuary by a technician. Dr Piers Holcombe was already hard at work, in full scrubs, facemask and white plastic wellingtons, at a stainless-steel examination table, dictating into a suspended microphone. The detective donned her face mask, inserting into it a small pad of tissue which she had earlier soaked in perfume, but even from a distance, the stench of putrefaction was more than a match for it. Her first glimpse was a handful of greenish goop which Holcombe was extracting from Jade Kernow's body, and slid into a dish for weighing. 'The liver, of apparently normal size, shows expected signs of deterioration from almost three days in a warm and humid environment,' he intoned into the mic.

Seeing Talantire, Holcombe stopped the recording. The stench was stomach-turning, but she forced herself to approach the body, and stand under the largest of the extractor fans. The bloated corpse was slit from pubic bone to sternum, neck, thorax and thighs distended from decomposition. Poor Jade looked like an obese doll, a rotting nightmare of humanity.

'Hello, Jan,' Holcombe said, drawing her attention back to his face. He was a Home Office forensic pathologist, not yet forty and highly thought of. He'd only been based in Devon for a year, but had quickly earned the respect of all. 'I've sent off plenty of samples for testing, but my hopes for DNA aren't high. The skin was damaged by a caustic agent, probably chlorine bleach.'

'I'm not surprised, as it seemed to be splashed all over the boot of the car she was found in.'

'Likewise, on the toxicology front, internal liquefaction has begun in earnest, there were plenty of purge fluids leaking, plus cascades of chemical reactions that rather mask some of the things that we might be looking for. However, all is not lost. I think I know how she was killed.'

'Yes?' Talantire asked, struggling to control her gag reflex.

'I think she was strangled. The hyoid bone is broken,' he said, pointing to an area low on the corpse's throat. 'As you know, this is a bit of a giveaway. There are also broken blood vessels, petechiae, on her neck, and a few I can still see in what remains of the eyes after the flies and maggots have been at them. I've taken a DNA swab from the part of the exterior neck where I think the assailant's hands may have exerted pressure. There are no guarantees, of course, given the conditions in which she was found, but there is a good chance we may get lucky.'

'Anything else of interest?' Talantire said.

'Evidence of contusions and lacerations on knuckles, knees and ankles. Although these may have been caused during her struggle, they could equally have been caused immediately ante-mortem if she was still alive when squeezed into the boot of the car. Certainly, there is no evidence of significant bleeding. As mentioned earlier, we found some potential evidence of fightback under the fingernails. We should have all the results first thing tomorrow, but, obviously, I'll need much longer for my full report.'

'Right,' said Talantire. 'I presume you also have the body here of Mrs Shona Roscoe?'

'Indeed I do and I think I may have anticipated you. I'm planning to conduct her autopsy as soon as I finish this one. Would you like to see her?'

'Yes.'

'She's a bit easier to look at than poor Jade. I'll not come with you because of the dangers of cross-contamination, but Steve will show you.'

Talantire followed the technician into the far corner of the room, where a drawer was opened and a sheeted figure slid out onto a gurney. Steve lifted down the sheet, so Talantire could see the face. Shona Roscoe looked peaceful in repose, finally safe from all of life's worries; from her son's behaviour, from shame. Even from Ofsted. Oh how I'd love to be able to see inside your mind, Talantire thought. What caused you to take your own life? Was it anxiety because of the pursuit of your son? Was it horror at the discovery of something your husband had done? How convenient for David that you are no longer able to reveal what you may have seen or heard. No suicide note, either.

That got her thinking. Was this the kind of woman who would pass out of existence without leaving a note? A woman for whom her legacy, certainly as an educationalist, was important. If she had found something significant, would she not have written it down for the world to see, or perhaps a reproach for her husband?

Talantire thanked the technician and said her goodbyes to the pathologist as she exited from the mortuary. She wanted to know what the CSI team had found at Roscoe's home, and to make sense of it she needed Nuala.

Nuala had agreed to meet her at the Roscoe home. Talantire spotted her from the car as she arrived. She was beyond the blue crime tape and the remaining members of the press, talking to members of the CSI team.

Talantire parked behind a BBC van, slipped on booties and gloves, then made her way towards the house. She signed in with the uniformed PC at the tape, then ducked under and made her way up to the group.

'Hello, ma'am,' Nuala said.

'Hello, and thank you for agreeing to meet me here.' Talantire was aware that specials were unpaid and only so much could be demanded of them.

'It's no trouble at all. The crime-scene people have already been through the room where she took her own life,' Nuala said.

The CSI head, Ragavati Venkatagiri, came over to them. A former pharmacist from Southall, Venka, as she was known, was now based in Exeter, enjoying a second career in her fifties. She had a reputation for being a tough boss. 'I know you asked for a diary, Jan, but so far we haven't found one,' Venka said.

'That's a shame. Still, I want everything from that house, and the garage, particularly male clothing – overalls, shoes, gloves that kind of thing,' Talantire said.

'I'll show you what we've got.' Venka led Nuala and Talantire to the large police van, where all the evidence was being stored.

The evidence officer had done a neat job, collecting household items, cross-referencing them to photographs, then stacking them in lidded plastic crates on shelves that ran on both sides of the long-wheelbase Transit. With her help, it didn't take long to find two crucial boxes: one which had been used to parcel up books and papers from Shona's home office, and another from the master bedroom where her body was found, which included the contents of her bedside cabinet. Venka took both boxes back into the forensic tent, where Nuala, now in gloves and booties, helped her lift them onto one of the trestle tables. Talantire took off the lids.

'Nuala, when you were here at the house and David Roscoe returned at 6:10 p.m., what did he do? Did he go in and see Shona?'

'He went upstairs, and I think he went to his home office. He did tell me, about twenty minutes later, that he hadn't been in to see her. He was more concerned about the car keys which I'd taken. Then I went into the kitchen and he and I had a conversation and when I turned round, he'd gone upstairs. That's when he went into the room.'

'Did you hear her bedroom door open?'

'Yes, I think it was that door.'

'And how long after you heard that was it before he shouted out about her.'

'Oh, just a few seconds. It was very quick.'

'This is very important, Nuala. I think she would have left a suicide note, if it was a real attempt to kill herself.'

Nuala nodded.

'Obviously, if David had been in there,' Talantire said, 'there would have been an opportunity for him to hide or destroy any incriminating suicide note.'

'Yes, that makes sense.'

'Now, from the paramedic notes we have, it seems that an empty bottle of antidepressants was found by the bedside, along with a half-empty bottle of gin. We don't know exactly what type of other drugs she may have taken.'

'When she came in, she did say she was going to take a sleeping pill.'

'And according to your statement, that was 5:30 p.m., forty minutes before David arrived?'

'Yes.'

'I'm just wondering, Nuala, whether David Roscoe might have killed his wife, or at least made sure she died. If he'd seen a suicide note, and at that point she wasn't yet dead, he might well have needed her to die to cover up for whatever it was she had discovered.'

Nuala blinked and looked shocked. 'Even when I saw her, there was vomit on the bed from her mouth, how could he fake that?'

'I'm not saying that he did. She may well have been dying anyway, but I have a feeling that he wanted to make sure it happened.'

'But how did he kill her? He wouldn't have had much time.'

'I don't know. I suppose it's just another piece of conjecture for which I don't have any proof.' Talantire shrugged. 'But if I have to, I'm going to look through every single evidence bag. David Roscoe may be clever and forensically aware, but he will have made a mistake. All we've got to do is find it.'

Her phone rang. It was Nuttall.

'Hello, Dave,' she said. 'Any progress tracking down Finlay?'

'Some,' he said. 'We suspect he was at Trelissick Gardens, which is just half an hour south of Truro, because we traced a phone call made to Mrs Roscoe at school this afternoon. The school secretary tipped us off. The call was made from a public phone box there. An hour or so later, his mother's hire car tripped an ANPR camera heading in the same direction.'

'What about Finlay's car?'

'No sign. He may have ditched it because it's too obvious, maybe stolen another one. He could well have an accomplice, hiding him.'

'It's certainly not Ellie Symmonds because she's at home. I've checked,' Talantire said.

'There have been a few vague sightings, but nothing that really checks out. We've got all the patrol cars that we can muster. But if he's managed to get another vehicle, he could be anywhere.'

'Right, keep up the good work. I must crack on,' she said, finishing up the call.

No sooner had she hung up when Moira rang her.

'Hello, Moira, sorry we crossed swords earlier.' Talantire had her phone tucked under her ear and was starting to flick her way through Shona's documents.

'It's all right, just been a bit stressful recently. We've now put out the minimum press notice about the arrest of a forty-seven-year-old man in connection with the murder, but it would help if you got some more that we can give out. I'm being besieged for details. Reporters are obviously asking neighbours and will get the name very shortly, if they haven't already.'

'I hear what you're saying,' Talantire replied. 'I've got nothing yet, I'm afraid, but will let you know.' She said goodbye and hung up, then turned back to the boxes in front of her. 'Ah, maybe I have got something.' She had found a hardback office-style diary, and it was full of very neat handwriting.

Talantire sat in the office at Plymouth Crownhill going through Shona Roscoe's diaries. She had several volumes in total going back twenty years, which had been found in a box in the garage. What she didn't have was the most up-to-date one. The last six months must have been in a new diary. Perhaps it was at her school, certainly there were plenty of educational thoughts and issues covered, as well as her feelings about difficult staff, ongoing vacancies and the inevitable anxieties about Ofsted inspections. If it wasn't at school, then perhaps David Roscoe had disposed of it. That was the kind of careful planning the man seemed to be capable of. At this rate, Shona Roscoe would take her secrets to the grave.

Talantire steepled her hands over her nose and glanced at the clock. Gone ten. The light outside had faded. She needed to think. If Roscoe had disposed of his wife's latest diary, he wouldn't be so stupid as to throw it into the household waste bin. She'd seen on the evidence file that these had all been logged. The 1980s-built house had no fireplace. It could conceivably still be hidden somewhere around the home, loft or garden, but she reckoned he would have taken it away to dispose of. It couldn't have gone far because clever Nuala had his car keys. She didn't see him leave the house after he got back to discover her suicide attempt.

This all seemed a long rabbit hole to go down. What else was there? She had already looked through everything that contained her writings, and flicked through those educational books she had kept in her home office in case they contained anything useful. All she had left was blank stationery. Talantire pulled out an A4 pad that she hadn't yet looked at. It was logged as being found in a bedside drawer in the master bedroom. It was about half used, the pages having been torn out. The last two had not been torn neatly, and left fragments by the spine.

And then she had a brilliant, though hardly original, idea.

She found a blunt pencil, and quickly swept it back and forth across the page to see if the impression of writing on the ripped-out page would come through on the sheet beneath. And it did.

It was dynamite.

Chapter Twenty-three

David, how could you? I went to see Finlay, who was hiding like a fugitive near Trelissick Gardens. I took him some things, I gave him cash, and I lied to cover up for him. I confronted him about the earring. I told him I recognised it as one of Jade's. I'd always admired those tiny little butterflies made from splinters of opal. We'd told Finlay before about using our marital bed with girlfriends, and when I found it on the carpet under the bed, stupid me, I assumed that's what he was doing again, and you agreed. I had vacuumed only a week ago and would have seen the earring, had it been there before. So, naturally, I assumed that Finlay had lied and that he and Jade were back together.

How stupid I have been. How very stupid. Once I confronted Finlay, telling him what I had found, he of course denied everything. So I just assumed he was lying. It was only when driving on the way home that I realised what was really happening. The truth to which I had been so blind. That you had seduced Jade, when she was at her most vulnerable. You, a married man of nearly fifty, with a girl of seventeen, screwing her on our bed, on my bed. You have destroyed me. You have destroyed our marriage, obliterated my trust and devastated our family. My blameless son, hounded over a murder he did not commit, is at his wit's end because of you. And now the only conclusion I can come to is that it was you who ended the life of this poor girl. How you did that, I cannot even bear to think.

If this is the truth, then I cannot live with it. We must all bear our burdens, and my guilt is to have trusted a man who would kill to stop the truth coming out. There is nothing for me now. No way out, no future; no one will know me as a head teacher, the woman who worked every weekend for three decades to build a better future for the children in my care. I will merely be a hapless dupe, a footnote, a witless appendage to the much more interesting story of a killer without shame or remorse.

I cannot live through that. I just can't.

Talantire put a hand over her mouth as she finished reading. Shona's agony was plain to see, a woman stabbed in the back by the person whom she most trusted. The betrayal was staggering. She fought to control her own emotions and assess this find forensically, evidentially.

And that was when she realised.

For all its emotional power, this testament was *still* circumstantial. That she and David Roscoe's wife had come to the same conclusion didn't stop it being conjecture. There was still no proof that it was David who was having an affair with Jade, no proof it was him with her in the car in pursuit of the Mercedes, no proof above all that he had squeezed the life out of the girl's body. The problem in some ways was quite simple: David Roscoe's

DNA and fingerprints were not in short supply: in the Mercedes which was his car, in the Vauxhall Nova which was his son's car and which he sometimes used, in their home, and undoubtedly in the office and warehouse that he used for his business. What they needed was to find David's imprint in a place it should *never* be. On the VW where her body was found, and on or inside Jade's body.

If they hadn't been obliterated by bleach.

Talantire had been promised DNA results by eight a.m. tomorrow. But she couldn't afford to wait that long. She needed more. The clock was already ticking on how long she could keep Roscoe in custody. Twenty-four hours without charge. She'd need West's agreement, or that of her own boss DSI Wells, to extend that period to thirty-six hours.

Her phone rang. Primrose. Talantire picked up, full of expectation that her talented digital evidence officer had made a breakthrough.

'Hello, ma'am. I've been working with the forensic accident investigator and managed to get some manufacturer data mapping the movements of the Roscoe family's hired Audi.'

'That's brilliant, Primrose. I thought there was no app?'

'The app, called myAudi, just taps into a signal that already exists, a GPS positioning system in the car. It's like if you turn off your phone's location service, it doesn't stop it functioning entirely, it just stops other apps seeing it. Anyway, Doug Blackstone has some senior contacts at Audi headquarters at Ingolstadt in Germany. Once I'd emailed him a copy of the warrant for the Roscoe home and property, they were very quick sending out the data file on the car.'

'So where did Roscoe go?' Talantire asked.

'I've just emailed you a series of maps for each day the Audi was used since it was supplied last Friday. I think you can ignore the simple house-to-school journeys which we assume were Mrs Roscoe. I did find one occasion when Jade's phone location corresponded to the Audi on the Saturday morning.'

Talantire thought about that for a minute before replying. 'That's going to be tricky. It may have been David Roscoe with her, but of course it could also have been Mrs Roscoe giving her a lift, or any other of a number of permutations.' She was aware that even if they proved the existence of an affair between the two it was no proof David Roscoe had murdered Jade Kernow. After thanking Primrose and hanging up, she opened the series of emails that Primrose had sent and the attachments covering Saturday to Tuesday – the day immediately before Jade was killed up until the arrest of David Roscoe. One journey jumped out to her immediately. Late on Sunday evening, the Audi was driven along the A30 to the town of Bodmin, stopped at a petrol station, then travelled on back roads along the southern edge of Bodmin Moor. Talantire zoomed in on the map, which showed that the vehicle had not only passed through the village of St Neot, where the body had been found, it remained there for three and a half minutes, from 11:47 p.m. to 11:50. She zoomed in closer. It was exactly at the site of the dumped VW, and at a time when it would have been dark.

This was significant, because it couldn't be construed as an act of curiosity. It took place a day and a half *before* the discovery of Jade's body in the car. Though circumstantial, it was clearly evidence that David Roscoe knew what was in the car. Why else did he go there? Was he just checking the vehicle was intact? Was he bidding some kind of emotional farewell? Or was it just a cold-hearted killer revisiting the scene of the crime?

Bleach.

That was it. He had driven there to clean up the body. Open the boot, pour bleach all over her, and head off again. Even though the car had been dumped opposite a home, the chances of being spotted were minimal. Three and a half minutes was bags of time for that: lift the boot lid, unscrew the bottle, pour. That could be done in thirty seconds. Probably most of the time spent there was reconnaissance, looking around to check the neighbour's lights were off before starting.

Reverting to the list of journeys, Talantire opened the map for the next day, Monday. The Audi left at 9:30 a.m., was driven locally within Truro for a short while, then parked near Roscoe's Truro office and the nearby warehouse for an hour. It then headed out twenty miles east to a remote rural area, where it remained for only fifteen minutes before coming back. She had an immediate hunch about this. After cleansing the crime scene the day before, the obvious thing for Roscoe to do was to dump any contaminated clothing, plus all the incriminating drug-making kit and supplies. How was she to be sure whether that indeed was the purpose of the journey?

Simple. Roscoe couldn't risk using the legal route for disposing of refuse. Most waste transfer stations and council facilities have CCTV or ANPR cameras, or at least some form of validation to prove that waste being disposed of isn't commercial. Illegal dumping was bound to be a temptation. But where? She interrogated the local police databases in Truro to find hotspots for fly tipping, and then, using Google Maps, superimposed those locations with the car's journey. There was a perfect match.

The car had stopped for a few minutes late in the afternoon at one of the worst fly-tipping hotspots in the county. There was a logic. There would be so much rubbish, a bit more wouldn't stand out.

Talantire checked the time. It was gone eleven p.m. It would be light at five, and she could be there with a full forensic kit. It meant leaving Plymouth at three. She was dog-tired and had scouted out Crownhill Police Station for somewhere that might be quiet enough to catch some sleep. By far the most enticing location was the rape suite: designed to put victims at ease while they were gently questioned, it was all soft furnishings and pot plants, and a settee big enough to lie full length on. She had a word with the night-duty desk sergeant, a big bluff Yorkshireman called Oldroyd. He gave her a wink, and said, 'You'll be safe in there, ma'am. I'll make sure that in the unlikely event we need it, you get awoken gently.'

She lay down on the sofa, under a blanket she had found in a sliding plastic box beneath the couch. It was probably the 'operational blanket' used by the rape team to cover the modesty of women and girls who had been found semi-naked or worse after an attack. With it were two unopened plastic packets of underwear and feminine hygiene products. She sniffed the blanket, and it seemed fine. She assumed it had been washed, though there was a faint brown stain that could have been dried blood. They should have used a cold wash. Still, it would do. She slipped off her trainers, slid under the blanket, and closed her eyes.

–

In the end, Talantire didn't sleep. At two a.m., a couple of noisy drunks were arrested and kicked up a fuss in the corridor as they were being taken to the cells. Their shouts echoed in her mind, along with the crash of steel doors and the jangling of keys. But, really, it was the search for evidence that kept sleep at bay. She was confident of getting proof that David Roscoe had been manufacturing ecstasy, but that wasn't the real prize. How could she prove that this slippery, forensically aware man had killed Jade and dumped her body in the abandoned VW?

At 2:45 a.m., she gave up the search for sleep, slid off the settee, slipped on her trainers and carefully folded the blanket back into its box. Feeling decidedly woozy, she jangled her keys in her pocket as she went out, thanked the desk sergeant and departed in her car.

Traffic was light on the A38 as she left Plymouth, past Liskeard and Bodmin and joined the A39 heading down to Snozzle. St Austell was quiet as a grave as she made her way round the numerous roundabouts of Cornwall's largest town. As she left, she could make out to the north the pale peaks of the china clay spoil heaps, dubbed the Cornish Alps. The satnav was taking her to Grampound Road, an obscure hamlet twenty miles east of Truro. That was where the Audi had been on Monday, close to Dolcombe Farm, a fly-tipping blackspot.

Realising she was going to get there before it was fully light, she pulled over in the lay-by and riffled through the glove compartment for the stash of cereal bars she kept for emergencies. The first thing she found was a wrapper, which indicated that Maddy had got there before her. Fortunately, there were three others and a net of satsumas, easily enough for an alfresco breakfast.

She got out of the car and peered towards the first spreading light of a rosy summer dawn. She could hear the hiss of a car in the distance, and see the lights of another cresting a hill a mile ahead. She did a few Pilates stretches, rolling her shoulders, circling her neck, and stretching her hamstrings. Tina, her Pilates tutor, would be impressed.

The buzz of her phone made her jump.

Primrose. 'Sorry to disturb, ma'am, but I thought you'd like to know that Finlay Roscoe's phone has just been turned on, two minutes ago. It pinged a mast at Portloe—'

'Portloe?' Talantire interrupted. 'The same place that David Roscoe went with Jade in the Merc three Wednesdays ago.'

'Yes, that's right, ma'am.'

'I'm only ten miles away! With a bit of luck, I'll catch him.'

Talantire thanked her and cut the call. It was 4:10 a.m. and just getting light. She jumped back in the car and raced off. There was no traffic and there seemed no point in using the blue lights. Best to arrive with the element of surprise. She called into the control room on the hands-free and asked for backup but knew even before they'd responded that she would get there long before. She was offered a firearms unit currently at the all-night café in Falmouth, with an ETA of twenty-five minutes. She accepted. Finlay had no history of violence, and though he was a big lad, probably thirteen stone, she reckoned she could handle him. For a dare, she'd bench-pressed 180 pounds before now, surprising many of the men at the gym. That must be about his weight.

The satnav took her on a B road through Tregony, then towards a campsite at Portholland.

No, that wouldn't be it. It didn't match the triangulated location that Primrose had messaged to her, which seemed to be right down on the south-west coast path. Two more minutes and she was roaring down the narrow winding road into the village of Portloe. She could see the cliffs ahead of her, against a pinkish light spreading along the horizon. She now realised that Finlay visiting Portloe was not a coincidence at all. This must have been a favourite place for Jade, who had been there with her two lovers, father and son, on separate occasions. The fact that Finlay was there now showed that he was probably thinking about her. Given that his phone had been on, at least for a few minutes, if he'd looked at the news or listened to local radio, he might now know his mother was dead. She could guess what his mood would be. All she could hope was that his grief and shock would paralyse him. The worst version would be anger, either directed at the world or himself.

She slowed at the narrowest single-track part of the road and headed to the harbour, close to the coastal path. And right there she saw him: beardless, in a woolly hat and rainproof stuffing a tent into the back of a green Vauxhall Nova. He looked up at her and realised immediately. She slewed the car right in front of the Nova, blocking its exit. He dropped the tent and ran back towards the path which led to the cliffs. She called in her location, and her sighting of the suspect, adding for the benefit of the armed response unit that Finlay appeared to be unarmed.

'I'm going after him,' she said and hung up, not waiting for the control room's inevitable cautionary advice, to wait for backup. There was a chance that Finlay would be suicidal, and there were some high and rugged cliffs not far away. She couldn't afford to wait. Not only to save his life but also because what he knew about his father could make or break the case against him. She grabbed PAVA spray and handcuffs and stuffed them in the pocket of her fleece, exited the car and locked it.

Finlay was already out of sight.

She sprinted along the edge of a series of terraced homes to the start of the footpath. It led uphill, parallel to the rising cliffs on the right. Finlay was now visible. He had a good 150 yards on her, but she was a seasoned runner, a school athletics champion specialising in middle distance as a teenager, moving to longer-distance running once she had joined the Black Bull Harriers. More importantly, she had always kept herself in shape.

The steep uphill section was sapping, and she could already see it in the lad's slowing momentum. He tore off his woolly hat and kept it in his hand, a clear sign he was getting hot. She could feel her breath coming hard too as she pounded uphill after him, closing the distance gradually. She wondered how long it would be before the crucial confrontation, that moment when he realised he couldn't escape her.

The slope slackened off a little, and he accelerated but so did she. When she was just thirty yards away, he turned to look at her. Scribbled in a frown across his youthful face was the massive disappointment that his best exertions hadn't left her behind.

'Fuck off, and leave me alone!' he yelled, his breath coming in bursts. 'I didn't do it.'

'Finlay, I know you didn't,' she shouted against the wind. 'Just stop, let's talk.'

He swore at her again and loped off, waving a dismissive hand behind him.

She caught him easily, ten yards short of the cliff edge, and he rounded on her ready to fight, fists up.

'Finlay, only you can help us find the killer.'

'My mum's dead!' Tears were streaming down his face.

'I'm so sorry, Finlay.' She moved within two yards, but he backed away towards the cliff.

'It's your fault! You accused me and she couldn't take it,' he roared. 'You police are bastards!'

She didn't dare tell him the full truth, that his father was under arrest. That would undoubtedly emerge with the morning papers.

'Come with me, Finlay. Bring the madness to an end. Let us sort everything out. You are not under arrest.'

'So what the fuck are you doing here?' He turned away and bellowed his anguish, his arms wide, looking up into the sky and then down to the sea, the roiling surf smashing into the cliffs a hundred feet beneath. His face hardened, jaw set.

No, don't. She knew what he was going to do and she lunged for him. He dodged, but she got one arm by the wrist. He dragged her with him towards the cliff edge. He had the weight, and she instantly gave up the idea of digging in her heels. Instead, using her grip on his arm for leverage she kicked at the back of his knees, and he toppled sideways, now only three feet from the cliff edge. She kept a grip on his arm and translated it into a wrist hold, his back to her.

'Aargh!' He elbowed her with his free arm, smack on the nose, a crunch of bone and she could taste blood. Now feeling less merciful, she tightened her grip, turned it into a thumb lock which immobilised him completely, and forced him, yelling in pain, face down. Kneeling on his back, she held the thumb with one arm, grabbed her spray with the other, and reached round to give him a long blast to the face. This seemed to infuriate him even more, and he attempted to crawl and wriggle his way to the cliff edge, so that now his chin was resting right on the edge, with a view down to the rocks. She had handcuffs, but was damned if she was going to cuff him to her and end up being pulled off the cliff.

'Just calm down, Finlay,' she said.

In response, he called her every name under the sun and then added: 'My eyes are burning! And let go of my bloody thumb.'

'I'm trying to save your life, and I won't let go until I get you somewhere safer.'

The sound of sirens cut into their conversation.

'That's the firearms unit,' Talantire said. 'Don't mess with those guys. Unless I stop them, they'll leave your body looking like a second-hand colander. Come with me now.'

All fight seemed to go out of him and he began to shudder, breathless tears and copious snot running down his face. She coaxed him gradually away from the edge, his wormlike progress retarded by the grip she still kept on his thumb and wrist. Only when she was a good twenty yards from the edge did she dare cuff him, and then gradually walk him down.

The firearms unit rounded the corner as she descended: four armoured hulks, sweating testosterone and bad temper, stared up at her, and the cuffs which connected her to Finlay. Automatic rifles were cradled across their chests, mothers holding their firstborns. They looked distinctly disappointed that they might not have a chance to use them.

She made sure she had her warrant card to hand. 'DI Talantire,' she shouted, holding it up. 'Everything is under control.'

'Don't shoot,' Finlay said, lifting his arms, and dragging Talantire's up too.

'You didn't need us then,' said the lead officer, dark beady eyes raking Talantire up and down.

'No, but thank you for coming.'

'So has he been a naughty boy then?' said a younger officer, who seemed about the same age as Finlay.

'He's a witness,' Talantire said.

'So why is he under arrest?' the sergeant asked.

'Technically, he's not. But he was about to bung himself over a cliff, which would have made cracking the case I'm working on a little bit more tricky.'

Two of the officers laughed at that, and they all walked back together. Once they were at the patrol car, and the weapons had been securely stowed, Talantire requested use of their first-aid kit, for her nose, which was dripping blood, and to deal with Finlay's eyes, which he said were agonising.

While most of the guys looked at her with considerable respect for the size of the bloke she had brought down, the beady-eyed sergeant, older than the rest, continued to stare at her. She released Finlay from his handcuffs and put him in the back of her car. As she was bending over tending to his eyes, she felt their eyes on her rear and heard the kind of male chuckle that only means one thing. In the wing mirror, she caught a glimpse of one of them pulling his arms back and forth at waist height, hips thrusting, face scrunched up in lust.

She whirled around and said. 'Sergeant, you must have seen that?'

'Seen what?'

'Seen what, *ma'am*,' she corrected him.

'Did any of you see anything?' the sergeant asked them.

'No, sir,' they chorused, grinning like loons.

'I saw it,' said Finlay from the car.

'Ah, we do have a witness,' Talantire said triumphantly. 'And you, I'll have your name,' she said, pointing at the offender, who no longer believed he was in the middle of a comedy. He turned to the sergeant for support, but he simply glared at Talantire.

Nice, a new enemy.

'Your *name*,' she said pointedly to the officer. 'And yours, sergeant.' She took a snap of the group with her phone. After she had got both their names, she got back in the car and dabbed her nose, which was still bleeding. They were all watching her.

She buzzed down the window just in time to overhear the sergeant announce to the group. 'She used to be one of Commander West's bitches. Gives good head, apparently.'

She drove off, furious. Right, the gloves were off, she was going to file a complaint about this as well as Brent bloody West.

Chapter Twenty-four

Talantire was still fuming by the time she arrived at Dolcombe Farm, the sun now breaking the horizon. The ten-minute drive with a monosyllabic Finlay hadn't produced any answers to the question that she most wanted to know: had he had a reconciliation with Jade? Had he brought her home? Her butterfly earring, according to Shona's suicide note, was found on the floor of the Roscoe marital bedroom. Talantire didn't want to refer to the note, but told Finlay his mother had mentioned the find. Although his eyes were much better, he was nursing his twisted thumb, and was in no mood to answer.

It could wait.

The dumped rubbish was easy to find, spread along fifty yards at the far end of a lane, where a public footpath diverged from the track leading to the farm. She parked ten yards away from a fridge freezer, on its side. There was at least a skip's worth of builders' rubble, hundreds of paint tins, some broken windows still in their wooden frames.

'Why are we here?' Finlay asked.

'Can't tell you right at the moment,' Talantire said. 'Stay in the car, and don't touch anything. I'll only be a few minutes.' She wasn't quite sure she trusted him not to start rooting about in the car, but at least he would be within sight.

She went to the boot and slipped on overshoes and a pair of blue nitrile gloves. She then made her way along the path, surveying the extent of the rubbish. Most of it had been here a while. There were dead leaves, bird poo and other evidence of the passage of time. Gingerly, she stepped amongst the garbage, looking for fresh footprints, or anything that might be relevant to the manufacture of MDMA tablets. She had made a list from Google. And there, among the paint tins, she found something. A can, very like the others, five pints capacity, but dark with soot. It had been used as a brazier. Dark gobs of melted plastic or rubber had been burned there, but some shapes survived in the burn mark on the inside of the tin: gloves.

She lifted the tin and tried to read the label. Safrole: concentrated sassafras oil.

A vital ingredient for making MDMA.

The other ingredients required included ephedrine, caffeine and amphetamines.

She went back to the car and picked up a collection of large plastic evidence bags from the boot and returned. Near the tin, she found an eyedropper, an empty five-litre container of bleach and a burned plastic bag which had contained shredded paper, the remnants now soggy.

Roscoe had been bloody thorough. Damn him.

She bagged up everything she could find. She then took a final scout around using a powerful LED torch. She was hoping to spot any metallic or reflective items in the undergrowth. There was nothing that seemed relevant.

She got back to the car and found Finlay curled up, fast asleep, his sore thumb in his mouth like a child. She felt an uncharacteristic maternal sense of caring for this poor young man. He already knew his mother had taken her own life and was about to discover that his father, or more precisely his stepfather, had killed his former girlfriend Jade. No one could ever get past all that. But there was always hope for a new life, a new beginning. And in this new dawn, with the light playing on his pale face, he looked shorn of all those worries. Not a man, but a boy still full of possibilities and potential.

She opened the boot, dumped in the evidence bags, then opened the rear door. He was awake.

'When did you last eat?' she asked.

'Last night. Prawn and pineapple crisps,' he said, yawning.

'Prawn and *pineapple*,' she repeated, incredulously.

'Yeah, disgusting. They were on special offer, by the till, end of line.'

'Not surprising,' she said. 'So are Wetherspoon's going to sack you?'

'Dunno, probably,' he said, shrugging.

She went to the glove compartment, retrieved a cereal bar and offered it to him. He opened it and ate it in two bites.

'I know a greasy spoon somewhere near Truro that does a better breakfast,' she said. 'Fancy bacon, sausage and egg?'

'Yeah,' he said, his face lighting up.

'It doesn't open until six, it'll be packed out with lorry drivers, but the portions are huge. I'll pay. But I've got some news I need to give you.'

'What's that?' he asked.

–

Molly's American Diner wasn't American in any obvious way, apart from the red-checked decor and Betty Boop paraphernalia. It was a former motorcycle showroom, just off a roundabout on Truro's ring road, with plenty of parking for even the largest trucks. Food was standard British fare, involving mugs of strong tea and plenty of grease. They sat in a secluded area. The food came quickly, but Talantire had to cut up Finlay's breakfast for him because his right thumb was now so painful and swollen that he couldn't grip a knife. She really hoped she hadn't dislocated it, but it was already the size of the bangers on his plate, and an interesting shade of purple.

She watched him then eat left-handed with a fork, perhaps the only American-style trait in the place, but it didn't inhibit the consumption of three sausages, two rashers of bacon, hash browns, baked beans, grilled mushrooms, two fried eggs and two slices of toast. She had the small version – still enough calories for a whole day.

He had taken the news of his father's arrest better than she expected. 'It had crossed my mind that he fancied her,' he said. 'He made a couple of comments when I first started seeing Jade. But murder, I just can't...' Tears ran unbidden, freely down his face, and a wordless sob escaped him. She offered him her paper napkin. His biggest concern was that any of the lorry drivers might see him, a full-grown man blubbering.

In some way, she was killing time until seven a.m. That was the first possible moment for any of the lab tests to be notified. These would include those from Jade's post-mortem, as well as some fingerprints. She had to hope against hope that David Roscoe's DNA defied bleach and turned up on Jade's throat. If it didn't, there would simply be nothing other than circumstantial evidence, and little hope of persuading the CPS to charge him.

She walked Finlay back to the car, and used the time to take a series of voice statements on her phone. She began with his movements on the night of Jade's death, with more questions asked about his interactions at home. There was nothing new that he hadn't already said, and no real insight into his father's movements.

It was 7:15 a.m. when her phone rang. Dave Nuttall.

'Morning, Jan. I am just opening the emails from the lab. There's also some notes from Dr Holcombe. Let's have a look.'

'Okay.' She stepped out of the car and closed the door behind her so that Finlay wouldn't hear the details.

'Shit,' Nuttall said. 'It says there was "little retrievable DNA from Jade's body".'

'He predicted that, because of the bleach. Were there any fingerprints on the throat?' she asked. 'Holcombe had already shown me the petechiae, you know, broken blood vessels from thumb pressure.'

'Nope. Body decomposition prevented it, it says here.'

'Anything else?' she asked, almost desperate.

'Cause of death was probably strangulation; it mentions the broken hyoid bone—'

'I knew about that.'

'You seem to have heard it all already,' Nuttall muttered. 'Are you interested in the post-mortem report on Mrs Roscoe?'

'I suppose so,' she said, cagily.

'Right, here we go. Cause of death is uncertain at this point. Toxicology indicates an insufficient quantity of prescription drugs to cause death in the average person of her weight. Examination of the heart indicates the presence of usual quantities of gases. An aspirometer was

301

used to extract them, and a gas chromatograph test is being undertaken.'

'That's all a bit mysterious,' Talantire said.

'It says all this is just the early results.'

'I'll ring Holcombe,' she said. 'He might tell me more. Though I know from experience he won't answer before eight. Oh, and Dave, I'm by a fly-tipping site near Truro, which Roscoe visited on Sunday. I think we have enough to support a prosecution for drug manufacture.'

'That's something, I suppose.'

'But not enough.' She hung up, bitterly disappointed. She desperately needed some strong physical evidence of David Roscoe on Jade's body or in the car where she was found. Otherwise, the CPS would not take a murder prosecution forward. But he had been so clever and so careful, coming back to soak the corpse in bleach. He couldn't have done that so easily if he'd buried her. Dumping her in an abandoned car that the police already knew about was an act of forensic genius.

She got back in the car, and saw that Finlay was messaging away on his phone, one-handed.

'I want to go home now,' he said simply.

'I'll check to see whether the crime-scene people have finished. You'll get a family liaison officer, and you might need to stay with a neighbour.'

'Can I stay with Ellie?' he said.

'If she and her parents approve,' Talantire said, putting the car into gear and driving away. He smiled.

–

Talantire was back at CID in Plymouth when the forensic pathologist returned her call, just after nine.

'I'm very disappointed that nothing turned up on the post-mortem to link David Roscoe to the murder,' she said.

'I wasn't entirely surprised considering the conditions in which the body was kept,' Holcombe replied. 'You wouldn't normally see this much putrefaction in two and a half days; the combination of the moisture level in the boot, and the unusually warm weather would have accelerated the breakdown of her internal organs, and the bloating. The flies and maggots massively accelerate the process too. Then there's the bleach. So I think we can conclude that the killer was very forensically aware, which ties in with the suspect's background, from what I've read.'

'Yes. I already have a bleach container which he might have used, and we might be able to find abandoned clothing which might have splashes,' Talantire said. 'Would you know if these products have a distinctive brand by brand signature?'

'I don't, but I can look it up,' Holcombe assured her. 'However, I do want to draw your attention to my findings on the other body, that of Mrs Shona Roscoe.'

'You don't think she took enough tablets to kill her?'

'That's right. Toxicology tests show an insufficient quantity of antidepressants to cause death to an average person of her weight. Now, there may have been some other drugs that she took which metabolise very rapidly and did not show. I have to say I cannot immediately imagine what those substances might be, and I don't as yet have the list of what was found in the Roscoe family drug cupboard.'

'I'm sure that's in the evidence file, I can forward it to you.'

'Good. I made a very interesting discovery,' Holcombe continued. 'Mrs Roscoe had an intravenous injection, not long before her death. One of the paramedics noticed it, when he was trying to find a vein for epinephrine to revive her and sent me a note. Medical records show no signs of diabetes or any other ailment which would require such a jab, and I have to say it didn't look particularly practised or neat.'

'Maybe that was the drug that you didn't detect?' Talantire suggested.

'Possibly, but that's not actually what I'm suggesting here. I'll expand upon this in the full report, but I don't think she gave this injection to herself. It was so soon before her death that neither contusions nor scabbing were in evidence. Jan, you might recall the trial of the nurse Lucy Letby who was convicted of killing the babies in her care.'

'She injected them with air, didn't she?'

'Yes, it was very controversial during the trial as it's so hard to prove. Veinous embolism is a very subtle killing technique, and not always reliable, as the survival of so many of the afflicted babies in Nurse Letby's care testifies. However, if combined with an overdose of medication that Mrs Roscoe had already taken, it could well be fatal. It's very hard to prove, but my suspicion is that this woman was murdered.'

'There was no needle recovered from the scene, nor drug containers, cotton wool or anything like that,' Talantire said, looking at the evidence list on her screen. 'Which reinforces the suspicion that Roscoe disposed of it. We know he arrived forty minutes after his wife had announced she was going to lie down. The special constable who was there said he claimed not to have gone into the room until the moment he discovered the overdose, at about 6:30 – an hour after she went upstairs. But, of course, he could have been lying. And probably was.'

–

Two floors below CID, in a large and rarely used meeting room, DS Maddy Moran and two CSI technicians were rapidly working away through bags of evidence that had been seized from the Roscoe household. They were wearing Tyvek suits to avoid contaminating what they had found. Maddy was slightly bemused to be spending a Wednesday morning going through a huge plastic bag labelled as the contents of a laundry basket. It was one of those occasions when her paid employment exactly mirrored her unpaid household chores.

She muttered to herself as she separated out the female and male clothing, and concentrated on examining the latter. Talantire had asked her to look for bleach stains, particularly on shirt and trouser cuffs. She found other stains, but nothing that had the characteristic white blemish she was looking for.

'Have you found anything, Sue?' she called across to a colleague.

'No. We've been through everything in the wardrobe,' she said. 'Mike's been through the overalls from the garage and the cloakroom. There's nothing.'

'Absolutely bugger all here, either,' Maddy said, checking the clock. Half an hour left. They had to find something by ten a.m. when the incident-room meeting was to take place upstairs, led by Brent West. An hour after that they had a Zoom meeting with the Crown

Prosecution Service and nobody was looking forward to that.

Brent West. Maddy felt for Jan on her dealings with this awful man, a sympathy intensified by what her boss had messaged her about the confrontation with the firearms unit. Poor Jan. Sexual gossip about her was clearly being passed around widely. And once it was out there, it could never be eradicated. Not even with bleach.

Maddy shrugged and looked across at the table where they had taken dozens of DNA samples from many of the male clothes. She was aware that finding Jade's DNA on any of them wouldn't be conclusive, but it looked like it might be the best they could get. She moved onto the shoes, and at least here it was easier to discern which were David's: Finlay was a size ten – two sizes bigger than his father. Maddy didn't see any sign of bleach stains, but took DNA swabs anyway. She couldn't imagine that these would prove anything, and she gradually got more dejected as she reached the end of the fifteen pairs. By a quarter to ten, she decided she had to ring Jan.

–

While Maddy was working through socks and under-wear, Talantire was making a last-ditch attempt to find something – *anything* – to connect David Roscoe to the location where the body was found. She had gone to the locker where Desk Sergeant Oldroyd stowed the property taken from prisoners upon arrest. There were half a dozen clear polythene bags there, each with a receipt itemising the contents. She picked out David Roscoe's bag and undid the staples. Inside it were his wallet containing £65, some coins, a kidskin belt, shoelaces and a Tissot wristwatch.

She reached in with a gloved hand and brought out the watch. It had a leather strap and a brass buckle. And then she saw it, and gave a whoop.

The duty sergeant peered over his spectacles at her, as she gave a little dance of delight. 'Won the lottery, have we, ma'am?' he asked.

'Yes, I bloody have. I'm signing this out,' she said, lifting up the bag.

Chapter Twenty-five

It was five past ten and the incident-room meeting hadn't started. There were plenty of cops in attendance: Talantire's team of Maddy Moran, Dave Nuttall and Primrose Chen, Sergeant Beatrice Dodds and two of her uniformed officers from Camborne Community Policing; and on Zoom, forensic accident investigator Doug Blackstone, media chief Moira Hallett, senior CPS lawyer Edward Weatherall and, last but not least, Police and Crime Commissioner Lionel Hall-Hartington. But there was no sign of Commander Brent West. He hadn't returned messages, and his phone seemed to be turned off.

'Does anyone know where he might be?' Talantire asked as she walked up to the whiteboards that were arrayed across the room, crammed with photos and writing.

'I've not seen him at Exeter this morning,' Moira said.

Just then, the door opened and a dapper Asian officer in full dress uniform walked in. 'I'm sorry, you are probably expecting somebody else,' he said. 'But let me introduce myself. I'm Hamid Sharif, as of today the new chief constable. And as this is the biggest case we have in the region, I'd like to see Devon and Cornwall policing at its best, first-hand.' Sharif was disfigured by what looked like a horrific burn on the left-hand side of his face, and despite obvious signs of surgery, his skin was mottled white, his ear just a stump.

'Welcome, sir,' said Talantire suppressing her surprise. 'Is Commander West on his way?'

'No. Commander West has been suspended on full pay while an investigation takes place. I'm appointing you SIO with immediate effect.'

'Thank you, sir.' She let go a slow exhalation of relief.

'And I think, seeing as you're all staring at my face, I should explain that I was disfigured with acid in an attack in Pakistan when I was fifteen, because of my sexuality.' His gaze moved across the room from one side to the other as he let this revelation sink in. 'Some say that I have made progress in the British police force because I tick three minority boxes: my ethnicity, my disability and my homosexuality. However, I will stand on my record, and the effectiveness of my action going forward. This case has been mired for far too long, and I want to see it resolved with charges and then a conviction.'

There was a muted murmur of agreement around the room. It wasn't just Talantire who felt Sharif's arrival was like manna from heaven.

'DI Talantire, the floor is yours.' He found a chair and sat down at the back of the room.

–

Feeling distinctly nervous, Talantire stood in front of the whiteboards, and summarised the original road accident, and the electronic and forensic evidence which indicated the locations of Jade from the Saturday evening. 'This case relies heavily on electronic and forensic evidence,' she said. 'The forensic evidence provides us with a list of *who* was in or near the car at the time of the accident, the electronic data is a vital cross-reference to allow us to establish exactly *when* certain individuals were present.'

She then listed all of the occupants of the crashed car, their current health status, and pointed out how limited the role of witness statements had been because of their injuries.

'Through mobile location, we can place Jade Kernow in a second vehicle in the minutes leading up to the accident, which corresponds to a witness sighting from the resident at the rectory, and is confirmed by handprints and fingerprints on the crashed vehicle.' She then described how the inverted prints proved that she had touched the car only after it was upside down. 'Forensically connecting the suspect to the victim has been much more troublesome.' Talantire caught Maddy's gaze as she said this. The sergeant was nodding gravely.

'We have a huge volume of forensic evidence connecting to David Roscoe: he was all over the crashed Mercedes, but then it was his car; his DNA was in his son's Vauxhall Nova, which we believe to be the pursuing car, but then, again, we know that he had driven it on other occasions and had worked on it with his son. His DNA has been found on an envelope bearing a Dutch postmark, found within the glovebox of the Mercedes, but again this envelope was concerned with his legitimate business. I will email you a chart of all this evidence, which points to the deficiencies of most DNA forensics: they tell us *who* but don't tell us *when*.'

She clicked a pointer and a slide appeared on a screen, showing the abandoned VW Polo.

'This is where we come to the vehicle in which the body was found. Now here, almost all of the

DNA evidence points to Tyler Darracombe, who has admitted to being the original thief of this vehicle. The victim's mobile phone was found in Darracombe's garage, although we believe that was planted by David Roscoe.' She pointed to the VW on the slide. 'There is absolutely nothing forensically to link David Roscoe to it. The fact that bleach was poured all over the murder victim has destroyed any evidence that we might hope to have had of his contact with her body.'

The chief constable shifted uncomfortably in his seat, perhaps wondering when some conclusive evidence was going to be shown. The CPS lawyer, likewise, was resting his head in his hand and visibly drumming his fingers.

Talantire let the moment draw out. 'However, thanks to tremendous work by our digital evidence officer Primrose Chen and Doug Blackstone, forensic accident investigator, we have managed to reconstruct a series of journeys by an Audi hire car, which was a replacement vehicle for the stolen Mercedes. Though not available to the hirer, the car's location was tracked, as are most high-end vehicles, by the manufacturers' servers. The next slide shows part of a near two-hour journey, taken on Sunday night, by this car, from Truro to the village of St Neot, and the site of the abandoned vehicle. We believe the sole purpose of this journey was a belated attempt by the suspect to remove his DNA from the body of the victim by dousing the corpse with chlorine bleach.'

'Yes, but can you prove it,' lawyer Weatherall muttered.

'I believe we can.' Talantire showed another slide. On it was the burnt can, and a number of the other items which she had found at the fly-tipping site. She described how she had discovered them by following the car location. 'Given the forensic sophistication of our suspect, I'm not expecting to find his fingerprints or DNA on these items, but they are evidence of a cover-up of an MDMA manufacturing operation. The details of how ecstasy tablets are manufactured is in the appendix that I will email to you after this meeting. However, it is the bleach that I think will give us the conviction we are seeking. We have worked very hard to find traces of bleach on any of his clothing, his footwear, and so on. He is, as I keep saying, a very careful and meticulous man.'

She clicked another slide which showed a wristwatch.

'This is David Roscoe's Tissot, which was taken from him upon arrest and examined by me this morning.' The next slide was a close-up of the strap. 'I spotted a tiny dot of bleaching, which you can just about see here.' The next slide was an even closer view. 'Using this specialist CSI camera close-up, I think you can see that the stitching on the strap, originally black, is now white, and there is an area of fade around it. A CSI specialist is going to extract a sample to see if we can match it to the splashes of bleach found on the inside of the VW boot, and those on Jade's clothing. Not all brands of bleach are identical, and if we can match the precise chemical composition between the abandoned bottle, the inside of the car and the wristwatch, we will secure a conviction.' She turned off the projector. 'So, in summary, this is what we have: a detailed set of journeys undertaken by the suspect's replacement car linking him to evidence of a cover-up for the murder and of the drug manufacturing facility. What this tiny dot of bleach does is prove that it was him.'

'What on earth was his motivation to kill this young woman?' the crime commissioner asked.

Talantire explained the theory about the affair, of Roscoe's determination not to let the girl remain at the scene of the accident even though her friends were inside the car.

He harrumphed, clearly not entirely convinced. He looked more like Bagpuss than ever.

Sharif spoke up from the back. 'DI Talantire, you are to be congratulated on the enormous amount of evidence that you have assembled in an incredibly short time, and despite the distractions over the organisation and leadership of the operation. We clearly have a very wily and devious murderer, and I can certainly see there is more work to be done. I'm happy to sanction a further day's detention of the suspect, and I will do my damnedest to make sure that you have the budget and resources you need to bring this to a successful conclusion. I've emailed you my direct line and please feel free to use it.'

At that, he got up and left.

Most of the other officers left at this point, while the meeting with the CPS began.

Talantire was aware that one of the Camborne officers, PC Nadine Lister, was waiting to speak to her as she began the Zoom with the CPS. In the end, Nadine left her Camborne business card, with a note on it saying 'please ring me.'

The meeting with the CPS went pretty well and a plan was laid out to interview the suspect again, present him with the evidence and try to elicit a confession. Talantire noted that there was still a chance of finding more traces of bleach, in the boot or interior of the Audi, which would further corroborate what they already had.

After they had wrapped up the proceedings, she rang PC Lister, who answered and said she was going somewhere where she could talk freely. Sensing what this was about, Talantire herself left Crownhill CID office and went into the fire escape, a blank concrete stairwell whose beige emulsion was dotted with decades of fag burns.

'What's this about, Nadine?'

'Brent West.'

'Ah, I see. Are you the officer who made the complaint?'

'No, I'm not. So it's not you?'

'No, though I have been considering it,' Talantire said.

'Brent came to see me, last Saturday night. He threatened me, if I made a complaint against him.'

'That's terrible,' Talantire said.

'He said he'd kill me.'

'Did you get a recording of it?'

'No. We'd been to a pub and it was in his car in the car park outside.'

'I've got a recording,' Talantire said. 'Not a very good one, but I have someone who can enhance it for me.'

'You should put that forward,' Nadine said. 'We've got to stop him. We should work together.'

'I'm not sure I should—'

'So what did he do to you, in your relationship?'

'Nadine, please. I don't think—'

'He raped me, Jan. Several times.' She sobbed, no longer able to control her emotion.

'Nadine,' Talantire said gently. 'I feel for you, but it's really important that we don't compare stories. We could be accused of collusion. When this becomes a disciplinary or even a legal case, it's largely going to be his word against ours. We've got to stay apart.'

'But I've got nobody to tell,' Nadine sobbed. 'I've not told Beatrice. I don't think I can go it alone. I've been off sick for three months and only been back a week. In fact, it's only having heard the complaint has been made that has given me the courage to stay with the force.'

Talantire realised that she couldn't just let this woman suffer alone. 'Don't you have family or friends who can support you through this?'

'My husband is in the force, and we live in a police-owned house. He doesn't even know I had a relationship with Brent, and I daren't tell him. Our marriage is falling apart anyway, because of my mental state, and I don't know what to do.'

'Nadine, I hear what you're saying, but we have to be really careful. Look, I have to go now, but I will ring later.'

Talantire hung up, feeling angry and helpless. It wasn't the greatest mood to be in when going to interview a murder suspect.

–

Talantire and Nuttall had Roscoe brought up from the cells. Apart from a day's growth of stubble, he looked tidy and relaxed. He was clearly convinced they had nothing on him. Once the brief arrived, Talantire prepped the tape and then began by repeating many of the questions she had asked previously. His replies were almost identical. She then told him about the bleach stains they had discovered, showing him a close-up photograph of the stain on his watch and pictures taken at the dump site of the empty bottle and the inside of the car.

'Did you pour bleach over Jade's dead body?' she asked him.

'No,' he said calmly.

'We have evidence that the Audi hire car you had as a replacement for your stolen Mercedes was driven to the site of the abandoned Volkswagen on Sunday night, the day after the killing, and then the following day was driven to a well-known fly-tipping spot, where we found additional evidence of your cover-up.'

'I know nothing about that. Those journeys were not undertaken by me. Perhaps my late wife would have been able to tell you something? Had she not been driven by police persecution of our son into taking her own life.'

'DI Talantire,' the solicitor interrupted. 'Can I please urge you, yet again, to release Mr Roscoe on police bail? He needs to see his son, and he has many arrangements to make following the tragic and untimely death of his wife.'

Roscoe nodded emphatically at this.

Nuttall intervened. 'Speaking of that, Mr Roscoe. We have evidence that you killed your wife.'

Roscoe looked shocked and turned to the lawyer.

'Kindly present it,' the solicitor said.

'We are still awaiting final pathology results,' Talantire said. 'We believe you gave your wife a fatal injection, while she was unconscious with the overdose.'

'This really is preposterous,' Roscoe said with all the wounded pride he could muster.

The two detectives took a five-minute break. Nuttall had seen a message on his phone which might be significant. They went to the oversight room which had a view of the prisoner through one-way glass. Nuttall was working his phone, and said: 'On Sunday evening when the Audi headed out to St Neot, it stopped at the Q8 petrol station on the A30. I had noted this before but could find no transaction on the financial order.'

'So if he stopped there he didn't pay by card,' Talantire said.

'Exactly. So I asked for all the CCTV they had from five minutes before to five minutes after the Audi was there. And guess what?'

He showed Talantire the screen. The footage was from an exterior CCTV camera underneath the canopy, with views over two vehicles and four pumps. It showed a man in a baseball cap and hoodie walking out of the kiosk. Given the overhead angle, it was hard to see who he was, but he had in his hand a five-litre plastic container. He pressed a key fob to open his vehicle and stowed his purchase in the boot. The car was a silver Audi and there was just enough of a glimpse of the registration number as it drove away to prove it was Roscoe's vehicle.

'That's fantastic work, Dave,' Talantire said. 'Even if we can't identify the bottle, we can get the merchant receipt from the till roll and see if it turns out to be bleach.'

Nuttall transferred the video to their iPads, then followed Talantire back into the interview room. After seeing the footage, David Roscoe slumped in his chair. From then on, he answered every question with a 'no comment'.

It was the breakthrough they had been waiting for.

–

In the weeks leading up to trial, as Talantire was preparing the Roscoe case with the CPS lawyers, she found time late in the evenings to prepare her complaints, both against Commander West and Sergeant Colin Donnelly of the firearms unit. She sent them off to the headshrinkers at Middlemoor, together with a sound file of the recording of the threats made to her by West. Primrose had done a terrific job of enhancing the first part of the recording, including West's offer to buy her off, which was now discernible.

Within a few days, she was asked to attend a meeting with Fiona Hendricks, Devon and Cornwall Police head of human resources. The woman was a very intimidating individual, with sharp eyes concealed behind her steel-framed glasses, and Talantire did indeed feel her head shrinking under that gaze. Mrs Hendricks assured her that her allegations and evidence would be assessed, not only for disciplinary action but against the higher evidential bar for a criminal offence.

'I assure you that we will do all we can to protect you,' she said, adding that the complaint against firearms officer Donnelly would be referred back to the head of Tactical Support. Hendricks told her the fact she had secured a witness statement from a member of the public, in this case Finlay Roscoe, would help hugely. When Talantire asked about whether West's suspension was on full pay, Hendricks was noncommittal. 'I can't share any information, for obvious reasons.'

'How many other complaints have you had?' Talantire asked.

'Yours isn't the only one, that's all I can say.'

West himself seemed to have disappeared, and even Talantire's friends at Middlemoor weren't able to shed any light on where he was. Hendricks certainly was playing her cards very close to her chest.

It was a week later when Talantire heard on the grapevine that West had indeed been suspended pending an investigation on the personal order of Hamid Sharif, and that Sergeant Colin Donnelly had left the police force. Whether he was dismissed or simply resigned wasn't clear. She also received a personal email from Sharif thanking her for having the courage to come forward. 'You are not alone,' he added.

She took that as a positive step.

There was one more thing to do.

She texted PC Nadine Lister. The text was two emoticons: one a thumbs up and the other a wink – a code they had agreed in advance. Nadine had yet to submit her complaint and said she probably wouldn't have the courage to do so until she knew Talantire had made her own. However, Nadine's reply lacked all subtlety. 'I'm so relieved, Jan. Hopefully now we can nail him.'

Talantire wholeheartedly agreed with the sentiment, but wished Nadine hadn't expressed it. The discovery of collusion was the one thing that could save Brent West, and Nadine's words were damning. She prayed that nobody would find out.

Epilogue

David Roscoe pleaded not guilty to both the murder of his wife Shona and of Jade Kernow. Halfway through the trial, he refused to come out of his cell but was found guilty on both counts and was sentenced to thirty years. Meghan Kernow, along with Gary Heaton, with whom she now seemed reconciled, watched from the public gallery, and they both shouted 'yes' and raised their fists when the verdict was read out. Alongside them were Leanne Moyle, Scarlett Jago and – with his prosthetic leg already in place – Aaron Darracombe. All had made remarkable recoveries, though neither Leanne nor Scarlett remembered anything from the time of the crash. Tyler Darracombe was charged with car theft, and a few other offences, but spared jail.

Finlay Roscoe watched from the public gallery. Talantire sat a row behind. When his father was found guilty, Finlay covered his face with his hands. An aunt was there to put an arm around him, but he seemed as damaged as if he'd been in the car with the joyriders. Finlay had the rest of his life to contemplate his own decisions, and the cascade of events which followed. The affair with Scarlett which had ended his relationship with Jade, the intensifying enmity with Tyler Darracombe, which had culminated in the theft of the family car. Above all, there were the consequences of young Aaron

Darracombe's harebrained desire to try to find the Beast of Bodmin, on a humid summer night, filling the stolen car with all his friends and driving off into oblivion.

–

Talantire did finally go to see her sister Bella. She and her elder brother, Richard, met in Bristol on a hot day in August, and went together to the specialist care home where Bella had been for decades. The identical twin was no longer identical; she was in a wheelchair, her legs were swollen, and her head sat on a thickened neck. They wheeled her into the garden and sat in the shade of a lime tree. From Bella, there were unearthly sounds but no speech, and no recognition of her visitors. Talantire grasped her sister's hand, and felt the warmth. She looked into Bella's blue eyes, so like her own. She silently promised her that she would live life enough for both of them. Was there a glimmer of a smile in return, or did she imagine it? Probably the latter. Nevertheless, a promise it was and she would come again to tell Bella her news.

–

Brigadier William Llewellyn didn't live long enough to give evidence at the trial. He died of a stroke, peacefully, at his niece's home just a few days after going to see the grave of his fiancée Lily in Nunhead Cemetery southeast London. Talantire attended the funeral and sat next to Stef Metcalfe, the first responder. In the row immediately in front of her, Leanne Moyle, Scarlett and Lily Jago sat together, arm in arm, flanked by Holly Skewes and Aaron Darracombe: a reunion of joyriders. This was in some ways an emotional substitute for the much earlier funeral of Jordan Bailey, which neither Leanne nor Scarlett had been well enough to attend. Leanne, Lily and Scarlett wept, leaning on each other and holding hands, when the vicar recounted the tale of the accident and Bill Llewellyn's heroic role as rescuer.

Bill Llewellyn's last request was to have his ashes scattered on Bodmin Moor, and after discussion with the family, Lily went along as a representative of the survivors. It was a cold blustery day in November, and the sky had a winter iciness to it. After leaving the warmth of their car, half a dozen of Bill's closest family made their way into the rectory garden, past an estate agent board flexing in the wind, and up to the broken telegraph poll which had become a makeshift memorial. Bunches of flowers, many of them fresh, were there, alongside messages to and photographs of Jordan Bailey, who had lost his life there. From there, they walked onwards over the moor, through the gorse bushes, watching the gusts tug at the yellow petals. In the far distance was the reservoir, a smudge of slate grey. Once they were a few hundred yards from the rectory, Daphne took out the small urn which contained her uncle's ashes. Some silent looks were exchanged within the family and then she handed it to Lily.

'Go on, Lily. I think he would have liked you to do it.'

She tentatively took hold of the blue aluminium canister and looked to Daphne for instructions.

'You just unscrew the lid and throw it into the air, over there, downwind from us,' she said.

Lily managed the lid, gave it to Daphne and then with the canister drew a rapid arc across the sky, as if waving goodbye. The ashes plumed, rising high into the air, before disappearing like smoke across the moor.

Afterword

This is a work of fiction. I have, as usual, taken liberties with the geography of the south-west, inventing hamlets and villages, and placing them among real settlements. Likewise, this is not intended to be an accurate portrayal of Devon and Cornwall Police or its officers, simply a believable scenario within a police force in modern Britain. However, research related to policing techniques, to accidents and vehicles, is as accurate as I can make it. This would not have been possible without the assistance of a number of experts, including Rob Parsons for his input on first responders and paramedics, Mark Crouch, head of forensic investigations and chair of the Association of Traffic Collision Investigators, and special investigator Noel Lowdon at Harper Shaw Ltd. Lucy Fulford of Start Safety helpfully provided the data about smiley face speed cameras. Dr Victor Calland's 2005 article on accident victim extraction techniques in the *Journal of Emergency Medicine* was invaluable too. My friend Kiat Huang provided me with much information about his Mercedes. Thanks are also due to Dr Neil Rushton, and my long-time sources Home Office forensic pathologist Dr Stuart Hamilton and retired detective Kim Booth. Consultant obstetrician Sarah Chissell's knowledge of twin births was invaluable. I'm also grateful to my beta readers, Jo Joseph, Valerie Richardson, Tim Cary and John Selfe, who between them spotted so many slip-ups and inconsistencies. They make this a much better book. Any remaining errors are my own.

Thanks also to Julie Davenport, Heather Harley, Murray and Dani Sharpe, plus Bill Allen and Sarah Milden. I'd like to thank my editor at Canelo, Siân Heap, and Craig Thomson and Julian Holmes at WF Howes. Jade Craddock did an excellent job on the copyediting.

Last but not least, I'd like to thank my wife Louise, for her boundless patience and support during the gestation of each and every book.

CANELO CRIME

Do you love crime fiction and are always on the lookout for brilliant authors?

Canelo Crime is home to some of the most exciting novels around. Thousands of readers are already enjoying our compulsive stories. Are you ready to find your new favourite writer?

Find out more and sign up to our newsletter at canelocrime.com